D1250927

THE
LILIAN S. BESORE
MEMORIAL LIBRARY
GREENCASTLE, PENNSYLVANIA
FOUNDED MARCH 20, 1963

Red Rosa

ALSO BY MICHAEL COLLINS

Minnesota Strip

Freak

The Slasher

The Nightrunners

The Blood-Red Dream

Blue Death

The Silent Scream

Shadow Of A Tiger

Walk A Black Wind

Night of The Toads

The Brass Rainbow

Act of Fear

RED ROSA

A NOVEL BY

MICHAEL COLLINS

DONALD I. FINE, INC.
NEW YORK

 Published in the United States of America
by Donald I. Fine, Inc. and in Canada by General Publishing Company Limited.

Library of Congress Catalogue Card Number: 87-46027

ISBN: 1-55611-052-9

Manufactured in the United States of America
10 9 8 7 6 5 4 3 2 1

To William Campbell Gault

1.

"I KNOW YOU ... *Wait for me, Hans! ... I know you! Say something ... Tcheka, Hans! ... Tcheka! ...* "

In the glare of the Intensive Care Unit at St. Vincent's the monitors flashed and beeped. Rosa Gruenfeld lay under the oxygen tent on the bed of steel and tubes and dials. An old woman so small and thin she was lost under the equipment that kept her alive. Red Rosa, the bag lady Lenin. Someone had shot her.

Lieutenant Marx asked, "She know what she's saying, Doc?"

"No," the doctor said. "But that doesn't mean it's not real. It could be memory or it could be hallucination. Complete nonsense, or the exact truth."

"What's Tcheka?" Marx asked.

"The Czarist secret police," I told him. "She must be back in Russia before the First World War, her childhood."

"How old is she, Fortune?"

"Late eighties at least."

"Who's Hans?"

"I don't know her that well, Lieutenant."

I didn't know any of them that well. The old, the demented and the solitary who lived in the Oneida Hotel over on Twenty-first Street near Ninth Avenue. Just well enough to recognize old Jason Reich when I'd found him in the downstairs vestibule of my office/apartment that morning on my way out for a paying job up at Six Sport Cable Inc.

"Hello, Jason. You want something?"

"You know me?" the old man had said. "Who am I?"

"Jason Reich. You used to own a clothing store."

"A good store, too." He stared at my empty sleeve in its duffel coat. "You got one arm."

"Just one, Jason. Did you want me?"

"Who are you?"

"Dan Fortune."

"What am I doing here?"

I took his arm. "I'll take you home, Jason."

"You know where I live?"

I thought he was going to cry. They do, the lost old people who are lucky enough to find someone who can tell them who they are and where they belong. But he didn't cry, and we walked the two blocks to the Oneida Hotel—and found the milling, buzzing crowd in the narrow lobby.

I pushed Jason through. There is no furniture in the dingy lobby, and no one is ever behind the abandoned registration desk.

This time someone was. "Fortune!"

Barney Ederer stood behind the empty counter. Nothing's wrong with Ederer except that he spent two years in Vietnam and has no interest in the society that sent him there.

"Back here."

On the floor behind the counter, Rosa Gruenfeld lay in a pool of blood. Her mouth gaped open, her eyes were closed and her pulse was weak. A tiny old woman in a ragged gray sweater, brown wool skirt, men's surplus army OD high socks, half-laced combat boots with a jaunty maroon paratrooper's beret on her head. Her short hair was hacked off with a knife just below her ears, never combed, and still had a lot of its once-dark color.

"Your territory," Ederer said. "I'm splitting. I can see the 'Crazed Viet Vet' headlines."

"You called the police?"

"Emergency," Ederer said. "You can have the cops."

On cue the sirens wailed a few blocks away. The

police would be with them. I looked at all the faces in the lobby. Tenants of the Oneida and neighbors from the block. Faces that ranged from violently excited by the thrill to pale and shaking from the terror, but mostly only confused.

"Anybody see anything? Hear anything?"

The silence was filled with the movement of heads as they all looked behind them, searched the narrow lobby of the cheap hotel for anyone who had seen anything. Anyone but themselves. This is not a time when people want to see what is around them, and West Twenty-first Street and Ninth Avenue is not the place.

The paramedics arrived, and the police. I gave my story to a patrolman, watched them work over Rosa Gruenfeld.

I'd known her on the streets of Chelsea and the Village for ten years, give or take, come and go. One year she was there, another year gone. One week here, another week somewhere else. Not a total street person by the grace of a single twenty-by–twenty-foot room in a derelict hotel that was half flophouse and half Bedlam. A bag lady, one of thousands.

The only difference was that in her shopping bags Rosa was more likely to have yellowed books and pamphlets than rags and scraps of food. Copies of *Masses and Mainstream, The Communist Manifesto.* Pamphlets by every version of the radical left from the almost-normal ADA, through Socialist Labor and Socialist Worker and Socialist Anarchist, to the most violent and wild-eyed fringe of The Maoist Shining Path and Symbionese Liberation Army. *Red Rosa,* as often on the benches of Union Square as in the trash cans of Fifth Avenue.

"*... slavery and injustice for all ... tell them,* cholo! *Campesinos! They give you nothing except it is good for them! Nothing ... Where are you, Cabrera? ... I know you ... The Good Gestapo ... what do you want? ... no ... no ...*"

"Who shoots a bag lady?" Marx said. "Why?"

She had been shot twice at close range.

"They don't always need a reason," I said. "Not one that makes sense to us."

"You know a Cabrera?"

"No."

The doctor said, "She could be telling us something, having hallucinations or mixed-up memory or some combination of all three. A pain-induced dream, nothing, or her unconscious speaking. Cabrera could be someone she met yesterday, or someone in the Gestapo way back in World War Two."

He was young. Way back to him was yesterday to me. Maybe that's why we move ahead so slowly. It takes half our lives to catch up to what's happened so far, and some never do catch up.

"We'll keep a man in the room," Marx said. "Wait for her to come out of it."

"If she does," the doctor said. "At her age it could be a week, it could be never."

2.

SIX SPORT CABLE INC. IS IN A warehouse on West Thirty-sixth Street and Ninth Avenue. The boss is a nervous six-feet-seven ex-basketball player who invested his profits from point shaving in the "riches" of cable television.

"You're late," he said.

When your world tells you to buy everything you ever wanted, and it's okay for governments to steal fair and square, those who don't have it are sooner or later going to steal it. That's what the former point-shaver figured someone was doing in his empire. Free enterprise a little freer than the founding fathers or Adam Smith had in mind. Pilfering was so common on the docks when I was a kid they figured it into the wage scale. The peasants have always been creative at swiping extra corn, and that's really okay with the lords. A little illicit venison keeps the proles distracted from thinking about why they're not lords, too. Just don't make the grab too big or threaten the manor.

"It's not just the boxes, Fortune," the TV tycoon told me when he hired me. "Every stolen converter they sell costs us the monthly fees as well as the installation."

"What do you want me to do?"

"Nose out the damn thief. The cops won't come in until I can give them solid evidence."

That's how I eat—jobs the police don't have time for. So I joined his workers, handed out tools and parts and watched for anyone to put a hot hand on a case or two of cable converter boxes. I'd been there a week, had two prime suspects. Neither of them did anything the rest of the day. I gave the former slam-dunk artist—make or miss depending on the spread—an extra hour until 6:00 P.M. and hung up my apron.

I walked east and south in the warm evening of a late March false spring down to St. Vincent's. The nurse on ICU told me Rosa Gruenfeld was unchanged, it wouldn't make any difference if I went in or not, and the patrolman at the door had seen me with Marx. Inside, the old woman lay like a mummy displayed under a glass case. A bored policewoman sat with a notebook, and a young blonde woman stood over the bed.

"Relative?" I said to the blonde.

No man on earth could have helped noticing her body first. A slim, hard, almost perfect body. In tailored charcoal-brown corduroy jeans, a tight tan turtleneck over large firm breasts, a wide cordovan leather belt low on her hips. Cordovan western boots. She wasn't tall, five-feet-five and a hundred twelve pounds, but she looked tall.

"Are you a policeman?"

"Just someone who knows her," I said.

When you got past the body, her face was almost as perfect. Not pretty—the nose too strong, the eyes too large and pale; the mouth too full yet immobile; the skin too smooth; the blonde hair too short—but almost beautiful.

"Lenny Gruenfeld," she said. "Her granddaughter."

"Dan Fortune," I said. "Any ideas of who shot her or why?"

She didn't answer, and I had the strange feeling she wasn't really in the room. Somewhere else, behind an invisible plastic wall. A beat out of sync in time, a micron displaced in space, her voice—when it came—from an infinitesimal yet infinite distance.

"The 'good' people. A dirty parasite of a bag lady." She looked at me. "What do you care? What's your interest?"

"Call it habit," I said. "I'm a private investigator. How about someone at the Oneida?"

She looked back at her grandmother, motionless under the tent. "They're harmless at the hotel. She helped them all."

"Outside the hotel? Did she have any enemies?"

"Red Rosa? She's eighty-eight, been an agitator all her life. She's probably made ten enemies for every year. But not to shoot her. Except maybe my father."

"Why would he want to shoot her?"

"Pure hate." She turned for the door. "Only I don't think even he'd go this far." She stopped at the door and looked back at the old woman. "She always said they'd get her in the end. I guess they did."

Alone with the old woman, I listened to the noises of the machines keeping her alive, the clicking sounds of the monitors. She moved restless under the tent. *"Cor-*

ruption and injustice ... Injustice for all ... They're afraid ... don't let them ... your brother's keeper ... "

Red Rosa, the bag lady Lenin who lived alone in one room, foraged in the trash and garbage of the city, harangued indifferent listeners from Union Square benches, gave out old pamphlets against long-forgotten evils, had no past or future anyone knew or cared about. Now the present was gone, too.

I walked out with a sense of being glad I was alive, went up to my loft/office, boiled a pair of eggs, made a pot of tea, toasted an English muffin and called California.

"Early modeling job," Kay Michaels said, explaining why she was home at such an early hour out there. "It looks like I can fly into New York Monday."

I'd met her a year or so ago on a case in California for my old flame, Marty Adair. End the old, begin the new. An old that had been a long time fading, and a new too long coming. But here now, and it was Kay I called when I needed to talk, Kay I wanted to come to New York.

"Six days is a long time," I said.

"Six months is longer," she said. "There's nothing to keep you from coming out here, Dan. If you wanted to."

New hopes and new troubles.

"I want to come out. I want to work, too."

"You can work here."

"Maybe I could. Tell me about *Wozzeck.*"

She told me about her new part: Marie in the German play so far before its time. It made me think of Rosa Gruenfeld. I ate my dinner and told her about Rosa. She saw the parallel between the bag lady and the lost soldier. I drank my pot of tea while she told me about her modeling job for the morning. The tea was gone before I let her get some sleep. Maybe I should move to California—my telephone bills were starting to make me take jobs just for money.

3.

"INJUSTICE FOR ALL . . . they're afraid, Hans . . . Don't let them stop us, Hans . . . your brother's keeper . . . keep your brother . . . they're afraid, don't let them scare you . . . go and keep your brothers, Cabrera . . . go . . . go. . ." It had been with me all night. Hallucination or the truth? Real or dream? Dreams are real, are what is on your mind. Were Rosa Gruenfeld's dreams what was on her mind?

I spent the morning at Six Cable watching the forty-odd employees. The clothes on any of them would pay my rent for a month: cashmere and silk; imported leather boots; imported handbags and hand-made belt buckles; Shetland sport jackets and the layered look. Rings, earrings, bracelets, watches. Radios and tape players, rows of earphones and tapping feet. So much to buy, so much to have. How could you not want it all?

My two suspects—Akira, a thin, smiling clerk in billing who had to go to the doctor a lot, and Greg, the athletic courier sent with needed supplies to the installers in the field—failed me again, and at 5:25 P.M. I headed home. The false spring was holding, the evening clean and warm. Lenny Gruenfeld leaned against the corridor wall outside my office.

"I looked you up," she said. She wore a full denim skirt now, sandals, a denim vest over a loose white silk blouse, her blonde hair catching the last sunlight. She had changed her clothes but not her detachment, her distance.

"Why?"

"I think I want to know what happened to my grandmother."

"You only think you want to know?"

"Does it matter?" The white silk of her blouse rippled when she moved, the sun almost flashed from her blonde hair. "I can pay you. If there's another reason, I suppose it's my business."

The detachment wasn't all unconscious. It was part of her relation to people, maybe the world.

"Three hundred a day plus expenses and extras."

"What are extras?"

"Bribes, payoffs, rewards."

She opened a large canvas and rope bag.

"How much now?"

"How much do you have?"

"Three hundred in cash. I'd rather not write a check until we're paid for our last gig."

"Gig?"

"We have a band."

"Three hundred's okay."

It was in twenties. Since every bank in the country opened automatic teller machines we've become a nation of twenties. She stood up. "Rosa was always good to me. She cares."

She left me with the three hundred dollars and the old woman's voice in my head: *"Corruption and injustice . . . Injustice for all . . . They're afraid . . . don't let them . . . your brother's keeper . . . keep your brother . . . "*

The Oneida Hotel was as good a place to start as any—one of those single-room warrens where an affluent society hides its invisible. The solitary old, the homeless and jobless, the socially wounded and mentally damaged we turn out into the streets the way they did in seventeenth-century England when "poore distracted men" were thrown out of Bedlam to live by begging. Everyone is on social security or a minimal pension or welfare, and it is never enough.

But places, too, that are the last hope for those who

have lived alone and independent, want to go on alone and independent. People who would like nicer rooms but prefer the freedom of squalor to the comfort of an institution. Want to decide what they will do all day, not sit bored in some home no matter how comfortable and properly fed. Don, a brain tumor removed, always waiting for his daughter. Grace, who spent her time away from garbage cans doing crossword puzzles in gibberish. The Dover brothers, addicted to everything known to man. The dishwashers and cleaning women who after eight hours of grueling work spent the few dollars left from food and rent to get drunk. Walt, 75, who ate eggs for breakfast and nothing but ice cream and beer after that, who knew every free admission and cheap ride in New York, and who would die before he couldn't ride the bus every day to anywhere he wanted.

They were out on the sidewalk in the warm March twilight. Barney Ederer sat on an orange crate against the gray brick wall.

"She gonna make it?"

"They don't know. Anyone remember anything yet?"

"Cops couldn't come up with a whisper."

Jason Reich told everyone about the fine store he'd had until his sons stole it and threw him out. "They should of shot me, too! I heard them shots. Two of 'em. Didn't look, nossir. Heard her talking, then the shots."

"She was talking to someone?"

"Hell," Barney Ederer said. "Old Rosa talked to herself all the time."

"Rosa talked to my little honey," Don said.

Crossword Grace said, "She's a Communist! Always talkin'."

"Communists! That's what my sons are!" Jason Reich said.

I said, "No one saw who she was talking to that morning?"

"They wouldn't remember if they did, Fortune," Ederer said.

"Do the names Hans or Cabrera mean anything to anyone?" They were all silent on the sidewalk in the last light before it was time to go back into their small dark rooms. "She's talking about the Tcheka, the Gestapo. About injustice. She keeps saying she knows someone. 'I know you,' she says."

"Rosa always talked about injustice," Jason Reich said. "I told her about my sons."

"The Tcheka sounds like way back," Ederer said. "Maybe she really was a Communist in Russia."

I said, "She's talking about being your brother's keeper, help your brother. Did she have a brother?"

They all looked at each other, shook their heads. I left them in the last of the light. Rosa's room was at the rear on the third floor. I climbed through the odor of urine and dirty sheets. Rosa's door was open, the light was on inside, and a man stood in the room.

He turned to me. "Look at it. Christ, this is what killed her. Her whole insane life."

"She's not dead," I said. "Who are you?"

He was trim and neat in a dark blue three-piece suit, white shirt, pale blue figured tie, black shoes. An even six feet, medium hands with clean nails, medium feet, nothing excessive. He carried a topcoat, had a tanned face that had been to California or the Caribbean recently, a nose too large and a mouth too small and reminded me of someone.

"Are you a policeman?"

"Private," I said. "Hired by her granddaughter."

"Arlene? I'm not paying any private detective! I don't give a damn who shot Rosa or why!"

I had a hunch I was seeing the other reason Arlene/Lenny Gruenfeld had hired me.

"You must be Lenny's father."

"Insanity skipped a generation. Like grandmother, like granddaughter." He looked around the room again and then back at me. "Not dead? I've seen her. This time she's dead."

I won't say he sounded happy, but he didn't sound unhappy. He sounded angry. Enraged as he looked at the room where Rosa Gruenfeld had lived. "Look at this sewer."

It was a single room piled from floor to ceiling with books, newspapers, magazines, pamphlets and posters. The piles were orderly, with chairs, a table and even a couch in open spaces between piles. The narrow bottom section of an army bunk was against the far wall in a kind of nest with an armchair and a coffee table. The furniture was old, but it was neat and looked clean. A battered manual typewriter stood on the table she obviously used as a desk. The room of someone who still worked, was very much alive.

"Garbage dumps look better!"

He saw chaos, clutter, trash and neglect. I saw a shabby room but spartan, exactly as she wanted and needed it.

"God, what a waste. Useless stupidity."

He wasn't angry at the dilapidated room, but at his mother for living there. He hated where she lived, and he hated her.

"Something got her shot," I said. "You have any ideas about who might have wanted to do that?"

"Anyone who ever met her." He brushed his hands together as if rubbing off the chaos. "You better get your money from Lenny up front." Then he walked to the door and out.

I looked after him for a time, then made a quick search of the room, found nothing and went back downstairs. It was full night on the street. An old black, George, motioned me to him like a conspirator. He'd been a janitor at a right-wing think tank, read all their reports alone in the night, became a staunch free-enterprise capitalist even if his pay had always been so low his social security was barely enough for him to live at the Oneida.

"You was askin' 'bout Rosa she got a brother?"

"She has one?"

"Nope, on'y someone does in this here hotel, 'n someone got trouble 'bout that there brother."

"What kind of trouble?"

"Police kind o' trouble," the old man said, dropping his voice even lower. "Maybe Rosa she done seen somethin'."

"Where do I go, George?"

"Top floor, back left. You watch yo'self."

On the top floor the feeble light of the single bulb at the top of the stairs barely reached the shadows around the last door on the left. I listened at the door of the rear left room.

The two men who exploded out of the door behind me hit high and low before I could half turn, had me down on my back with two guns pointed at my eyes.

4. "WHERE'S AGNEW!"

"Don't shit us!"

One had his knee on my chest, his pistol still aimed at my eye. The other held my one arm, looked for the other.

"The bastard's only got one arm."

They were young: black-haired and brown-haired. Black-hair had a dirty Navy pea jacket, heavy work boots and chino pants. Brown-hair was in a sport jacket, brown slacks, white shirt and tie. They were both nervous. That scared me. Pistols and nervousness is a deadly combination. That's why no one except trained cops should have guns. They're dangerous enough.

"Just one," I said. "Sorry about that."

My missing arm and lack of resistance seemed to make them relax. Black-hair took his knee off my chest. Brown-hair found my wallet and my ID in my jacket under the duffel coat.

"A goddamned PI."

"Shit," black-hair said.

They were cops.

"What do you want with Regan, Fortune?"

"You working for Johnny A, Fortune?"

It's hard to be tough lying on your back, but it was time to assert myself. I sat up against the hallway wall, asked, "Who's Johnny Agnew, and who the hell are you two? You have ID?"

If they didn't identify themselves they could be in trouble later in their case against whoever Johnny Agnew was, or if I brought charges against their conduct. Brown-hair finished frisking me, shook his head to black-hair. I had no gun. Black-hair put his away reluctantly.

"Detective Fanelli," he said. "He's Mason. Center Street Fugitive Squad. What the hell you doing with Regan, Fortune?"

I waited. Fanelli swore under his breath, showed me his shield. So did Mason. I got up, brushed off my duffel.

"I'm on a case. Marx at the precinct knows all about it. An old woman named Rosa Gruenfeld was shot down in the lobby yesterday. The old woman's been babbling about a brother. One of the tenants told me this room had a brother in trouble with the police, maybe Rosa knew something about it that got her shot."

You tell the police everything you can. You may need

them, and that way they trust you more for when you have to hold back.

"You think maybe she saw Johnny Agnew and he blew her away?"

"Or Regan did?"

"That's what I came to ask," I said.

They both looked at me in the hall's dim light.

"Where is this old lady?" Fanelli asked.

"St. Vincent's," I said. "But she's in ICU and doesn't know who she is or where she is or what happened. She's been raving all over, maybe I heard something could help you. What's it all about? Who's Regan, and who's Johnny Agnew?"

Mason said, "Johnny Agnew's a Hell's Kitchen hotshot wanted for pushing H and a couple or three killings. Kevin Regan's his half brother out of the same mold. Fifteen out of forty years inside."

"Regan's on parole," Fanelli added, "but we figure he's helping Agnew. We've been after Johnny A for three years. We was just getting close when he faded right near here."

"Regan knows where's he's hiding," Mason said.

"We didn't even know Agnew had a brother until we found a letter in the room up the street where Johnny A slipped us."

"Where's Regan now?" I asked.

"In the Tombs, where else?" Mason said. "He's aidin' and abettin', and he busted parole."

"You don't figure this old lady can tell us anything?"

"You can try," I said. "You have any evidence Regan helped Agnew, gave him money, knows where he is?"

"They're brothers," Fanelli said. "They come from the same place, spent their lives in jail, are going the same place."

"Crook helps crook, brother helps brother," Mason said. "If Regan didn't help Johnny A, he'll have to prove it."

"How?"

"By helping us," Fanelli said.

Kevin Regan was guilty until he proved he was innocent. It's a pervasive belief deep in all of us, especially if the suspected criminal disturbs our own peace. The great concepts of English law are not natural to a fearful humanity concerned with itself, must be learned and learned again. Our advances can be frighteningly skin deep.

I waited until their footsteps faded away below before I knocked on the door. It opened a crack.

"Are they gone?"

It was a woman's voice.

"Yes."

"Are you a friend of Kevin's?"

"Dan Fortune, a private investigator. I'm investigating the shooting of an old lady down in the lobby yesterday."

"That was an awful thing. Poor Rosa."

She was a small thin woman in a yellow print dress, a long brown cardigan sweater, stockings and worn blue tennis shoes. A friendly face that was meant to be cheerful, but dark circles in the hollows around her brown eyes weren't cheerful now.

"Can you tell me anything about it, Mrs.—is it Mrs. Regan?"

"Yes," she nodded. "No, I don't know anything about it."

The room was identical to Rosa's, with the clutter replaced by bareness. A double bed hidden behind a folding screen, a table with two straight chairs, two worn armchairs and another table used, like Rosa's, as a desk.

"Where were you and Mr. Regan when she was shot?"

"I don't know when it happened."

I told her.

"We were right here at home." She sat down in one of

the armchairs. "I'm just scared he'll lose hope, get bitter. I mean, he can't help loving his brother, they'll see that. It'll be okay. I mean, they'll understand, let him go."

Her voice had that combination of fear and hope only the desperate know. I didn't have the heart to tell her what the chances of the police understanding were.

"Tell me about Kevin and Johnny."

"I don't know much about Johnny. He was in jail when we got married." She wrapped her thin arms around herself. "They grew up in Hell's Kitchen. Kevin says they both decided early they were going to survive and get out any way they could. Kevin joined the army in 1960 when he was eighteen. I guess Johnny was already in jail. Kevin served four years and came back here. He tried to get work, but he didn't know any trade. He got into fights, killed a man, went to prison. In prison he impressed everyone with his good behavior, was paroled."

She shook her head as if debating with herself somewhere inside. "He still couldn't get any decent work, drank, kept getting into trouble. It's hard to grow up fighting and clawing to survive, and then learn not to act the same even when you don't have to. He kept going back to prison. Then five years ago he looked at himself and knew it just had to stop, he was better than that. Some people in the prison believed in him, helped him go to a community college, and he did very well."

She smiled at me. "I met him at the college. I was a student-tutor. He was so eager to learn, we fell in love. When he was paroled we got married, and he started classes at NYU. He's got a job in a lab there, and he studies full time. He wants to be a psychologist, do prison rehabilitation work." She stopped smiling. "They walked in on a class at NYU and arrested him. They say he helped Johnny escape them. They say he knows where Johnny's hiding."

"Does he?"

"I don't know. His court lawyer says Kevin hasn't broken any laws, but they want to send him back to prison."

"Did Johnny come here, Mrs. Regan?"

"Yes, but Kevin only gave him some money, sent him away."

"Did Rosa know about Kevin and Johnny?"

"I don't know. She did talk to Kevin sometimes."

"Could Kevin have shot her?"

"Kevin never even owned a gun!"

"Johnny Agnew?"

She was silent.

"Can I talk to Kevin, Mrs. Regan?"

"I suppose so. Mr. Walter Eimold is his lawyer."

She rocked silently in the shabby armchair in the bare room as I left. The night had taken on a March chill. It was too late to call Eimold now. Kevin Regan would have to keep until morning.

5.

IN A PRISON I FEEL AS IF I'm in the engine room of an old Liberty with a hurricane outside and the fear that she is going down with me inside and no hope of ever reaching the air to breathe again.

"Somebody shot old Rosa?" Kevin Regan said.

The visiting room at the Tombs is spanking new and modern. Counselor Walter Eimold breathed down my neck as I talked to Kevin Regan. Eimold was a graying man who'd had bad acne as a boy fifty years ago and was the best of the court-appointed lawyers in the city. A quiet determination seemed to be as much a part of him as his rumpled brown suit. There was determination about Kevin Regan, too, but it wasn't quiet—rage and a lurking violence in Regan. Maybe it was only the difference between growing up on Long Island and in Hell's Kitchen.

"You think I shot Rosa?" Regan said. "Are the cops going to pin that on me, too?"

He was stocky, slow-moving, in his early forties. A pale Irish face quick to color. His nose had been broken, both eyes had thick scars over them, one cheek and his neck showed knife marks. His hands, clasped on the visitor's table in front of him, were scarred and battered. His voice was quiet and well spoken, with a faint trace of an Irish lilt. The violence was held in but still there behind the slow movements and soft voice.

"Why would I shoot a nice old lady?" Regan said.

"Could your brother have been around the hotel in the morning two days ago?"

Regan looked at Eimold. "You're sure he's not a cop?"

"I have to ask the questions," I said. "I'm just a private investigator hired by Rosa's granddaughter to find out who shot Rosa."

"And I have to tell you what I told the cops. I don't know where Johnny is. He called me, I sent him some money. He came around once. He was hungry. I gave him money. I didn't give him a lot of money, I don't have a lot of money. Food money and flop money, not escape money."

"What if Rosa saw him? Maybe recognized him. Did she know about you and your brother?"

Eimold said, "You don't have to talk to him."

Regan ignored him. "We'd talked about Johnny. She's smart, might have put two and two together if Johnny came around, and if she saw him. So what, Fortune? Unless she walked right up to him, he wouldn't have known she knew who he was."

"Maybe she did walk right up to him," I said.

Regan stared at me for almost a minute. He sat back in the hard chair, his eyes half closed. "My mother raised us together, me and Johnny. She was no nun. We had different fathers, and we weren't two years apart. Men and going to confession, that was all the fun she had. What else do you do after working all day for a dollar an hour? The men came and went, my mother worked, and we stayed poor. Johnny and I grew up close, and maybe we're going different ways now, but I won't help anyone catch him and put him back in prison."

"Does that mean the police are right?"

Eimold bristled. "I think this interview is—"

"I won't help them," Regan said, "but I won't try to stop them either. I owe Johnny as a brother, that's all, and that's all I've done. I haven't helped him escape, or hidden him, and I don't know where he is."

"That's a pretty narrow distinction, isn't it?"

"Sometimes narrow distinctions are all we have, Fortune. The difference between being human and being an animal."

Eimold said, "He hasn't broken any laws. All he did was give his brother some money to eat with, maybe a place to sleep for a night. What anyone would do for a brother. For that they want to crucify him, take away five years of hard work trying to rehabilitate himself from a wasted life. In prison the last time the warden said in twelve years he'd seen about a hundred and seventy-five men really break away from the cycle of crime and return to society, and Kevin ranks in the top three."

"I got lucky," Regan said. "I was over forty, I couldn't just keep going back to jail, and I ran into people who were really interested in helping me."

"They're out to make him catch Agnew for them," Eimold insisted. "They walked right into a class to arrest him."

"When they questioned me, they said all I had to do

was come up with an address and they wouldn't file charges," Regan said, his hands slowly opening and closing. "They told me if I didn't give them Johnny they'd finish me, and they're doing it."

"And you can't give them Johnny?"

"No," Regan said, "and I don't know anything about Rosa. There's plenty of trouble in that hotel, out on the streets, and Rosa was always into everyone's business."

"Even yours?"

He smiled a thin smile. "Even mine."

"Who else's business?"

"Everyone's. Last time was with the old man in the garden apartment. Mr. Abraham Roth, our rich man. He got in a shouting match with her maybe a week ago. She even went around telling Don and Barney Ederer how to run their lives."

"Who shoots an old woman for butting into their business?"

He said nothing. He didn't have to.

"You're sure you don't know where Johnny is?" I said.

Eimold stood up. "That's it, Fortune. End of interview."

6.

THE WAY THE EX-DRIBBLER'S EYES FOLLOWED ME as I passed his office at Six Sport Cable I knew I had to produce soon. Neither of my suspects cooperated. By quitting time I was tired from doing nothing, and the cable tycoon looked like a man tired of paying me for doing nothing. It's a hazard of the profession.

I gave him my best reassuring smile and went down to St. Vincent's. Rosa's angry son was arguing with someone on the business staff. He was wearing a banker's gray chalkstripe suit this time, and from what I could hear he was making sure the city or state or anyone but him would pay Rosa's bill.

"I'm damn well not responsible for my mother's bills, and I'm damned if I'll pay a red cent for her!"

There was more than anger in his voice. The Gruenfelds were not a happy family, or any family at all. A businessman, a bag lady and an isolated girl who made her living playing "gigs."

At the ICU station the nurse talked to a short swarthy man in a Mets baseball jacket and a longshoreman's earflapped cap. He had alert eyes that glanced at the empty sleeve of my duffel coat as he left. I had the sudden feeling that this man would remember everything about me. Or already knew.

"Who was that?" I asked the nurse as I watched him go. He didn't wait for the elevator, took the stairs.

"He didn't say. Some friend of Rosa Gruenfeld's, like you."

"Rosa?"

"He asked how she was, looked in her room for a moment."

I went after him. In the stairwell there was only silence. I went all the way down to the lobby. He was gone. The nurse looked scared when I returned.

"He only peeked into her room. The officer was there."

"What was his name?"

"I . . . I forgot to ask."

He hadn't told the patrolman on duty his name either.

"He never went in, Fortune, just looked. I think maybe he was here yesterday, too."

"Yesterday? You think?"

"He was wearin' a suit an' topcoat, but it could of been the same guy. Just looked in. I frisked him." Then he remembered he was a policeman, I was only a private eye, and bridled. "Hey, I know my job, Fortune."

"Sorry. Can I go in?"

He thought about it just long enough to make me remember his authority. "Okay, go ahead."

In the brightly lit ICU, Rosa Gruenfeld lay as if she hadn't moved in two days. The nurses worked, the woman police officer sat with her notebook. The angry son stood in grey chalk/stripe. He still wore his hat, looked down at his mother.

"*... Hans! ... run Hans! ... the police ... the police will do nothing ... look out Hans! ... they're coming with horses ... they're coming ... they're coming ...*"

"Who is Hans, Mr. Gruenfeld?" I said.

"Grenfell," he said. "Nicholas Grenfell. I changed it when I was eighteen, and she was in prison. Hans was Johannes Gruenfeld, my father. Her first husband. He was killed fighting against everything America stands for, everything we believe in. I was four years old, I never really knew him. He worked all day, went to meetings all night and died in a street brawl without even thinking of his son, what a son needed from him."

"When was that?"

"Nineteen twenty-eight. I'm sixty-four, that woman in the oxygen tent is eighty-eight. She hasn't changed in sixty-four years, hasn't thought of anyone but herself longer than that."

He went on looking at his mother with the same coldness in his eyes he had in his voice when he talked about the father who had died without thinking of him. Somewhere in the hospital a radio was on, a soprano, probably Sutherland, singing. *Norma*. It's absurd, *Norma*, but true. The plot is absurd, but the music holds one of the truths, the truth of loss. A man who can't feel loss isn't quite human. There was no sense of loss in Nicholas Grenfell's eyes or voice.

"Your daughter changed her name back?"

"Obviously." He turned to look me up and down. His eyes showed no particular expression, not even when he looked at my arm. "Look Mr. . . . Fortune, is it? Look, Fortune, my mother and I live in different worlds. We have since I was eighteen. It was my choice, I've never regretted it. To be quite honest, I don't much care who attacked her or why. She chose her way of life. She turned her back on the normal world for the sake of insane ideas. She didn't care about me in the past, I don't care about her now. Is that honest enough?"

"I don't know, Mr. Grenfell. Is it?"

Anger came into his eyes again. An anger that lurked even closer to the surface in him than violence did in Kevin Regan.

"Remember, I'm not paying you a nickel."

For him, that was a parting shot. He walked out of the bright room of dials and beeps and blinking lights.

7.

"A SWEETHEART, RIGHT?" Lieutenant Marx stood in the doorway.

"He sounds like he has his reasons," I said.

"So did Jack the Ripper. We're checking into Mr. Grenfell, but so far we don't place him in the city that morning."

He came through the glare of the ICU to the bed, looked down at Rosa Gruenfeld.

"They say she's getting better," Marx said. "Damned if I can see it."

"Who was in the city that morning?"

"The granddaughter, the people in the hotel. A couple

of the flea-baggers admit to hearing the shots, stuck their fingers in their ears and ducked back under the covers. Closest we can reconstruct it, the attacker was waiting behind the desk. There's a door back there down into the basement. From the basement you can go out the backyard or the front areaway up to the street."

"The gunman was waiting for her?"

"Looks like it. Weapon was a thirty-eight, no empty cases, probably a revolver. She was behind that old hotel desk when she was shot. The M.E. says about eight-thirty that morning, half an hour before you got there. In that dump anyone who works is gone by eight-thirty, all those who don't work are still hiding in bed. Ederer's the only one there out before eight-thirty and not working. We've turned him up, down and sideways, and he still saw nothing. No trace of the gun."

Someone had not only shot a bag lady, but it looked like had come to shoot a particular bag lady. Neither random nor chance. We were still thinking about it when Rosa Gruenfeld opened her eyes and slowly turned her head to look at us.

"Is it over?"

Marx moved in closer, "Is what over, Mrs. Gruenfeld?"

"The pogrom. The *goyim,* are they gone?"

Marx said, "Can you tell us who shot you, Mrs. Gruenfeld?"

"The Germans. *Goyim* bosses, they're afraid of us. Of the strike. They shoot us, put us in prison."

I said, "Rosa? Do you know who I am?"

"Of course."

"Who am I?"

"You're Sam."

"Sam who, Rosa?"

"Sam Bronstein, my husband."

Marx said, "Your name is Gruenfeld, Mrs. Gruenfeld."

She blinked, the dark eyes clouding as if a film had

slid over them. The bright, empty eyes of a bird.

I said, "Who are you, Rosa?"

"You don't know who I am?"

"I know who you are. Do you?"

"Rebecca Bronstein. Who are you?"

"Dan Fortune, Rosa."

She peered up at me like a blind person. "Rosa Bronstein. When the war's over, they have to let us go home."

"Who has to let you go home?"

"The Germans. It's always the Germans."

"The war's been over a long time," I said. "One ended almost seventy years ago, the second over forty years ago."

"They have to send prisoners of war home."

"You're not a prisoner of war, Rosa."

"Of course we are! All prisoners of war! We're soldiers! We must fight for our rights!"

Her voice rose, and she thrashed the bed with its tubes and bottles and dials. The nurse hurried over, lifted the oxygen tent to hold the old woman, glared at us. She must have pressed a signal before she came. A doctor hustled into the room. Rosa had fallen back and closed her eyes the moment the nurse touched her. The doctor looked at the dials, felt her pulse, listened to her heart. He straightened up and turned on us.

"You two trying to finish the job?"

Marx said, "She woke up and started to talk."

"So you had to—what do you people call it—grill her?"

I said, "She doesn't seem to know who she is or who we are, Doctor. Is that normal?"

"After you've been shot twice at the age of eighty-eight nothing is normal or not normal," the doctor said. He pointed to the door. "I've tried to cooperate because I want you to catch whoever did this, but I can't have you disturbing her. We intend to keep this lady alive, so out you go."

Under the oxygen tent, the old lady began to talk again. *"The Revolution!* ... Es ist Siegen, Vater! ... *We've won ... in Russia, soon here ... The new world, Papa ... Can you hear me, Papa ... Mama does not understand ... I love you ... it wasn't all for nothing, Papa ..."*

The doctor turned to the nurse. The nurse released something into the glucose drip tube. The old woman calmed almost immediately. The doctor motioned us out.

Marx said, "Who do you think she thought she was when she was talking to us?"

"Her mother, I'd guess. Sounds like her father was the radical and her mother didn't go along."

"She was raving about the Russian Revolution there at the end? Telling her father the Commies had won? You think we've got a political shooting?"

"At her age?" I said. "How important could a bag lady be?"

"She was important to someone," Marx said.

8.

THE REAL-LIFE VARIATIONS OF 007, *Theirs* or *Ours,* don't kill a bag lady for making speeches in Union Square or distributing ancient pamphlets. Not even the CIA. I decided that over kidney stew—Thursday's special—in the Hudson Diner.

It was a cold clear night over the city, the false spring gone, and by the time I reached the Oneida Hotel stars were visible high up between the buildings.

"You should of seen 'em in Dakota," a Dover brother said. "Like the whole fuckin' sky was pushing you down into the dirt."

I'd never been able to tell the Dovers apart. They were always drunk, or stoned, or both. This one was drunk.

"Work your ass off ten hours pickin' 'n diggin' 'n nothing damn all to do after." He giggled. "'Ceptin' get drunk."

"Where's your brother?"

"Al? Up to the Strip. We got some boxes o' Mets caps."

I didn't ask where they'd gotten them. He was Larry.

"Did Rosa act scared of anything recently, Larry? Maybe from the past? Foreigners, political enemies?"

"Never saw old Rosa scared o' nothin'."

"Was anyone looking for her? Asking questions about her?"

He shook his head, leaned back to look up at the stars. He was short and scrawny and almost bald, his gray pants and shirt hadn't been washed in months. He sneered up at the stars.

"You know an old man who lives in the rear room, ground floor? The rich man."

"Old Roth? Ain't worth shit."

"Did he have a fight with Rosa?"

"He done fight with ever'body."

"Which ground floor room is his?"

"Left. Four locks 'n a peephole. Two rooms. The royal damn suite, you know? Even got bars on his fuckin' windows."

The four locks and the peephole were obvious on the door at the end of the first-floor corridor, but Larry Dover hadn't added that the door was also covered with sheet metal. Maybe he hadn't noticed. I knocked. Knocked again. And again. I heard a soft, almost furtive movement inside, and the peephole seemed to move.

"Mr. Roth?"

The voice was almost a whisper. "Who asks?"

"Dan Fortune. Could I talk to you?"

"Come to store."

The peephole was closed.

"It's not about the store, Mr. Roth. It's about Rosa Gruenfeld."

With the peephole closed the voice was even more muffled.

"I know nothing of Gruenfeld woman."

"You were heard arguing with her."

"She puts nose where has no business."

"So you did fight with her."

I could almost hear the angry stare behind the door. I felt out of focus, even unbalanced, in the silent hall talking to a blank door, imagined the glare of his eyes on the other side.

"I fight with no one."

"The police are interested in anyone who fought with Rosa."

It had to be dim and airless in there, fussy and dusty, the curtains drawn and old furniture that hadn't been used or dusted in years. It was in his voice.

"You are the police?"

"A private detective. The police come after me."

I heard the locks open one after the other. The door swung inward, and the old man looked out at me. A tall man in a gray cardigan that reached below his hips. Gray wool slippers on his feet, the trousers and vest of an old brown suit that bagged at the knees. An unironed white shirt and narrow brown tie that had been knotted too often. Tall and bald, a fringe of white hair above a bony face, and deep eye sockets like a skeleton.

"I talk with you, the police do not come?"

He saw my empty sleeve, looked at me curiously, even with hope. His seamed face was not one where hope had come often or for a long time. All downturned, inverted, sliding away into expected disappointment.

"I'll do my best," I said.

I went past him into a room as airless as I had imagined behind tightly closed drapes. Dusty old furniture unused for years. A straight chair and an enameled kitchen table next to a counter with a hotplate. In the second room, through an open door, a narrow twin bed was unmade.

"Rosa Gruenfeld is bolshevik with big mouth. Always long nose in other peoples business. Stupid *yenta.* I tell her keep nose out of my business."

"What business?"

"Tell me how to think, run store."

"What kind of store do you have, Mr. Roth?"

"Clothing. New and used. Down Hudson Street."

There was no television set, not even a radio, but there was an expensive stereo tape deck and turntable, even a compact disc player that had to be new. A long cabinet crammed with records and tapes. One wall was all books, most of them from the Nineteenth Century by the look of the bindings.

"You must do well," I said. "That's an expensive stereo."

"I do not lose money."

"Then why live here?"

"Rooms are rooms. I have nice garden outside for good vegetables like from village where I grow up." The old man's voice grew animated. He seemed to see that far-off village somewhere in Eastern Europe. "My father has best garden in village before Cossacks come and we go to America. City food is not good. Landlord here not care I have garden."

He explained it all logically, but there was uneasiness in his voice, and his large gnarled hands moved nervously. Maybe he was just another of the millions of old people who had come to America from other countries and never really felt at home, never really stopped being afraid of the strange land.

"What do you think happened to Rosa Gruenfeld?"

"Happen? What has happen?"

"You haven't heard about it?"

He shrugged again. "Never talk to *gonifs* in hotel."

"Somebody shot her in the lobby two days ago."

His gray indoor pallor went even grayer.

"I know nothing of shoot! Go away! Leave from me!"

He lunged and pushed me to the open door. He had a violent strength I hadn't expected, and before I knew it I was in the corridor again, looking at the closed door.

The arm clamped my neck. The knife flashed in the feeble light of the corridor. I caught the knife wrist, twisted.

"Ahhggg!"

The knife clattered on the tile of the corridor floor, the arm held on. A skinny arm. Tight . . . darkness and a narrow face . . . wolf face . . . teeth skinned back . . . no air . . . weight on a hanged man to get it over faster . . . pain . . .

He was a handsome man. Blue suit neat and pressed. Blue suit and gun. Running. Pale woman . . .

9.

"ARE YOU ALL RIGHT, Mr. Fortune?"

She looked down at me.

"Tell me where I am."

"What?" Lenny Gruenfeld said.

"Tell me where I am."

"You're in the Oneida Hotel. Should I get a doctor?"

"No," I said. "Describe everything around me."

"You're on the floor of the first-floor corridor. You don't appear injured except for some marks on your throat and a cut on your hand. The emergency door into the back yard is open."

"What did you see?"

"I didn't see anything. I heard noise, someone running—two people, I think. I came back to look and found you."

So it made sense. The dark face had jumped me outside old Roth's door, and the gun with the blue suit had chased off the thin arm. I sat up. Lenny Gruenfeld clucked. The switchblade had been on the floor under me. I took out a plastic evidence bag, picked up the knife by the tip of the blade, worked it inside the bag with my lone arm. I slipped the bag into my pocket. Aside from a sore throat, a queasy stomach and some lightheadedness from blacking out, I seemed all right.

I stood. "What are you doing here?"

"Going up to Rosa's room. She's conscious, she'll need some clothes." She sounded happy, but not that happy. "She still doesn't know where she is, what happened."

The stairs and corridors were as empty as usual, no one wants to be seen when strangers pass in the Oneida. But a lot of them would be listening. I held on to the bannister and walls all the way up to steady myself. Lenny Gruenfeld unlocked her grandmother's room. Nothing had changed in the room, as cluttered and piled with books and newspapers as earlier, and as silent.

"She's lived here so long," Lenny said, "no one else could live in it without stripping all of her away."

"Your father thinks it's a garbage dump."

"He would."

I sat down, still shaky. Lenny opened drawers and the single closet. In a slim khaki canvas skirt and high fringed moccasins, a striped shirt of some stiff material like cotton ticking and a short jacket with a big sheepskin collar. I watched her as she moved around the chaotic room. She found a single tattered blue robe, a pair of canvas running shoes, some torn cardigans, one red flannel nightgown.

"Clothes are always the last thing she thinks about." She sat down across the room from me, all but her face hidden by a stack of books between us. "Clothes and comfort."

"Tell me about her and your father. About her husband Hans, your grandfather."

"I don't know a lot, neither of them talked much about the past or each other. My grandfather died long before I was born." She looked around the room, more to not have to talk than for any other reason. Her distance from everything included not talking much. "She was born in 1899. That seems so long ago."

"Not to everyone."

"To me it's the Dark Ages. Horses and wagons. Immigrants and labor fights. Political rallies in the streets. Workers and police fighting. That's how Rosa grew up. Her father was a radical immigrant from Germany, a socialist. Angry and violent."

"Sam Bronstein," I said. "Your great-grandfather."

"I can't feel anything that far back. A man who was Rosa's father, that's all. Her mother didn't care about politics, wanted her children to be rich and safe. The two boys thought like her, but Rosa listened to her father."

"She had two brothers?"

"Joel and Isaac, they're both rich."

"They're still alive?"

"As far as I know. My father would know."

"Why did he change his name? He says Rosa was in prison. You know what for?"

"Some labor trouble somewhere. I don't know where.

All I really know is he hates Rosa. I never even knew I had a grandmother when I was growing up. When I did find out he said she got his father killed, didn't care about anything except herself and her stupid ideas. He didn't want me to have anything to do with her, so I didn't. I was a good little girl back then."

"Aren't you now?"

"Not to him."

"But you know nothing about your grandfather, the trouble back then, enemies they had, your great-grandparents?"

There was something almost ridiculous about talking of those old world political passions, the nineteenth–century struggles when the workers were going to inherit the earth, to a slim, isolated American blonde of the late Nineteen Eighties.

"My father never told me anything, and Rosa never talked about the past. When I first found her she told me her parents had both died young just like her husband, but that's all. Her father died of tuberculosis from too much work and not enough food, and her mother of some kind of anemia that doesn't kill you today. The only reason she told me, I think, was that she wanted me to know she was surprised she'd lived so long, still expected the bosses, the Cossacks, to get her. But there wouldn't be any enemies alive from those days."

"People have children," I said.

She only shook her head as if memory that long was beyond not only her comprehension but her imagination as well.

"If she was born here, and her parents came from Germany, why does she rave about the Tcheka, talk about Cossacks?"

"I don't know." She stood up, the clothes in a bundle in her arms. "I better take these to her, the doctors say she could come back to normal any time."

"When did you change your name back to Gruenfeld?"

She turned back from the door. "How much time do you have?"

"As long as you need. Over some drinks?"

She looked at her watch. "All right. Two drinks."

I wondered about the precise number of drinks. Did she have an appointment or a low capacity?

10.

McNEELY'S IS ONE OF THOSE NEW SALOONS the owners have worked hard to make look like a refurbished landmark from the city's elegant turn-of-the-century past. We sat near a window, the clothing for Rosa under Lenny Gruenfeld's chair. I had a Beck's. She had vodka on the rocks. Rock music played somewhere.

"I always liked music," she said. "Had a three-girl band when I was still in junior high."

Outside the window the city passed in all its shapes and colors. It was on these streets that Irish and Italians and Jews had teemed and multiplied at the turn of the century when the real saloons like McNeely's had needed their cheap labor. The river that had brought them was only a block to the west, but they were gone, spread across the nation in seats of power and affluence. Those who teemed now were even more alien.

"We were pretty good. Even made some money. But my father hated it, and I believed what he told me then."

She looked out the window at the black, Latino and Asian faces that would bring change. Unpleasant change for believers in the old ways, but change that *will* come, and that when the new faces settle in and spread in their turn, lose their fears and defenses and anger, could be for the good.

"He doesn't believe in ideas or education, so he got me a job as an airline stewardess. I thought it was wonderful. Glamorous. Flying everywhere. Making money. I was important."

I watched the faces—Anglo; old immigrant; new black, brown and yellow—pass in the night. Someday it would be for the good, the mix, but not yet. A time of change, and in such times there is always hate and silence, fear and violence. A time of opportunism, of the valueless man, of the Colombian dope dealers with their savage methods and no values at all except to win.

"How did you come back to music?"

"I opened my eyes," Lenny said. "I' was peddling phony comfort, phony friendliness, phony sex, phony emotion, and I was being paid to do just that, taught to do it." She drank her vodka almost viciously. "I was offering drinks in a fake 'home,' always smiling as if you were the most important person in the world to me and I just loved you to pieces, swinging my tits and ass at the men, selling an illusion—that you were having a swell time, that you were in a safe home, that I was your sister, mother, girl next door and private whore."

She waved for the waiter. He had a badge on his jacket: *Hi! I'm Fred.* Lenny ordered another vodka.

"Was it good? Hey, great! Are we having another brew, too?"

The waiter looked at me, all wide eyes and smiling teeth.

"Not yet," I said.

"Hey, no hurry, right? One vodka on the rocks for my lady."

Lenny watched him walk away. "Airline attendants, waiters, salesclerks in expensive shops, travel agents, social workers, nursery school operators, television emcees, a hundred other kinds of jobs—all paid to sell phony emotions and fake feelings. To hide real feelings, their real emotions. Actors, that's what they are, all of them, and that's what I was."

The waiter, Fred, brought her vodka. We waited in silence until he left. His smile had the faintest dent around the edges. We weren't playing the game, but he was trained. He'd go on smiling through almost anything we did.

"We were hired for our ability to act. Taught to use our smiles every second, to always act as if the trip was a wonderful experience and we were part of it, even hint that afterwards, on the ground, maybe . . . *wink*. We were even trained to get rid of real emotions. Classes on how to not feel anger. There were no bad passengers, only ones who were 'mishandled.' Even if we lost two engines, hit an airpocket, we were supposed to go right on making everything seem safe and homey, never telling the truth."

Out on the avenue the cars honked and squealed brakes, the drivers shouted, and the pedestrians walked oblivious. No smiles out there, real or phony. Smiles were for the family, the tribe, the familiar. Private smiles. For the public face only anger. Maybe phony smiles were better.

"I was making a living as a liar," Lenny said. "I didn't know what my real feelings were. On the job I would go into robot, and off the job I felt emotionally dead. I didn't know what I really felt anymore, if I felt anything." She drank her vodka, and I didn't think her limit of two had anything to do with her capacity. "So I quit and started the band again. My father was furious. He didn't throw me out, but he charged me room and board until all I'd saved at the airline was gone. The band was getting some gigs, but we'd always be small time. I needed to study music, study guitar, learn theory. So I told my father I wanted to go to college. He said okay, but I had to go to Rutgers and live at home and major in something solid. He wasn't giving me a free ride while I majored in rock and men."

"Was that when you broke with him?"

"Them. My mother and brother, too. I came here, got a job and an apartment, started studying music at night at NYU." She looked at her watch. "I was a puppet in that airline job, selling fake emotion, living with a father and mother who don't know the difference. In the city, sharing a rathole with three other girls, working a two-bit job, studying all night, I felt real." She drank half of what was left of the second vodka. "Funny, it was then I found out what a real phony I was."

"Phony?"

"I'd always thought our name was Grenfell, then one day this old bag lady walks up to me on the street and tells me she's Rosa Gruenfeld and my grandmother."

"How did she find you?"

"I tried to get some money from my great uncles. My father told them to say no, of course, but Rosa found out I was in the city from them. She knew where I'd have to live if I had nothing and went to NYU, and found me."

"Rosa keeps in contact with her brothers?"

"She used to call them on the phone all the time, mail them pamphlets, drive them crazy. They were afraid to cut her off completely. Maybe Jehovah wouldn't forgive them."

"Where do they live?"

"Out in Great Neck, if they're still alive. Big houses side by side. They were younger, my father admired them. Younger and a hundred years older than Rosa." She was nursing her vodka now. I wished I'd had another beer. "She came to help me out, teach me about the city, show me the ropes, recruit me for the Party, for her causes." That almost-smile again. "She always had a cause. That first year it was the poor and old kicked out of their rooms and apartments around here by gentrification."

"What year was that?"

"Nineteen seventy-eight. I was just twenty. Out of the emotion-peddling business and New Jersey and the Grenfell lie, too. That's when I changed my name back to Gruenfeld. Rosa was happy, put me to work on the gentrification front." She looked at her watch again. "You know that two and a half million Americans are displaced every year, most of them old and poor, because landlords convert cheap rooming houses and apartments into luxury co-ops and condos?"

"Is that what Rosa talked about?"

"Rosa doesn't just talk. She had me working against tax abatements that encouraged the owners to gentrify. For more subsidized housing, shorter waiting periods, no age restrictions. Rent control and tough condo conversion laws."

"That's a lot of work for an old bag lady."

"Rosa was younger then, but she never slowed down." She drained her vodka. "I remember when Reagan's Health and Human Services Secretary told a conference on aging they could cut Medicare costs by taking better care of their health, like making sure they had a good, substantial breakfast. Rosa got up and told that well-fed fathead he was speaking to people lucky if they could afford one meal a day. People who were always hungry, usually cold and often on the streets. She suggested he should get the Marie Antoinette Award, preferably the same as Marie got." This time the smile was a real smile.

"She was still as active before she was shot?"

"Right up to the last time I saw her."

"When was that?"

"The morning she was shot."

"You were there?"

"Upstairs waiting for her. Maybe if I'd been downstairs—?" She stood. "We start playing in an hour. You want to hear us? We could talk more later."

It sounded like more than an invitation to music. I went with her.

11.

A LONG, CROWDED CAVERN NORTH OF HOUSTON STREET. We'd left the clothes at St. Vincent's, where Rosa was still in ICU. Lenny pushed me through, sat me at one of the tables on the edge of the dance floor facing the bandstand and disappeared. On the stand, technicians plugged in wires.

NoHo some called it these days. It had once been the Ghetto, where the Jewish immigrants came off the boats and started the last great flourishing of the Yiddish theater. Then the East Village with its jazz joints, dixieland and spillover of the Beat artists and hippies who couldn't afford the real Village. (With the Poles and Serbs and Croats coming between with Slovenian R.C. churches and Dom Polska halls.) Now the lair of the Colombian drug dealers and, inevitably, the artists and the musicians and, even more inevitably in New York, the latest hot crazes in saloons. The East Village, NoHo, it never changed.

A mixed crowd but without the artists. The prices were too steep. Packed with the quick, bright and empty young affluent, price their only standard. (A joke going around had it that when the Army paid $600 to a defense contractor for a toilet seat, the generals tried to cover up, Congress called for an investigation, and the

Yuppies wanted to know where they could buy one.) Almost innocent in their clean faces, three-piece suits, striped shirts, slim dresses, high-heels, narrow gold chains. Rubbing shoulders with the sleek Latino dope dealers with their depthless shark eyes and thin mouths, their flat-faced Indian bodyguards, their gaudy women. The grasping peasant mind and the pushing middle–class mind, both with no values beyond displaying their success to the world and to themselves, unconcerned about their countrymen in South America or Seattle.

I ordered an overpriced Amstel Light. A skinny black in camouflage fatigue pants and a T-shirt crossed the dance floor. He held a five-year-old girl by the hand and sat at my table.

"You a private eye?"

"So they tell me."

"Yeah." He needed a shave, the black T-shirt had an ape's head in a top hat on it. "It gonna hassle Lenny?"

"Hassle?"

"Cut her time. Blow her mind. Shoot the gigs."

"Ask her, Mr.—?"

"Matt. The Preps don't need a hassle."

"The what?"

"The group. The Monkey Preps. Lenny, me, Cap and the drummer. How long you known Lenny anyway?"

"Not very long."

"Yeah." He scratched his stubble. "This here's her kid. She says you should watch her."

He walked back across the dance floor and through a door at the left of the bandstand. The technicians were checking lights now, staring up into the dark of the ceiling. An emcee appeared to test the level of the center microphone. I smiled at the small girl. She wore jeans, the same T-shirt with what had to be the band's logo and blue tennis shoes. She didn't smile.

"What's your name?" I asked the child.

"Margo."

"Mine's Dan. Danny if you like it better."

The child blinked.

"Margo what?" I said.

"I don't know."

"Do you know how old you are?"

"Sure. Five."

The emcee had finished testing the microphone, put on a vast synthetic smile, raised his arms wide, asked the crowd if they were ready. There was a roar of response, and I realized the Monkey Preps were about to perform.

And perform they did.

Lenny was lead guitar in a skintight black satin body suit, white calf-high boots, leopard short jacket, French Army khaki bush hat with chin strap and brim jauntily pinned up on one side and oversize sunglasses. Her guitar was a red electronic synthesizer flashing in the stage lights. She played without expression, without movement, and I had the sensation that the dark glasses weren't to hide her eyes from the packed audience in the smoky club, but to hide the audience from her where she played alone inside her insulated bubble.

Two men moved violently on either side of her. The skinny black dressed now in a full American camouflage jungle uniform with a bright yellow bass guitar, yellow helmet liner, wide yellow rhinestone belt and yellow combat boots. And a sandy-haired Caucasian on keyboard in the black pajamalike uniform of the Viet Cong, a white headband with red oriental characters, an old-style cartridge belt and thick-soled thong sandals. Both of them pounded and gyrated around the almost motionless Lenny, with the drummer behind half hidden by his drum set, dressed all in white, his motionless face painted to look like a skull.

The effect was chilling. Violence on each side, frozen

time and a pale skull in the center.

Yet isolated. The motion of the violent men related only to Lenny in the center and never to the audience, as if that wall Lenny Gruenfeld carried was between them all and the screaming audience. As if they wanted no contact with their audience, with anything. Only the music.

I'm more Stravinsky than Sting. Mahler and Shostakovich instead of Belew and Fripp. Prokofiev, not Pink Floyd. But they were good, and the best rock, especially the guitar work—and Lenny's guitar work was the best—reminds me of Steve Reich, Terry Riley, John Adams and the other minimalists. Ornette Coleman and Chick Corea, the guitar of John MacLaughlin, the crossover between classic and popular.

Their drive was inescapable. The power. Lyrics sharp and clear. In complete command of their instruments. In complete control of their audience. The pound, the beat, the relentless drive all enhanced by sudden unexpected changes, marvelous instrumental work, the blending of the three voices as good as anything I'd heard from opera singers. And all isolated from the audience, alone amid the screaming crowd.

The set went on for thirty minutes, they filed backstage expressionless. Only the drummer stopped to sign an autograph book thrust at him. I ordered another overpriced beer, sipped. The club owner was glaring at me. I was at the performers' table, and I wasn't drinking expensive enough or fast enough to add much to the take. The little girl, Margo, sat in silence.

The skinny black appeared. "Come on back."

Lenny lay on a couch in the cramped cubicle of her dressing room, still wearing the black stage costume without the boots, leopard jacket or hat. There was a mirrored dressing table with the usual bulbs all around it, a rack for hanging her costumes and street clothes, a toilet and sink, some battered suitcases and a single straight chair. I sat.

"You're good," I said. "All of you, but mostly you."

Her eyes were closed, one arm over them. "I know."

"Couldn't you do better than this club?"

"Maybe."

She didn't seem terribly interested.

"Afraid you'd have to change style, play to the audience?"

Her arm still lay across her eyes.

"There's that," she said.

I was aware of her body. Of her. Of the couch and her blonde hair and her mounds and hollows.

"The name Kevin Regan mean anything to you?" I asked.

She moved her head, worked her neck side to side as if it were stiff. "Something about politics."

"A different Regan. He has a brother. Johnny Agnew. Did Rosa ever mention those names? Anything about them?"

I could hear her neck creak as she stretched it, watch the play of her flat belly muscles, the swell under the black satin body suit where the slim thighs joined. "I've been away a lot. Out of town."

"What about old Abraham Roth?"

Her arm came off her eyes, she looked up at the ceiling. "King of the slum. The rich hermit. Rosa knows him, tried for years to get some of his money for her work. He hates her, won't open the door to her. You think he shot her?"

"He's scared," I said. "I'd been talking to him when I was jumped in the corridor."

"He's always scared," she said. "You don't know the attack on you was even connected to Roth."

She turned her head, looked at me. From the corridor, a voice called five minutes to the next set. She looked away, sat up. "I wish I knew more, anything. That was the first day I'd seen Rosa in months."

"What about the Communist Party? Anything wrong there?"

"I'm not sure she even still belongs."

She stood, put on her slouch hat, boots and leopard jacket, slung her guitar around her neck. She smiled before she left the room. A smile for me? Kay Michaels was due in town next week, and I was getting too old for uncertainty.

12.

AFTER THE SECOND SET, Lenny, the child, the skinny black bass man and the keyboard player came out to sit at the table. Only the drummer was missing.

"He goes to college," the keyboard man said.

They were all still in costume, Lenny wearing her oversized dark glasses. The child, Margo, sat close to Lenny, touched her.

"He got plans like for the future," the black said.

"Don't you?" I said.

"He got your kind of plans."

"How do you know what my plans are?"

The keyboard man said, "Big bucks, big score, big rep, big house, big insurance, big headache."

I laughed. "Have you got the wrong guy."

"Whatever."

He gave me the same almost-smile as Lenny Gruenfeld. The same sense of distance as if in another time warp, a parallel but different universe. The two men reminded me of soldiers in Rome on leave from the front during World War Two. Alone in groups in the cafés, not talking much and then only to each other. Their bodies on the Via Veneto, but their minds still at the front.

"Dan Fortune," Lenny introduced as if she'd heard nothing at all, "Matt and Cap. Dan's working on who shot my grandmother. Matt's on the bass. This is my daughter, Margo."

"I've met Margo," I smiled.

The little girl moved even closer to her mother.

"Whose payin' him?" the black, Matt, said.

"I am," Lenny said.

"Why?" the keyboard man said. He was Cap.

"She's my grandmother."

"What's the matter with old Nikolai?"

Lenny raised an eyebrow. "The original cave man?"

"We got our own hassles to get down," Matt said. "Time 'n money back in the band."

"I hold up my end."

"The band's supposed to be first."

"It is!"

"Not all the time now," Cap said. "Maybe soon not enough. We all have grandmothers."

Lenny sat silent. Margo looked up at her. Lenny absently tousled the girl's thick hair. "That brain-dead father of mine doesn't care."

"The band," Cap said. "That's all there is."

Lenny went on stroking her daughter's blonde hair. It seemed to be an ongoing argument—Lenny Gruenfeld's time spent on something other than the band.

"You've been busy outside the band," I said, "but not with Rosa?"

"Charity work."

"Charity start at home," Matt said.

"Rosa's bleeding heart's big enough for both of you," Cap said.

I said, "You two know Rosa?"

"We met the old lady," Cap said.

"She got some powerful mouth," Matt said.

Lenny said, "It's hard getting old in this country. Old and poor and out of sight."

"It hard gettin' old anyplace," Matt said.

"Or poor," Cap said.

Time for the third set was coming close. Lenny looked down at Margo. The child smiled up. But Lenny wasn't really looking at her daughter.

"We send two messages to the old," she said. "The Golden Years, enjoy your grandchildren, the wars of life are over, take the satisfaction of what you've earned." Margo leaned close to her mother, held her arm, afraid of the tone of Lenny's voice. "But everything we do says if you're not young you don't count. If you don't work, buy, you're nothing. Get out of the way, die. If you're poor *and* old, don't have stocks, bonds, real estate, then die fast and disappear."

"Four-hundred-fifty a month and eighty percent of some of your medical costs," Cap said. "Live it up, grandpa."

"A nice one-bedroom only cost you four hundred a month," Matt said. "Three-fifty if you knows where to look."

"The *barrio* of beautiful downtown Tulsa," Cap said.

Lenny rubbed the child's thick hair, her voice as hidden as her eyes behind the dark glasses in the loud, crowded club. "The out of sight. Not crazy, or black, or brown, or foreign. Just poor and old. That's all Rosa is. Old and poor and out of sight, and someone shot her."

The little girl said, "Momma?"

Lenny patted the child's head. "It's okay, honey."

"You better find out then," Cap said.

"Shit," Matt said. "We got new songs to learn, out o' town gigs we could get."

I said, "She wasn't out of sight to someone."

Lenny said. "Enemies, yes, but killers? I can't believe

that. Even Neanderthal Nikolai needs a reason. Revenge isn't enough. What does he gain? They haven't even talked in years."

"Her politics? The Party?"

"The Party's dead, no danger to anyone. Not even itself."

The drummer stood over the table. "Time."

Lenny nodded to me. "Keep looking. I want to know."

They walked back across the empty dance floor and through the side door to the dressing rooms. I left the crowded club as it was turning into a madhouse. Enough booze in them, warmed up by the first two sets, they were ready to howl, rage, explode.

Outside it was dark and windy. I caught a taxi, told the driver to stop at St. Vincent's. The patrolman at the door of ICU nodded me through without even looking up from his magazine. He knew me now, and we all assume too much. Inside, the nurses were busy. Rosa lay in the same narrow bed, but the tubes and oxygen tent were gone. She opened her eyes, reached up to clutch my arm.

"Oh, you're here! I've had two men in my room all night!"

"What two men, Rosa?"

"Cabrera and him. The Gestapo. I told them to leave, but they wouldn't. They walked all over my room, Hans."

"I'm not Hans, Rosa. I'm Dan Fortune, remember?"

"Oh don't go on about that. I know who you are. I told them if they didn't go I'd throw water on them. But I didn't have any water. I must keep a bucket near the bed. That'll make him go, douse him with water. I know him. They hate water."

"Who do you know, Rosa?"

"I don't want men in my room. I'll throw water on them. Yes." Her bird eyes looked up at me. "That's what I'll do. Throw water on him."

"Who, Rosa?"

She seemed for an instant to struggle to answer, to know what I was asking. Then her eyes closed, and I'd lost her. She lay breathing quietly, asleep almost instantly. If I awakened her again, she wouldn't know what I was talking about.

As I went uptown to my own bed, I wondered if she ever would.

13.

THE WINDOW SMASHED, and I rolled off the bed in the same instant. We hit the floor together on opposite sides of the bed—whatever had smashed the window and I. It made more noise. I was bigger, but it was denser. Something hard, compact. About the size and weight of a 60-mm mortar shell or a large grenade.

My bed is a king box spring on the floor with a mattress on top. As good as a steel bulkhead. Maybe better. Six feet of mattress can stop more than sheet steel. I pressed tight to the bed. It hadn't exploded on impact, and you don't throw a bomb with a delicate timing mechanism through a third-floor window.

Nothing hissed or smoked.

Sooner or later you have to look. I took a breath. My lone arm down behind the bed, I raised up and looked.

A brick lay on the floor, shards of broken glass all around. An old brick with a piece of paper tied to it.

I put the brick on the kitchen table, swept up the broken glass and poured a cup of coffee from my automatic machine before I read the paper. *Man stay out of old man you don't gonna get hurt bad. You better heer reel good you no man? Reel bad shit.*

Illiterate, by someone who spoke English as a second language, it was meant to sound tough and sounded only juvenile. It didn't connect to the well-dressed blue suit in my vision in the hallway outside old Roth's door, but it could fit the skinny arm with the dark face and the knife.

I finished my coffee, dressed and went up to the precinct to give the note to Lieutenant Marx. It was another of the cool but sunny March days that make the city seem as clean and crisp as Montana. The crowds hurried. It was Friday, and the faster they got to work the faster they could get out and get home and enjoy life. It wasn't logical, but it seemed to make New York sense. Even Marx looked out the window of his office, watched some soaring pigeons as if they were eagles.

"Rosa could have seen something around Roth."

"We'll check."

"Anything else?"

"Not a flicker."

"Johnny Agnew?"

He shook his head. "Probably out of the city, state and maybe country by now. His kind don't worry about ruining a brother's new life. Regan should have known better."

"His penance for deserting the old ways."

"Yeah," Marx agreed, "a guy should act the way he's supposed to or it confuses us."

A cop who thinks that way won't go far. I reported in at Six Sport Cable and settled to watch. The morning went by, but when the office emptied for lunch my suspect number two, Greg, appeared carrying a case of converter boxes balanced on his incipient beer belly. He set the case down near the loading dock door, covered it with a canvas, went back into the main office.

It was all so matter of fact. Stealing from where you work was a routine matter of making an extra buck, no big deal. I watched him leave the front way, checked the loading dock door. It was locked on the inside. If there was a pickup, it would be made after lunch. I had at least an hour.

14.

THE HEADQUARTERS OF THE COMMUNIST PARTY U.S.A. is on the seventh floor of a building on Twenty-third Street. They own the whole building, publish a magazine and newspaper, still act as if they are a force in America. They cite figures to show how they help elect leftists and prolabor and antinuclear and anti-intervention candidates all across the country. They cite the power of labor. They aren't convincing.

When I asked to talk to someone about Rosa Gruenfeld the receptionist acted suspicious, but she finally sent me to a big craggy man who smiled from behind a desk in a small cluttered office.

"You don't look like FBI, *Newsweek* ain't interested in us no more, so maybe you want to join up? I like a guy that crazy."

He had the body and voice of an old bear, the wool shirt, work pants, boots and union button of a longshoreman. Gray hair, and a thick, crooked nose. The face of an Irishman and a drinker. Big hands. Most of the fingers had been broken, and more than once. His nose had been broken. Scars over both eyes. A bullet scar in his left cheek and half an ear gone.

"Dan Fortune," I said. "I'm a private detective. Rosa Gruenfeld's granddaughter hired me to find out who shot Rosa."

"Yeah, I heard about that. Who the hell wants to shoot

an old lady like Rosa?" He looked more closely at me. "I know you from somewhere. Ever work the docks? Ship out?"

"Merchant marine in the war."

"I remember the arm. You was just a kid, I was a premature anti-Fascist. Cops watched us both. I never forget a face." He stood, held out his hand. "Joe Kennedy, the other one."

He had six inches over me, and close up I saw he was in his seventies at least, with the wrinkles and lines and sagging neck, the slightly stooped shoulders. An old man, he'd worked hard all his life, and his body was ten years younger. But he moved stiffly as he came around the desk to clean books off the other chair in the office, a heavy limp in his right leg.

"Who does shoot Red Rosa," I said, "the bag lady Lenin?"

"Politics? You think we still worry someone that much? I mean, maybe we're doing somethin' right?" He grinned.

It was a cheerful grin, and his speech was pure blue-collar American without the trace of an accent. The great majority of Communist Party members his age had been immigrants or the children of immigrants raised in the Party, but Kennedy had all the marks of a native-born New York blue-collar working man.

"When did you join the Party?"

"The Depression. Breakin' heads at Ford." He studied me. "What you really want to know is how a good American got to be a Commie. Well, I looked around me when I was a kid, and I saw what was right and what was wrong, what got to happen to make it right, and I ain't had no reason to change my mind since."

"Spain?" I said.

"Jarama and Brunete. Seemed like a good idea at the time, still does. Maybe saved the big one and fifty million dead if the so-called democracies had joined us." He shrugged. "Old history. You didn't come around to talk about me."

"Tell me about Rosa and the Party. When did she join?"

"From the whistle. Busted from the old Socialist Party with Jack Reed and the others after the October Revolution. Stayed most of the run, too. Took it all."

"She was a leader?"

"Too independent, a maverick. Leaders got to do paperwork, compromise. Besides, when she was young she had the kids, let the men do the leadin'. We wasn't so different about the sexist stuff in them days. Like Russia ain't today. A lot of ideas don't go with a damn-all repressive bureaucracy like we had 'n they got." He laughed. "Hell, she stays through all the shit, 'n quits over the best thing we done overseas—Vietnam invadin' Cambodia, or whatever the hell they calls it now. I mean, we booted that crazy Pol Pot. But she says no way, 'n quits."

"Hard feelings? People don't like defectors. Especially when times are bad for the group."

"Christ, she was over eighty then! We didn't even collect dues, just kept her on the rolls. She'd gone her own way for years. Protested where and when she wanted. Told us all off at meetings. I mean, hell, she was like a mascot. The last of the old days. We was sorry to lose her."

"So she quit politics six years ago?"

"Just the Party. She went right on demonstrating, marching, protesting. Maybe the Party got too small for her. Real politics is dull as hell, even Lenin found that out. Rosa's too much a dreamer. Impatient to see heaven, right? Maybe that happens to all of us when we gets older. We ain't got a lot of time, we want something to change before we die. Leave a mark, no matter how small, you know? That's why old anarchists end up fightin' for a two-bit city park. People been fightin' in the streets all their lives turn into dreamers 'n start talkin' like they was Lenin himself gonna change the world with a speech."

"Is that what Rosa turned into?"

He shrugged. "Could be."

"What can you tell me about the past? Her husband Hans?"

"What do you want to know?"

"Anything and everything."

"You ain't got far, have you?" He grinned that cheerful grin. He hadn't let being the tool of an evil empire get him down. "Okay, that's a hell of a long time ago, but I know most of the story up to her goin' west."

He swiveled around in the ancient desk chair, looked out his single window at what he could see of the sunny city through a narrow space between buildings. "Her dad was an old socialist from Germany, her mother wanted to make a pile in the land of opportunity. They both died young of overwork, bad eatin', no health care. I guess the bosses didn't know the mother was on their side. Her brothers took after Mom, Rosa after Pop, right? The brothers wanted to help her, but she never had nothing to do with them, worked with Emma Goldman, Reed, everyone. Met Hans Gruenfeld on some barricade, I guess. They got married around nineteen-nineteen. They had two kids, Nikolai and Karla. Hans got killed in a labor riot in 1928, kicked in the head by a police horse in a charge."

The big Communist looked at his broken hands, remembering other riots, other police charges. "Rosa took it hard. Why not? She had a pair of kids, no husband, and the Party couldn't do a lot to help in those days. She was kind of sick for a couple of years but never thought of working for anyone except the Party, the Revolution. She had real hard times, I guess they all did. Then the Crash, the Depression, and things got better. For the Party, that is. Bad for the country, good for the Party, right? Folks get a lot more militant when they get laid off or locked out or the bosses move the plant where the labor's cheaper."

He shook his shaggy head as if he never would understand his fellow men. "It was a great time for organizing, a lot of people joined, we had more money. They sent Rosa out to California to help the farm workers 'n canneries 'n migratory pickers, used to be IWW before it got broken up 'n Haywood went to Moscow. Seems she did pretty good organizing out there for a year or so, then got married again to another organizer named Cabrera, and New York didn't hear much about her for a long time. She landed in prison around the start of the war, didn't get out until forty-six. She came back east, worked for us in New York right into the McCarthy shit, got married again and kind of dropped out of sight. A lot of us went underground around then."

"She got married a third time?"

"Ben Douglas. A newspaper man, wrote for *PM*, *The New Republic*, *Masses and Mainstream*, the *Guardian* overseas. Probably blacklisted. I was out o' town those years. Douglas died in the Sixties, Vietnam heated up, Rosa showed up again. She worked until maybe the mid-Seventies, goin' her own way, raisin' all hell at meetings." He laughed aloud. "She was a pisser when she got going on the leadership, factionalism, old fogies runnin' things. Hell, most of us was ten, twenty years younger, but she was right. I had my fights with the fogies myself." He shook his head again, maybe over the problems men think up even when they agree. "So she went her own way, an' in Eighty quit cold over the Cambodia invasion."

"You can't tell me more about the last two marriages?"

"Nope. Except marriage 'n the Party never seemed to mix too good for Rosa."

"And she hasn't worked with the Party in recent years?"

"The new members don't even know her. Not that we got that many new members these days." He gave me the cheerful grin.

"What keeps you going?" I said.

"The Party or me?"

"You."

He leaned back in the chair. "Hell, the cause was here long before me, it'll go on long after I'm gone. Men been fightin' for a fair, human society since before history started. Since the first guy grabbed more'n he could use because he was bigger 'n stronger, started livin' off other guys working. For a world that don't institutionalize injustice 'n corrupt human potential. A world in the interest of all the people, not just the few."

"Most people think they've got that now."

"Most people believe what they got told when they was born, don't ask no questions. Even Americans got to wake up to the shit they been fed someday."

He grinned again. A man who didn't easily discourage.

"But you don't think politics could have had anything to do with Rosa's shooting?"

"Not today politics. But Rosa been a socialist longer than the Party. Maybe someone got a long hate. It happens."

"Even in the rational world of true human potential?"

"Until we're all a new human being, you know it."

"Why would she rave about the Tcheka, Cossacks? She's native born, her parents came from Germany, not Russia."

"Just symbols of all political police to someone her age."

"The way Gestapo means any ruthless police?"

"Like that, yeah."

I got up. "Thanks."

"Sure you don't want to join?"

"I'll think about it."

He laughed. "Sure. Wait for bad times 'n the next crash."

15.

THE CASE OF CONVERTER BOXES was still at the loading dock door when I reopened the stockroom. Greg was taking a long lunch hour. When he finally showed, he was as hyper as a stoned teenager. He might as well have advertised.

I told the ex-basketball player I had an errand, hired a car at Fugazy's, parked it with a view of the loading dock and returned to the stockroom. Closing time came, and Greg went, but without the case of boxes. Was I wrong? No, petty thieves are as predictable as politicians in an election year.

The office emptied. Even the boss went home, with a glare at me. One man didn't go. A young salesman Greg's age, with the same mandatory macho mustache. I closed up shop and punched out. On the street I sprinted to the rented car and waited. It was a short wait. Amateurs are always in a hurry.

The dock gate slid up, the case of converter boxes slid out, the gate slid back down. Clever. In two minutes a panel truck turned into the alley, Laser Electronics painted on the sides. A real smooth operation. Two men got out, looked around in cool Hollywood fashion. One of them was Greg Mertz himself. Their eyes told me the cool look around was all an act—they were too nervous to see anything, were just playing out a game like kids making believe they were soldiers.

They grabbed the case, dropped it, dragged it to the panel, shoved it in, damn near caught their hands in the rear door, tumbled fast into the cab and hit the curb getting out of the alley. The truck made a beeline downtown, east across Fourteenth Street, and moved onto the East River Drive. I stayed pretty close. These two wouldn't spot anything short of a patrol car with its lights flashing.

They got off at Houston, did a loop around some blocks in one more shrewd move to throw off any pursuit their alert operation might not have prevented, then drove straight to a Fifth Street tenement. The salesman I'd left in the office appeared from the tenement. He must have run all the way. The three of them carried the case of converter boxes into the building. They'd left the doors of the truck open, so I waited. Sure enough, all three hustled out again and piled into the truck. They were laughing like hyenas, pleased as hell with their daring caper.

They drove away. I went into the building. The mailbox of the first floor rear apartment showed the names of Greg Mertz, Steve Downey and Warren Cochran. Pros all the way. The inner door was unlocked as usual. I knocked a few times at their apartment. No answer and no sounds from inside. I used my keys. The first worked on the main lock, the fourth worked on the deadbolt. The stuff was piled everywhere. There must have been six hundred converter boxes, fifty boxes of camera lenses, two dozen TV sets, cases of stereo components and ten computers complete with CRT screens and even printers. The boys had been busy.

I found the telephone under a coffee table, called Lieutenant Marx and got out of there. Marx and the East Side Precinct squad appeared in ten minutes, listened to my story.

"Okay, Dan. We'll need a written statement, and one from the guy who hired you. When we charge 'em we'll need your ident, and you'll witness at the trial if they don't cop out." He looked slowly around the apartment. "Cute kids."

"Anything on Rosa Gruenfeld?"

"Not a thing."

They were taking inventory when I left, had a call out for the panel truck, one man meeting the ex-basketball player to see if Six Sport had a different address on the third man or Greg Mertz, and a detective on his way to Laser Electronics. I drove my rented car back to Fugazy's and walked on to St. Vincent's in the fading March twilight just starting to chill. The Six Sport job was over, except for the statements, testimony if there was a trial and getting my money out of the ex-basketball player.

A doctor or orderly in white pants under a brown topcoat came out a side entrance of St. Vincent's. His face under a brown fedora was swarthy, his build was stocky, and his quick eyes saw me as soon as I saw him. He went around the corner, and I went after him. Up the avenue he was getting into an illegally parked car. A dark blue Ford sedan that pulled away before I could get the number or the state.

I went up to Rosa's floor. The same nurse was on station. She'd had time to establish her correctness in her own mind.

"No, that man wasn't here again, and if he had been I'd have let him visit Mrs. Gruenfeld. He was a friend, and she needs to see people if she's ever going to come back to normal."

The patrolman on guard had never doubted his actions.

"No one looked in on her today, Fortune, except the docs and nurses and the Lieutenant."

"Marx talk to her?"

"He don't report to me."

In the narrow ICU bed Rosa was propped up, saw me

with those empty bird eyes and reached out one skinny veined hand.

"Oh, thank goodness you're here! Has he gone?"

"Has who gone, Rosa?"

"Him! I saw him."

"Who, Rosa. Tell me."

"Oh you know. Don't pretend. You always knew."

Her eyes had darkened, clouded, the brightness replaced by a petulance. Turned darkly inward, the empty bird stare gone.

"Who am I, Rosa?"

"I married you, didn't I? I must have been crazy." Cunning came into her small watery eyes. "You thought I'd forget you, didn't you, Flaco? Cabrera the skinny one."

"Cabrera's dead, Rosa."

Anger now. "Of course you're dead! They sent me to prison. Traitor! Cossack! Liar!"

"Why was Cabrera a traitor? Why did you go to prison?"

She glared up at me. "Money! Is that what you want? Go away. You've done enough." She closed her eyes, lay back.

"What did Cabrera do, Rosa?"

She breathed there in the bed, her eyes closed. "Handsome Flaco. Skinny one. So many of them are fat, Mexican men. Dark and handsome. Corrupt. So corrupt." Her eyes opened. "I know you! What do you want?" Seeing not me or the room but some vision inside her mind. "Go away! Go away!"

The nurse pushed me aside again, calmed the old lady. The doctor stood beside me.

"You don't have a therapeutic effect on her, Mr. Fortune."

I said, "It's like trying to break through a transparent wall. You can see her, but you can't reach her."

"That's exactly what it's like. A one-way crazy mirror.

Distorted, and you don't know what she can see or hear, what's real or dementia. What really happened, what didn't and when. Difficult for you and the police, but now she's had enough."

"When will she be rational?"

"I wish I knew, Mr. Fortune."

I called Lenny Gruenfeld's home number from a pay phone in the lobby. She agreed to take me to see her father over in New Jersey tomorrow morning. I walked through the packed Friday evening streets, everyone having a hell of a time. Even the businessmen on their way home had their ties loosened. That's why I noticed him. He was walking behind me as I reached Fourteenth. Three-piece blue suit, striped tie, shined black shoes, briefcase. So neat, cool, impervious.

Then he turned on Fourteenth as I crossed, and I forgot about him. Until I saw him again across the avenue. Or someone a lot like him. I walked over to Eighth, did some twists and turns and came back to Seventh. He was nowhere around. It could be something, it could be nothing. I opened a Beck's in my office and went back to thinking about Cabrera. I wanted to know a lot more about Flaco Cabrera, about his death and Rosa going to prison.

16.

"FRANCISCO CABRERA," Nicholas Grenfell, once Nikolai Gruenfeld, said. "Pancho the Great. Flaco. My wonderful stepfather. God, Rosa could pick them! A wispy dreamer who cut cloth for someone else ten hours a day, read books all night instead of looking out for himself and his family or giving his son ten minutes, and couldn't even get out of the way of a horse! And a crooked *cholo* who drank all day, beat her, treated her like some Indian squaw, was away half the time and in jail the other half. At least he knew how to take care of himself. I'll give Flaco that much. He was a man, not like Saint Hans, my angelic father."

"What about the third husband? Ben Douglas?"

He was casual now, informal. A cream-colored Egyptian cotton safari shirt open at the collar, gray golfing slacks pleated in the fashion coming back these days, black half-boots.

"Never met him. I don't think he was any better. A writer no one wanted to read, a journalist who couldn't even hold a job. Not a good word for his own country! Right on target for Rosa."

We were in the antique living room of the large house just south of Dover. Grenfell's wife sat watching us. I was in a pale green brocade wing chair with an antimacassar on the back for greasy heads. The wife wore a darker green dress that set off her silver blonde hair, looked as if she wasn't sure I was clean enough for the chair even with the antimacassar. Grenfell leaned against the ornate marble mantle above the wrought-iron decorated fireplace with its brass andirons and firetools.

Lenny wasn't with us.

"I'm not going in," she had said when we parked in the gravel turnaround beside the big house.

I'd picked her up that morning in the car I'd re-rented. She lived in a renovated brownstone on Perry Street just off Hudson, was waiting for me on the sidewalk in the dark corduroy jeans, turtleneck and western boots. She carried an acoustic guitar in its case and a backpack, tossed them into the back seat of the two-door Ford as she got in.

"You going to sing for your father?" I asked.

"A rally in North Paterson."

She sat silent as I drove through the Lincoln Tunnel to New Jersey. Not sullen or preoccupied, alert to what was passing as we climbed the Palisades and drove out across the Jersey Flats, but silent. She simply had no need to talk.

"A rally for what in North Paterson?"

"Isaiah Monroe."

If you were under thirty-five, hated sports, never watched or even owned a TV set, maybe you wouldn't have heard of Isaiah "The Wind" Monroe. But if you were over thirty and did any of those things, there was no way you could have escaped Monroe. Or if you were a cop anywhere in the country. Or a politician, especially a black politician.

"I thought he lost the second trial."

"He did."

"Then why a rally?"

"For a third trial, and a fourth, and fifth and however many it takes to finally get an honest one and free him."

She turned back to look out the window before she'd even finished talking. The subject wasn't open for discussion. It would make no difference to her what I said or thought.

"What can you tell me about Rosa's second husband, Cabrera, or her third, Ben Douglas?"

"Nothing."

"Try."

It must have been my tone of voice. She looked at me instead of at the scenery of the outskirts of Passaic as we approached the junction with U.S. 46.

"I'm sorry, Mr. Fortune. Going out to the Dover house does this to me."

"Dan," I said. "Okay?"

She watched me as if not sure "Dan" was okay.

I said, "Was growing up in Dover that bad?"

"Not then, no. It is now. Now I know how obscene it was. How obscene my father is."

"And Isaiah Monroe is good?"

"He's the future. The refusal to make ourselves robots."

Isaiah Monroe had come out of the ghetto of North Paterson on a double track. A magnificent athlete in every sport and a juvenile militant in trouble with every authority. Convicted at twelve of the savage beating of a white teacher who had attempted to eject him from a class, he was sent to Jamesburg State Home for Boys, an institution that looked like a college campus complete with "house mothers and fathers," but that was a place that took difficult children and broke them into mindless animals or hardened them into total enemies, started them through the system: Annandale Reformatory, Bordentown, Trenton State Prison.

"I'm sorry, Dan. I don't know anything about Cabrera or Douglas. I didn't know Rosa then, my father never talked about her or them, and she doesn't talk about them now."

She was facing me instead of the houses of Troy Hills where I switched to Interstate 80 and headed on west. A small crack in that shell of distance she carried with her.

"How'd you become involved in the Monroe thing?"

"Matt knew Monroe at Rutgers. Before Matt went to the army and Monroe went to prison. His people asked us to play at a fund-raiser last year before the second trial."

"Is Rosa working for Monroe, too?"

"I don't think she ever heard of him. It's not her kind of fight. No socialist theory, no international politics. Just one man's right to be himself, do what he has to."

"It's more than that, Lenny."

"No, not really."

She turned away again. We had reached Denville and

U.S. 46 to Dover, I had to pay attention to the road. She said nothing more until she took me off the highway to her parents' house.

It was a giant, sprawling brick and fieldstone Colonial with peeling white trim and an authentic center section that must have been there when Washington marched on Trenton. On three or so acres of oaks, maples, birch and other trees I couldn't name, with very little lawn, a circular gravel driveway and smaller houses crowding out from Dover all around it.

"I'm not going in," Lenny said, laid her head back against the headrest and closed her eyes. I didn't argue with her.

As I approached the house I sensed an uneasiness about it. The small houses were too close. The Cadillac inside the open doors of the four-car garage a little old and unkempt, the only other car in the garage a Honda. The grounds a little ragged, the brass on the front door unpolished. Like a grand old lady who was neglecting her appearance. Even the brocade chair where I sat and listened to Nicholas Grenfell, once Nikolai Gruenfeld, was overdue for a cleaning, and all the brass of the fireplace wasn't polished.

"How long have you hated your parents, Mr. Grenfell?"

"As long as I've been old enough to hate, Mr. Fortune."

"That's a long time."

"I only wish it was longer." He came away from the fireplace. "I wasted a lot of tears when I was a boy before I understood I didn't want the love of people such as my parents."

His voice had that tone of violent challenge that says—you think I'm unreasonable, excessive, vicious, paranoid? Ask me why I hate them. Go ahead, ask me!

"I'm sorry," I said.

He reddened under his tan, the small mouth set in a hard line. It wasn't what I was supposed to say, and his pale brown eyes had to calculate—was I sorry he hated his parents, or sorry they had been so bad? Should he explain, or tell me to go to hell? The wife saved him from the dilemma. It was something I expected she had done many times before. They were a team.

"A father should think of his family before he goes out and risks his life for an abstraction, Mr. Fortune. He is risking their lives, too, their future. A mother should stop a man from risking his life, abandoning his duty, neglecting, in the end deserting, his son for a chimera of an idea."

They'd talked about it, thought about it, had it all down. Grenfell had thought about it for fifty years, and now he talked with his hands in the antique living room. "I was four when he died, barely remember him. He was never home even before he got killed. Wherever home was. Some one-room walkup on the Lower East Side with no heat and the toilet down the hall. But I don't really remember, we were never in one place long enough. We grew up with strangers, my sister and I. Babysitters from the Party, communal day care by the Party, shop stewards, neighbors, anyone, so they could demonstrate, march, riot. I wasn't raised by Rosa, I was raised by the Party. Whenever she had to go somewhere on Party business, which was all the time, she dumped me with some Party member. In the summer we went to Party camp in Peekskill. Every Party member was my parent, and no one was my parent. I never knew who my mother was, never knew who I was, never had a private friend or a real friend. Talk about lonely in a group. I was lonely and miserable surrounded by every little Communist in New York. And all because of a Party that wanted to destroy the country I was part of. My country!"

The late March afternoon was warm in the stuffy living room, and Grenfell sweated as he raged over the wounds of a boy almost sixty years ago. Yesterday was as real to him as me sitting in his elegant living room. The wounds that had dominated, even determined, his life. Ugly sweat stains under the arms of the rich cream shirt like the blood of memory.

"Your shirt, dear," the wife said. "It's warm in here."

Grenfell stiffened as if she'd told him the house was on fire. She got up and opened the windows. Methodically, one after the other. Grenfell sat down on the antique couch, held his arms out to dry the shirt. We both waited. They were like a prizefighter and manager. Grenfell went into the ring, the wife managed, manipulated, handled the public relations.

"She should never have had children," Grenfell said, almost to himself, arms out like wings to dry the sweat from his shirt. "Both of them."

"That wouldn't have been too good for you."

"Being alive isn't enough, Fortune. It's how you're alive."

"You got even with them," I said. "You changed your name, pretended you didn't have a mother."

The wife finished with the windows. "You sound hostile, Mr. Fortune. Have you ever experienced the terrible abandonment a child feels when parents give their lives to something outside the home, outside the family? When they neglect, ignore, don't even consider the needs of the family, the children. Parents whose whole lives are devoted to themselves, to an abstraction? Something the child has no part in, no understanding of, but sees himself abandoned for."

Partner, manager and maybe trainer, too.

"My father was a cop," I said. "That's something like what you mean. It hurt my mother, I don't think it hurt me."

"Perhaps because you did have a mother," the wife said.

She had a point. My father eventually caught one of the men my mother turned to because he was away and in danger, beat him to a pulp and was booted from the NYPD for his trouble. Then he was gone for real and for good, and my mother wasn't alone much after that when I needed her, but she was there.

"She had no time for either of us even when we were teenagers," Grenfell said. "Out there in California where we knew no one, lived in a migrant labor shack ten miles out of town, waited in the dust for the school bus. Most of the migrants were wetbacks or *braceros* or from ten other states. Single and alone. No children out there to play with. No wonder Karla got into trouble. Rosa didn't have time to raise a daughter. Too busy organizing, talking in the fields. They loved her—*La Gringa.* If she wasn't making speeches she was waiting on Flaco. Cooking, sewing, washing, fixing the shack, anything and everything for *Senor* Cabrera like any *pachuco* wife." He shook his head, arms still spread wide to dry his sweat. "I took it until Flaco got killed and she went to prison. I waited a year, then I went. It was nineteen forty-one. I faked my birth certificate, enlisted, came home a captain and never looked back. Captain Nicholas Grenfell, an American instead of an enemy of the country."

"Fighting the economic system isn't fighting the country."

"You sound like the Party," Grenfell said.

"Sorry," I said. "I don't change what I think because someone unpopular agrees with me. Where is your sister now?"

"She died years ago. An abortion. Rosa wasn't there."

"Is there any chance Flaco Cabrera's still alive?"

"Alive? Flaco? My God, what an imagination. Flaco

was killed by the police in California forty-eight years ago. The same day Rosa was arrested." He leaned forward, hands clasped and elbows resting on his knees, a man about to tell a story.

The wife stood. "If you're going to tell that story, we should have coffee. I'll take Arlene some, too. She won't talk to me, but she'll drink the coffee."

Grenfell still leaned forward as if he hadn't heard any of what she said, already back somewhere in 1940 with his mother and Francisco Cabrera. Flaco, the skinny one.

17.

THERE ARE FOUR OF THEM. In their khaki cavalry twill uniforms they tower over her. Their trooper hats, holsters, guns, billy clubs, black boots. They look at her as they always do, cold and insinuating. She is the Anglo woman who sleeps with the god-damned greaser. One of our women who lets one of them fuck her.

"What have you done to him this time," Rosa says.

Small, she wipes the steam and sweat from her face with the sleeve of the faded green print dress. She has already stood up from her knees beside the tub of soap suds and boiled water where she does the laundry. Twice a week. Monday and Thursday. This is Monday. Stands and glares at them, dries her hands. Flaco had been home, sober, for the first Sunday in months. There were no rallies or meetings in the fields today.

"It ain't what we done, Ma'am," the oldest says. "It's what he done. He home, maybe?"

He wears a tie, the older one. His uniform is neat, clean, tailored. Not like the three red-necked men around him with their hands on their pistol butts, eyeing her as if they can see every inch of her body through the print dress. Two boys and a narrow-faced man in his thirties, their shirts open, uniforms ill fitting and wrinkled, and Rosa knows this time is different. The older man is the Sheriff himself. Serious, even solemn, calling her "Ma'am" even though she knows he knows who she is, not only a whore who sleeps with a *pachuco,* but a Commie, too.

"I haven't seen him since this morning. You can look."

"We will, Ma'am," the Sheriff says, nods to the deputies.

The three deputies spread out through the three-room shack. It won't take them long, the two bedrooms barely large enough to turn around in, Karla and Nikolai still in school or waiting for the bus with all the other farm children.

"You have a new lie to tell about him?" Rosa says to the Sheriff.

"No lies, Mrs. Cabrera."

Then she knows it is serious. No one has called her Mrs. Cabrera since she married Flaco. Red Rosa, Commie bitch, Hey *Senora,* other less genteel names, but not Mrs. Cabrera.

The three deputies return. The weasel-faced older one shakes his head. The Sheriff motions them outside and circles a finger—they will surround the shack and watch. The Sheriff sits down, nods to Rosa to sit also. There is no doubt who the host is, who owns the castle. It might be Rosa's house, but it is the Sheriff's county. Rosa remains standing. The Sheriff seems to think for a time. Then he takes off his trooper hat, wipes his balding head, shakes his head as he watches her.

"You're alone now, you and your kids. Ain't no time to be hardhead. Sit down."

She stands. Defiant, belligerent. She's been fighting

this corrupt society too long to bend now. No matter how scared she is. No matter what.

"What have you done to Flaco? We've got lawyers. The union. The Party."

"That's the trouble with you radical people," the Sheriff says. "You got no give. Give and take, that's what gets you ahead. Folks don't like people know the way it all got to be."

"We'll beat you. No matter what you've done to him!"

The Sheriff continues to sit and watch her. She realizes that he is really watching her. As if there is something he does not understand. But when he speaks again it is only a statement. Flat, simple.

"He's killed Mr. Bannister."

A simple statement that carries a weight of overtones, the finality of a death sentence. It is a death sentence. Rosa is as cold as she has ever been. Colder than when they told her Hans was dead. In this county, this state, no one kills Mr. Bannister. Hans died fighting the Cossacks, not murdering someone. Hans fought the murderers, did not join them. She resists.

"Flaco couldn't get close enough to Mr. Bannister to even recognize him," Rosa says.

The Sheriff stares at her, a fixed gaze as if there is still something he can't believe, yet is beginning to believe.

"You don't know about him, do you?"

"Know about who?"

She says it, still defiant, but she knows who.

"That's a Mex for you," the Sheriff says. "Thought you Commies were different, liberated and all. Guess the Mex comes first, the Commie second."

"Is he dead already? All this window dressing so I'll think you haven't killed him already?"

"How do you think he got close enough to Mr. Bannister?"

"He didn't."

"He was working for Mr. Bannister before you ever come out here, Miss Gruenfeld. You should have stayed in New York."

"No."

"For Bannister, the other owners. Even for me when I needed someone on the inside to tip me off."

"No."

"A Mex got no politics when there's money around. Someone should have told you and your New York people that."

She could go on saying no forever, but each time she says it she knows with greater certainty that it is true. It is Flaco. She has lived with him too long, knows him too well. She becomes aware of eyes, movement, and turns to see Nikolai at the bedroom door. His face is as neutral as ever, but she sees the shock in his eyes. She does not know how long he has been there. Lately he has taken to climbing in the window, not speaking to her or his sister when he comes home.

"The boy," Rosa says.

The Sheriff looks. "He's got to know sometime."

Rosa looks at the boy's expressionless face. He doesn't like Flaco, but he respects him, imitates him.

"Where is Flaco?" Rosa says.

"He ran out after he shot Mr. Bannister. That's all anyone's seen of him. He won't get far on foot."

"He knows you'd come here."

The Sheriff shrugs. "Guys on the run do crazy things."

He gets up wearily. He is not a young man. Rosa wants to offer him a cup of coffee, tell him to sit down again, rest. It is her weakness, mothering, so she says nothing. She hates this man, everything he is or stands for. He adjusts his pistol belt, walks to the door.

"If he comes here, don't help him. Call us."

Rosa says, "You think these shacks have telephones?"

"Just yell. We'll hear you."

Then he is gone. The boy comes from the bedroom. Together they listen to the Sheriff's car drive away. They both know there are other cars out there, and at least one will not drive away, will sit hidden where the deputy can watch the shack.

"He's lying, isn't he, Mom?"

"No, that's Flaco."

"Then he had a reason! He was spying."

"Money. That's all Flaco needs to betray the Party."

"What's the Party ever done for us! I hate the Party!"

The boy runs out of the shack. Sixteen is a difficult age for a shy, bookish boy who feels himself "different" from the other sixteen-year-old boys. She knows it is her fault, hers and Hans's and even Flaco's, but there is nothing she can do about it. She made her choice long ago. She sits for a time, listens to the sounds of the fields all around the shack, cars passing on the blacktop highway to the west, distant voices. She is waiting for the sound of guns, screams. They do not come, so she gets up and finishes her laundry.

Karla comes in two hours late, says she went home from school with a friend whose father just drove her out. Karla says Nikolai cut the last half of school and that is why he was home early. He probably walked all the way. At another time there would be lectures and recriminations, but not today. Rosa tells the girl about Flaco. The girl doesn't like her stepfather, but she is afraid of violence and has to lie down she is so afraid.

Rosa makes dinner, setting a place for Flaco out of habit. She looks at the place for some time, leaves it. As she is getting dinner, setting the table, moving around the shack, she is listening. For what she is not sure. Flaco would be a fool to come to the shack. He will know that the deputy is outside waiting for him. That the Sheriff has told Rosa the whole story. That Rosa will want nothing more to do with him. That her choice was made long ago. Yet she listens. Perhaps for the sound of the gunfire that will end it.

Only it is not gunfire that comes to the shack. It is Flaco. Long after dinner. The children are in bed. The deputy outside is a new one whose car drove up to replace the first some two hours ago. Flaco comes, not to the door, but to the window of their bedroom. A soft rubbing against the sheet of heavy cellophane he nailed up himself. Rosa lies there listening until his voice finally whispers, desperate.

"Rosa? It is Flaco. Rosa?"

She gets up and pushes open the window. Flaco climbs in hurriedly, as quick and lithe and muscular as a cat. Even now she remembers and feels his body. On her. Inside her.

"Traitor!"

Flaco grins. "Slick, huh? Nobody tumble."

He is tall for a Mexican, over six feet, and slim. Flaco. He is still grinning as he goes to the broken and scarred bureau where he keeps his possessions. Murder sits lightly on him.

"You killed a man."

"Hey," rummaging in his bureau, "the old bastard tried to cheat me, say he not pay me for a job, gonna tell the union about me. I hit him, *ay*? He got a gun in his desk. I grab, you know? We fight. The old son of a bitch."

He turns. He has his pistol in his belt. His rosary, the one his mother gave him before she died. The picture of his mother and father in the silver frame. His dead sister's gold crucifix, his vaquero belt with the silver conches. His decorated vaquero vest. He grins under his thin mustache.

"I send for you, okay? In Mexico. Soon."

He comes to kiss her. She turns her head. He shrugs.

"You won't get far. Who's going to help you around here?"

He grins still. "That deputy, he sleep in his car, *ay?*

"The police, the union and the Party."

He scowls, close to her. "Fuck the Party an' the union! You got a dream world, you know? You an' your fucking Party. A man he got to look out for hisself."

"The money. We never saw it. You never spent it on us."

"Sure I spend on you. Some." He laughs soundlessly, leans down close to her face. "Nobody look out for Flaco Cabrera 'cept Flaco Cabrera. I show you money, you want to know where it come from. I tell you, you turn me in. To the Party. So I don' tell you. I take care of Cabrera. When I get to Mexico, I send for you. You come, you don't come, what the hell."

"The children?"

"Sure, why not? I got plenty money."

"Judas! *Cabron!*"

Half smile, half scowl in the dim bedroom, his decorated vest on, his vaquero silver belt around his waist, the pistol in his belt, the rosary and silver frame in his hands, the gold crucifix around his neck.

"You'll never get to Mexico. All I have to do is scream."

"No, you don't do that, Rosa, *ay?*"

He is gone. Out the window as soundless as he came in. She does not scream. She will not go to Mexico, but she does not scream. She remembers his body, and it would not help the Party, and the Sheriff is still the enemy. So she does not scream, and there are no shots, and no distant gunfire long after he has gone. Only Nikolai who stands in the bedroom door.

"He's gone, isn't he."

"Yes."

"He's not coming back. He took his rosary and his pistol."

"And his sister's crucifix."

"I hate you."

"Go to sleep."

It is two days later when the Sheriff comes to the door with his trooper hat in his hands. The deputies behind him all look pitying. Flaco is dead.

"My men caught him trying to get through a roadblock in the back of a pickup. He got into a field, wouldn't stop, had a gun. They shot him. He's out in the truck."

She's thankful the boy and girl are in school as she walks out to the pickup where the deputies wait. She tries to know what she feels as she goes. Loss? Some, she has lived with Flaco for seven years. Grief? Sorrow at least? She tries, but there is only a kind of indifference. He was her husband, they had loved, but he had been a cheat, a liar, a traitor the whole time. He betrayed her. Betrayed the union, the Party and so her. Life is too short to fight for more than one truth. She has her truth, she and her father and Hans, and she will live for it and, in the end, for it alone.

Hate? Yes. And fear. She has always had the fear when the violence came, but you can't let fear stop what you have to do. She looks into the truck. The body is covered by a canvas, blood on the truck bed. A deputy pulls down the canvas so she can see Flaco's face. The dark eyes are closed, the mustache streaked with blood, the gaunt brown face narrow. The face of a wolf.

"What will you do with him?"

"We have to have an autopsy, an inquiry," the Sheriff says. "Then we'll send him back to Mexico to his family."

"I should bury him."

"You got your own problems. Accomplice to murder. Aiding a fugitive escape. Anything else I can think of."

"That's all lies!"

"We don't want you here. You, the union, your Party.

Killing Mr. Bannister gives us all we need to get rid of all of you."

"My children?"

"Tell your Party friends to take care of them."

He takes her to his car. The truck and Flaco's body and the deputies drive off. The Sheriff takes her to the school to get the children before they go to the jail.

18.

NICHOLAS GRENFELL LEANED IN THIS CHAIR. "They sent her to prison for ten years. Karla and I were taken by the Party. They didn't love us." His smile was as wolflike as his description of Francisco Cabrera. "I told them Flaco had been better than any of them. Flaco was a patriot, they were traitors. It didn't go over well. I stayed until I was seventeen because I didn't have anywhere else to go. Then I changed my name, joined the army."

"What happened to your sister?"

"She got involved with some soldier. He was shipped out." He looked up from where he sat, his hands clasped in front of him. "I was in the army, Rosa was in prison. Karla died alone in a motel room in San Diego."

The wife took it up like a Greek chorus. "I think you can understand now why Nicholas wants nothing to do with his mother, Mr. Fortune? Why, yes I'll say it, we don't care who shot her. Her total devotion to an evil idea injured her family terribly."

"I can understand it."

"But not approve?"

"I'm not much on hate. Everyone has reasons, even Hitler."

"How noble, Mr. Fortune."

"Your daughter doesn't hate her, Mrs. Grenfell. She has her reasons, and so did Rosa."

Grenfell almost jumped up. "My daughter's as sick as her grandmother! Just ask Isaac and Joel. Rosa turned her back on her dying mother, turned her back on them!"

"Do you have their addresses?"

"Addresses? You don't think they know anything about Rosa?"

"Someone shot her, Mr. Grenfell. Maybe you don't care, but your daughter does, the law does, and I do."

He sat there, and he didn't like me. "My uncles live at 204 and 206 Sycamore Drive in Great Neck. They're very old men, they deserve to be treated with respect."

"I'll do my best," I said.

"I hope you're getting paid for all this snooping."

"Your daughter makes good money."

He shook his head in disbelief. "For that noise she and those cretins make! We've lost all sense of values."

"I'll give Lenny the message," I said.

It was my exit line. I turned to leave, but the wife wasn't going to let me get away with it. She said, "Arlene and we heard each other's messages long ago, Mr. Fortune."

Outside the big house Lenny was still seated in the car. A cup and saucer stood in the gravel driveway. She hadn't even carried them to the front door. It was her message.

"What's your mother's name? He never introduced us."

"That sounds like my father. She's Alette. That's how I got Arlene," she said. "Take 46 back to 80 going east."

"Don't you want to know what I found out?"

"About them and Rosa? I've heard it all."

"About Flaco Cabrera."

"Okay. Tell me."

I told her.

"So that's why Rosa went to prison. What kind of men, human beings? Cabrera and that Sheriff?"

"A man out for himself, and a man doing his job. Human beings who believed in what they were supposed to do."

We reached Interstate 80 East at Denville and pulled on into the traffic. She watched the cars that passed. With one arm I'm not about to be a cowboy. She didn't seem to care.

"Monroe says they give up nothing they don't have to, and nothing will change without violence."

"Black, brown, yellow and poor should carry guns, stand up for their rights," I said. "That didn't help at his trials."

Isaiah Monroe had spent three years in Jamesburg, came out determined not to end up in Trenton State Prison, to never again do anything they could arrest him for. He became a great high school and then Rutgers athlete. He joined a radical black party that marched, protested, carried guns to the state house. But Monroe didn't carry a gun or do anything to be jailed for. He made speeches, wrote articles, told the poor and minorities to arm themselves. And wherever he went he had bodyguards to protect him so that he would never have to even bend a law.

"Nothing could help at those trials," Lenny said. "Go off on 287 north past Paterson."

"You're so sure he didn't kill those men? You weren't out of high school when it happened."

"I never knew anything about Monroe or the murders when I was in high school. I know now."

"And now you're sure."

"Now I'm sure."

When he finished at Rutgers, professional teams in four sports drafted Isaiah "The Wind" Monroe. The radical party got into riots, armed conflicts. The FBI wanted them outlawed. But Isaiah Monroe was too good for the pros to lose—FBI, violence, treason or whatever. Money was money, and Isaiah Monroe was money. Big money. He chose football *and* baseball, National Football League and National League. Both leagues had to bend rules to let him try out for both, but money is money. Publicity is publicity. Publicity *is* money.

"You ever meet him, talk to him?"

"Get off on 504 past Preakness Hills. The next exit after is North Paterson, " she said. "Yes, I've met him."

"Is he what they say? Violent behind the education. A volcano. Insane behind the charisma?"

"He's fifteen years older. He's in prison. He's polite."

"That's hard to believe."

She turned her head to look at me. "Why? They took the whole world away from him, locked him up for fifteen years. You don't think that might affect a man?"

The uproar was in and out of sports. The rules shouldn't be bent even for Isaiah Monroe, no one could play two pro sports. An anti-American hate-peddler shouldn't be allowed to make money out of the country he attacked. Sports heroes should be examples for the young, not advocates of treason, violence. A juvenile jailbird shouldn't be allowed to get rich on the public's money. Loud but local. Monroe wasn't yet a national name, only a possibility. Then five men were gunned down in the bar of the White America Club of North Paterson. By two blacks. Monroe and another member of the Black Liberation Force were identified by two survivors and two witnesses, sent to prison for life.

"There were four witnesses," I said as I took the North Paterson exit.

"Left to Courthouse Square," she said. "Two survivors on the critical list for weeks, and two white thieves. You want me to laugh now or wait until I get out?"

Courthouse Square in North Paterson could have been

in a thousand towns of northeastern America. A pre-Civil War gray stone courthouse with two four-story wings and a central tower with a darker gray slate dome, fire escapes on the outside added at the turn of the century when safety for workers began to be considered. Flat-fronted gray stone and brick buildings on the other three sides. Storefront and columned office entrances. Neon signs and old painted signs. A grass park in the center crossed by concrete paths, benches along the paths, the statue of a Union soldier on a pedestal in the center flanked by Civil War and Spanish-American War cannon, a lower statue behind the tall Union monument for World War One, a P-51 Mustang fighter plane for a memorial to World War Two.

In front of the P-51, facing the back of the Union soldier, a bunting-draped platform had been erected, seats set up all the way back beyond the cannon of past victories. Banners above the platform and across the corners of the square announced: Isaiah Monroe Justice Crusade. Lenny Gruenfeld's name appeared, along with other entertainers I recognized, most of them black, and various politicians, most not from North Paterson or New Jersey. It was not exactly a popular local cause. I parked in an open spot on the square. A North Paterson patrolman advanced on us. Lenny showed him her credentials as a performer at the rally. He looked her over and walked away. Anyone who took part in this rally was no friend of the NPPD.

"Miss Gruenfeld. I'm so glad you could come."

The man stood over our car, beamed as if he'd been watching for us. Tall and thick-chested, with a wind-reddened face and the small regular features of popular movie juveniles in the forties. The bland oval face of everybody's next-door neighbor in white, middle-class areas. Hatless, his graying hair almost polished.

"You've brought us another performer?" He looked at

my empty sleeve.

In a soft gray tweed Burberry, he smiled and waited for the introduction. A patient smiler. A gray suit with white shirt and striped tie under the expensive coat. Black shoes. An American Legion pin on one lapel and an NAACP pin on the other. A politician. North Jersey variety. The American Legion pin would always be there, but the NAACP would become Knights of Columbus, Sons of Pulaski, depending on the event attended.

"Dan Fortune," Lenny said, "Mr. Francis X. Keene, North Paterson Democratic Party chairman, former state legislator, city councilman, et cetera. He likes to be called F.X. or Frank."

She did not like Mr. F.X. Keene. But it looked like Mr. Keene liked her. He'd certainly been watching for her, and he wasn't happy to see me.

"You're joining us at the rally, Mr. Fortune?"

"Just a chauffeur," I said.

"Too bad." He smiled. It was part of him, the smile, as automatic and meaningless as a nervous tic. "The Wind can use everyone and anyone who could help."

"Watch my stuff," Lenny said, got out. "I'll check in, see when they need me."

She walked off toward the people milling around the draped platform in the center of the square without even glancing at Keene. That distance again, the private bubble of detachment she moved inside. Keene's gray eyes watched her go without his smile. But when he turned to me, the smile was back in place.

"Are you familiar with the Monroe case, Dan?"

"More or less," I said. "Not the details."

His smooth face expressed strong disapproval and concern at the same time. "The details, I'm afraid, are what count in a murder prosecution." His shoulders hunched in the expensive Burberry. "I hope you're not one of those people who decides from a distance that a man is guilty or innocent according to your own interests and prejudices."

"Aren't we all?" I said. "Unless it's something personal?"

"I'm not, Dan, and I somehow don't think you are. You look and sound like a man with convictions, not prejudices."

Now the shoulders relaxed, and the face became benevolent, comradely. It was an amazing face, mobile and flexible with any expression he needed at any time. He talked with his face and body as much as with his voice, and not at all with his hands. The big hands in his pockets the whole time, immobile, a center of tranquility a listener could focus on and feel calm.

"Thanks." It seemed called for. I guessed Keene made a lot of people respond the way he wanted them to. "I'm surprised to see you at the rally. I thought everyone in the Establishment figured Monroe guilty as sin."

"I'm not sure a local party chairman qualifies as Establishment, but even so it may not be as monolithic as you think, Dan. I find Isaiah Monroe's politics anathema. Violent confrontation can only tear the country apart, won't help the minorities gain their rightful place in the society. We must work within the system. Winston Churchill said democracy isn't perfect, but it's better than any alternative. Monroe would destroy democracy, the rights of individuals. But I admire the great athlete, and this is a murder case, not politics. I feel there is a very reasonable doubt as to his and young Johnson's guilt."

"You testified at the trials?"

"The second. I admit I was as sure of their guilt as anyone else at the first." He looked across the square toward where Lenny was talking to two young black men dressed all in black except for light green berets with bright yellow badges on them. "Then I came to doubt the veracity of the two witnesses. They both have criminal records worse than Monroe's, and there's some question of a deal between them and the police. Of course, the testimony of the two victims is damning. While the weapons were never found, Monroe was known to advocate carrying guns. His car fit the description of the car used by the two killers, but at least two of his witnesses say he was nowhere near that clubhouse. A very reasonable doubt, and that's why I'm here. I believe in our system, Dan."

He had to be a lawyer. No one else could so neatly suggest innocence and guilt at the same time. Only a lawyer could waffle that well while acting so righteous. To Monroe's adherents, the evidence was either useless or a lie, including the testimony of the survivors. To the police of North Paterson, the evidence was solid gold and utterly true. Keene seemed to come down square in the middle. And in a murder case the middle is against. Did he know that, or was he just a normal lawyer?

"I seem to remember the witnesses said the car had an out–of–state plate, and Monroe's had a Jersey plate."

"Yes, that too. More reasonable doubt. Even if those witnesses later said they weren't sure about the license, there's certainly more than enough to ask for a third trial."

"Just ask?"

"The law can't be rushed, Dan. That's how mistakes happen."

"At the rate they're going he'll die of old age in prison before they decide if he really did anything to be put in jail for or not."

Lenny Gruenfeld and the two young blacks came up to us. Close, I saw that one of the blacks wasn't all that young. A short, muscular man in a black turtleneck, black jeans, black calf-high boots, and pale green beret with the yellow hat flash. In his early thirties, he looked like a featherweight boxer. There was a clenched fist emblem on the yellow flash, with the black letters BLF—Black Liberation Force. The skinnier one wore the same flash on the same beret, was in his early twenties, and his black uniform was topped by a leather jacket.

It was F.X. Keene who introduced us. "Mr. Dan Fortune. This is Smoke, chairman of the local Black Liberation Force, one of the sponsors of the rally, and Loren O, a BLF member."

"Mr. Smoke," I nodded. "Mr. O."

The older one curled a lip. "Just Smoke. A revolutionary name, not a slave name."

The younger, Loren O, nodded firm agreement. Lenny reached into my car, took out her guitar and backpack, slung the pack over her shoulder and started toward the speaker's platform.

"I'll get back on my own," she said as she walked away.

The two BLF men followed her. F.X. Keene shook his head, shrugged to me and joined the parade to the platform. I got into my car. I had no interest in the rally, and Lenny had no more interest in me for today. Inside that shell she lived in a world of her own.

As I hit the Interstate and turned east for the Lincoln Tunnel and the city, I thought about Mr. F.X. Keene. He hadn't asked me what I did. I'd never met a politician on his own territory, who, like a prospective Irish mother-in-law, didn't want to know what a new man did.

19.

IT WAS STILL EARLY AFTERNOON so I drove I-80 into I-95, took the George Washington Bridge and the

Cross-Bronx Expressway to the Throgs Neck Bridge and Queens and on around to Great Neck. Sycamore Drive was in an older section where large houses stood on a manicured acre or two of big trees, mostly oak and maple with various evergreens thrown in. Not estates but mansions, comfortable.

Numbers 204 and 206 were side by side and totally different. The Mount Vernon colonial had an iron weathervane on a garage that looked like colonial slave quarters. The vane was a giant "J-B." Joel's house. It was white with front columns, fanlight over the front door, glassed-in porch on the side, the works.

The other looked more like a bank than a house. Massive red brick with a center dome and two front columns all in white wood. A cross between the Pantheon and Monticello. There were even marble front steps and marble window sills. The brothers weren't exactly original, but they knew what they wanted—display that no one could possibly miss.

At the Colonial I waited a long time for someone to answer my ringing. The small man who finally opened the door could have been a male impersonator as Rosa Gruenfeld. In a gray cardigan, wrinkled white shirt, baggy brown trousers, gray alpaca wool slippers with the toe out of one and almost white hair.

"Mr. Joel Bronstein?"

He started to close the door. "He don't buy nothing."

I put a foot in. "You're Isaac?"

He looked down at my foot, then up at me. "Who are you?"

"Dan Fortune. Lenny sent me."

"Arlene? Haven't seen her for years. She never calls." He shrugged. "You get old, no one calls. What's she want? Money?"

"Can I talk to both of you."

"Joel's sick." He looked at my empty sleeve suspiciously, seemed to decide that a one-armed man was somehow more trustworthy or, at least, less danger. "Okay, come on back."

He led me into a large rotunda-like foyer with the enormous living room to the left, formal dining room to the right. All the floors were polished bare wood, the foyer painted a pale robin's–egg blue with white woodwork, the rooms papered with blue and white small-figured colonial wallpaper. Neither room looked as if it had been used in years, a thin layer of dust on all the surfaces touched by the sunlight from outside.

I followed the old man back to a door at the rear. It was a wood and leather den as hot as the boiler room of some of the old buckets I'd sailed on. A portable TV had been set on the mammoth mahogany desk tuned to reruns of some detective drama. Another little man sat in a high-backed leather lounger like a child lost in an adult bed, a quilt over his legs, an elegant plum velvet lounging jacket around his narrow shoulders.

"This fellow wants to talk to us, El," my escort said.

"Didn't you tell him I was sick?" Joel Bronstein said.

"I told," Isaac said. "He come from Arlene."

Joel was as small as his brother, both of them thinner than Rosa and not much taller. Joel had less hair, dressed better, from the elegant velvet jacket down to the soft black pull-on high shoes of another century, and spoke far better. He was probably the youngest, got all the education Rebecca and Sam Bronstein could afford before they died. He looked at my arm. The one that wasn't there.

"What does she want, Mr.—?"

"Dan Fortune. She wants to know who shot her grandmother."

They both stared as if I'd spoken in a foreign language.

"You mean Rosa?" Joel said at last.

"Someone shot Rosa?" Isaac said.

"You didn't know?"

"How would we know," Isaac said. "We ain't seen her in thirty years."

"We haven't talked to her in ten years," Joel said, shifted angrily under his blanket in the lounger. "Except when she calls on the phone with her filthy politics. Asking for money, making speeches to *us!* She lives in a sewer and makes speeches to *us!*"

"She give us the back of her hand sixty years ago," Isaac said. "Picketed our factory shops herself! Who needs her?"

The dismissal of Rosa seemed to hang in the room like a radioactive cloud as they relived a lifetime of indignities and anger. A cloud that didn't lift until Joel said, "She's dead?"

"Not yet." A little guilt can loosen tongues. "Your nephew, Nicholas Grenfell, didn't tell you?"

"He don't call much neither," Isaac said. "He don't care about his mother. Maybe shot her himself. Wouldn't blame him the way Rosa and Hans raised him. Or didn't raise him's better."

"If she isn't dead," Joel said, "why don't you know who shot her?"

"She's incoherent. Irrational."

That shook them. Rosa had never been anything but coherent and rational no matter how crazy her ideas were.

"You think we can tell you something?" Joel said. "What can we tell? For thirty years we don't know what Rosa does."

"I thought you might know some particular enemies from the past? Someone with a reason to want her dead? Someone afraid of her? Of what she might know or say?"

Isaac's eyes rolled to the ceiling. "Who ain't her enemy? Friends she don't make so easy, but enemies?"

Joel heard the one question I hadn't asked. The question my visit to Great Neck had to imply.

"She is family," Joel said. "Of her life outside we know what we read in the newspapers. We couldn't help you, unless you think it is a family matter. You think one of us shot her?"

"Did you?"

"Us?" Isaac said, incredulous. "What do I know from guns? Which end is business already!"

"You've got the money to hire a hundred guns."

"Why, Mr. Fortune?" Joel said.

"Hate. Anger. Some last straw."

Isaac said something in Yiddish, then to me, "So find the straw, big detective."

Joel moved again. I could see he was in pain. "After so many years? At our ages? Anger and hate don't mean so much."

"I've seen it work the other way," I said. "Maybe she was going to do something that would really hurt you this time."

"What could hurt two solitary old men?"

"Some family secret, horror, guilt. You have children?"

The pain, whatever it was, was getting to Joel, and so was I. "We had no reason to shoot Rosa. Perhaps years ago because of the trouble she caused us with the authorities, the unions, our customers, our competitors, even our friends. But not now."

"Who gets your money?"

Both of them just stared at me. For an instant I saw Rosa standing with them like a ghost of the distant past. Three immigrant children on the Lower East Side, their frightened ambitious mother behind them, their militant father standing angry and a little apart, his thick European mustache defiant.

"Not Rosa," Joel said.

"You could bet your life," Isaac said.

"Talk to our lawyers," Joel said, closed his eyes. "I'm

tired, Mr. Fortune. Rosa hasn't been part of our lives for a long time. It's not easy to live on alone in an empty house, I don't have the strength to care about Rosa. I'm sorry."

Behind his closed eyes the bald old man in the velvet jacket seemed to go instantly to sleep under his blanket. Isaac put a finger to his lips, quietly turned off the TV, motioned me to follow him out.

"El gets tired easy," Isaac said as we went along the hall toward the front foyer. "He ain't strong like me."

"Who does get your money, Mr. Bronstein?"

"Call me Isaac. So you should forget the money, I tell you. Joel's goes to his two kids. They should burn they ain't got a good word for their father, but, they're blood, they get. I never married, mine goes to Brandeis University, a couple Talmudic think tanks so scholars should survive, some other charities. Rosa gets one dollar. I got good lawyers. It's iron."

"Nothing for Nicholas Grenfell?"

"We don't like Rosa no more than he does, but she's his mother, he got responsibilities. He hates too much. He changed his name. He don't go to temple." The skinny old man's eyes had hardened. Now they softened again. "Arlene I forgot. She gets some from both of us. I don't think she cares."

I didn't think Lenny would care about inheriting their money either. But Nicholas Grenfell would. Only I didn't see how that could relate to Rosa or her shooting.

"Thanks," I said, "I'll let myself out."

"I walk out with you. Got to get home."

"You don't live with your brother now?"

Isaac looked surprised. "I got my own house. Joel don't do so good since Annie died, so I come over, cook him something he don't eat junk. Watch TV, talk, then go home, right? I got a better house 'n Joel. Used to have all kinds of people take care of the place, but who needs to pay 'em to do nothin', right? I can open a can, put a TV dinner in the microwave. A cleaning company twice a year. Most o' the rooms we don't even look in. Gardeners got to come, the neighborhood watchdogs gets on you. The rest we lives in two rooms."

He walked me to my car, stood in the circular drive of Joel's house looking not that different from Rosa in the afternoon sunlight. He waved until I could no longer see him in the rearview mirror. Then he would turn away and walk across the two vast green lawns to his enormous brick and white wood mansion where he lived in the kitchen and the den, make a TV dinner, turn on the tube, go to bed early.

I picked up the bumper-to-bumper Long Island Expressway straight on into Manhattan through the Queens-Midtown Tunnel. It was getting dark when I reached Six Sport Cable, but the ex-basketball player answered my banging. He wasn't happy to see me. He was busy in his private office checking the police report of all the stolen property found in the Fifth Street tenement.

"Busy boys," I said. "Must have ripped off fifty places."

He said nothing, went on checking off everything swiped from him, a few extra items if he thought he could get them past the police. His word against some other cable company, screw a competitor. I dropped my time and expenses on his desk.

"My lawyer'll go over it, mail your check."

"When?"

"It looks right, a week. Maybe two."

He was in no hurry now. I left him still searching for anything he could claim. His lawyer would knock my bill down by a third. That was okay, I'd padded it that much, maybe a little more. It all works out once you know the rules.

I stopped at Bogie's for some beers and dinner. Fettuccine with clam sauce and three Beck's inside me, I turned the car in, walked up Eighth to my loft. I had my hand on the door when I heard the noise inside. Someone was moving around.

There were no marks on the lock, no sign of forced entry. My gun, as usual, was in my desk drawer. I was thinking about what to do when the door opened and she climbed all over me.

"Flew in early," Kay Michaels said, grinned down from where I found I was holding her up with my lone arm.

I carried her inside, staggering a little, she's a big woman, and kicked the door closed behind us.

20.

LONG AND LEAN, she moved against me, her head on my shoulder, her face touching my neck. The thick dark hair and her small breasts were heavy on my chest.

"I couldn't wait for Monday," her lips said, her breath against my neck.

It's one of the moments when I miss the arm. She lay on my left, half on top of me, her face and heavy hair and long body against me from shoulder to toes, and I couldn't hold her. Could only reach over, touch her breast with my right hand. Touch her hips, the mound of dark, wet hair.

"There was nothing I had to do out on the Coast, nothing I wanted to do, so I caught a flight this morning."

"If you'd called, I'd have met you."

"I like looking around your apartment."

"What for?"

"You."

Searching for who I was. I'm not sure I know that myself. I thought of Marty—Martine Adair, the woman I would always think of the way I will always think of my lost arm. There are events, moments, that become part of you. If I found Kay, I wondered who I would find a part of her?

"There's not that much to look for."

"I want to know what keeps you in New York."

"You won't find that in an apartment."

"I might in your office."

Her hand moved lightly against my belly all the while. My hips, lower. Moved and stroked.

"If I can find you, maybe I can find why you have to stay."

"Fear of change," I said. "The unknown. The comfort of the familiar."

"There are other kinds of comfort, Dan."

I listened to the night sounds of the city, looked up at the ceiling of the old loft with its tracery of cracks like a yellowing road map. Her teeth touched my ear.

"Is it a difficult case this time?"

I summed it all up for her and came out where I had gone in—with a gun there had to be a motive, and I had no motive.

"Street people get attacked all the time. Mostly by each other. But not with a gun."

"Couldn't some sick person have a gun, Dan? One of those berserk veterans? Men who shoot their whole families? Run amuck and kill innocent passersby?"

"They don't shoot one person and hide. They shoot up the neighborhood out in the open, don't stop until they run out of ammo or the cops corner them."

"You're sure it's not a mugging? Some random anger?"

"Two shots? Waiting in the lobby?"

We lay close and listened to the night. The day sounds

of the city are surging, busy, driven by need and greed and the aggressiveness of millions of people climbing over each other. A cacophony of motion, going, going, going, if no one really looks to see where. The night sounds are slower, distinct. At night we look and see, and the night sounds are different. Distant drunken laughs. The cries of fear. The sudden mad roar of a car engine speeding uselessly from shadow to shadow. The siren wail that echoes in a silence of ears that listen to be sure it doesn't wail for them. The brave songs of weaving youth on its way to or from the night of determined fun. The hiss of doors on empty buses. The shuffling of solitary feet.

"I can't see a motive for the family. Grenfell hates her enough, but what does he gain after all these years? Why shoot her now? The same for the brothers. What motive after all these years? All three of her husbands are dead, and what danger could she be to the Party or any other political cause?"

"What about Isaiah Monroe? His black revolution people?"

"Lenny says Rosa doesn't even know who he is. I believe her, it's not Rosa's kind of cause. Too ethnic, too personal. She's an idealogue, a socialist."

"The people at her hotel?"

"It's always possible. They're all a little unbalanced, someone could have hated her for some reason we can't even guess. Or she could have seen something, been a danger to Regan or his brother or old man Roth."

"The granddaughter herself?"

"She was there that morning, but she hired me, and what possible damn motive could she have?"

We both thought about it in the dark of my shadowy loft, the midnight city sounds reaching us from near and far. Feet and voices, machines and concrete. Manmade sounds.

"The answer's in her mind," I said. "Present or past, and no way now to tell what's real and what's imagined. Whoever shot her locked the answer inside her, too."

"What if she never comes out of it, Dan?"

"Then we'll have to find out the hard way or not at all."

She shivered against me. It happens all the time. People live and die and no one ever finds out what happened to them, or even who they were. But Kay shivered for Rosa locked in the unknown. We all need to know what and why.

The telephone jarred me out of a half doze. Kay snapped beside me like a tight spring. All our nerves are shot these days. My clock read 12:37.

"Yes?"

"Fortune?"

"Who's this?"

"Johnny Agnew. You make me?"

Kevin Regan's half-brother sounded excited, almost euphoric. High on something. Emotional or chemical or both.

"I make you. Where's Regan?"

"Where you think, mister? In the fuckin' slammer. In for nothin', you dig? Johnny A's gonna get him out."

"I don't arrange jailbreaks."

"Shit." Johnny Agnew didn't appreciate humor. "I got a deal for you to take to the Man."

"Why would I do that?"

"Because you want to know who blew out the old broad as much as the cops do. Maybe more."

"You've been watching too many TV movies," I said. "The cops can't be blackmailed by me or anyone else to let two hard cases loose for the attacker of one old lady."

"Kevin's straight now, they know it. I ain't talking a deal for me, just him. They drop the heat on Kev, I give 'em what I got. No strings on me. They grab me if they can."

"You trust them?"

"Hell no, that's why you're gonna front it. I heard you look honest. You talk to them, I got a witness I made the deal."

"Who told you I looked honest?"

"Kevin's old lady. She's right here. Angie, tell the man."

I heard moving and shuffling. The thin female voice was scared but hopeful. It sounded like Mrs. Regan.

"Can you help us, Mr. Fortune?"

"Does he mean what he says?"

"I think so. He wants to help Kevin."

"What does he know about Rosa?"

"He didn't tell—"

More shuffling, and Agnew came back on. "You want what I know you come down. Right now. No talkin' to cops first."

I held the receiver. "All right."

He hung up. I started to dress. Kay watched me from bed.

"Don't go, Dan."

"If I called the police, Angie Regan would be in danger."

There is something very alone about getting dressed again in the dark after making love. In the morning it seems right, but at night, the woman still in bed, there is something isolated.

"Make him come here."

It seemed colder than it was. I put on my old duffel coat.

"It's as safe as I can make it," I said. "It's my city, not Agnew's." I got my old cannon out of the desk, slipped it into my pocket. "Okay?"

"That doesn't make me feel any better," Kay said.

It didn't make me feel better either.

"Give me two hours, then call Lieutenant Marx. The

number's on the phone pad."

21.

THE COLD MARCH WIND BLEW along the silent block.

At the far end jukebox music played in a narrow stream of tavern light. No one sat in front of the Oneida. I watched from the corner. There was no sign of the small figure of Mrs. Regan. A bent bag lady shuffled through the distant shaft of saloon light. Twisted by the weight of her stuffed shopping bags, she disappeared down into the darkness of a sunken areaway.

I walked toward the hotel. Voices carried from somewhere high up in the darkened tenements. A man staggered from the saloon at the far end of the block, swayed toward the river, and a young black woman ran out of the tenement directly across the street from the hotel. She ran in the direction of the river, overtook the drunk and vanished into the night.

I watched for a man to come after her, but the man who did appear came from the Oneida itself. He stood in the night, adjusted his light navy-blue topcoat, brushed some lint from the sleeves. He wore a navy-blue homburg, striped tie, breathed deeply in the cold March air, walked toward me.

"Got a match?"

He looked at my empty sleeve, at the burning match I'd lit with one hand, bent to put his cigarette to the flame. Short, thick-faced, with the soft pale pinkish skin men get when they are shaved by barbers. A coarse face. Too well fed, a little bloated. Manicured fingernails with clear polish.

"Thanks."

He smiled at me and at my missing arm. He had bad teeth, stained and crooked. He walked off up the street away from the river. I looked after him until he turned the corner. He walked easily, unhurried, and looked back from the corner before he went around it into the avenue and was gone. He was too well dressed for this block, too self-contained for the Oneida Hotel.

A single bulb burned just inside the Oneida. No one was in the narrow lobby. The stairs went darkly upward to the light of the second floor. I went up. The corridor was as deserted as the lobby. Muted voices and movement behind the closed doors as if from far off, but the corridor itself was silent and empty.

"Mr. Fortune?" Angie Regan stood below, down in the dim lobby. "He told me to watch."

The thin wife of Kevin Regan wore the same yellow print dress. Wrinkled and not as bright as it had been. The brown cardigan had been replaced by a thick gray down jacket in the raw return of March. The dark shadows were still under her eyes, but the eyes were hopeful as she came up the stairs.

"Where is he?"

"In our room. Can he get Kevin released, Mr. Fortune?"

"Maybe."

Sometimes you have to lie. My job was to find who'd shot Rosa Gruenfeld. I worked for my client, not truth or justice. Only I can't live that way. Maybe that's why I'm not rich and successful. Agnew's chances of getting Kevin Regan off the hook without turning himself in were just about zero.

"No," I said, "his chances are almost nothing, Mrs. Regan. Unless whoever shot Rosa Gruenfeld is a serious danger who'll kill again, Rosa's shooting the tip of the iceberg. The police have to get more than they give.

That's how it works."

The hope weakened in her eyes, but it was still there. It isn't always the strong who survive, it's the hopeful, the tenacious who hang in no matter how bad it gets.

"He's sure, Mr. Fortune. He says what he knows is really important. Prime merchandise, he says."

"Important how? Who to?"

"The police, I guess."

The top-floor landing was as dim as the rest of the shabby hotel, but it wasn't silent. Voices came from the far end. The door to the last room on the left was open.

"Agnew have someone with him?"

She shook her head. "Nobody came up from the lobby. It must be someone from the building."

Whoever it was sounded angry. I put my hand on the old cannon in my pocket. That always made me nervous. I hadn't fired the gun in years, but I kept it in good condition. It would operate if I did.

"Johnny?" Angie Regan said. "It's Mr. Fortune. He—"

The angry voice was the radio. An all-night talk show host shouting at some lonely listener who had called to berate the host about the state of the Western world. Johnny Agnew wasn't listening. He sat in an armchair, blood from the small black hole in his forehead joining the other stains on the worn cloth.

Angie Regan moaned and pressed her face against the wall of the corridor. A moan of pain from the edge of the hope she held to so hard. I needed all the will power I had. Few people see much death today, but I've seen my share. The death of the old, the inevitable death I still have trouble coming to grips with. Hot and violent death that doesn't hit you until later. Even heroic death for something that seemed important at the moment. But this was cold, calculated death—the radio on, the door open to be sure no one observed unseen, a silenced pistol placed against the forehead and the trigger squeezed. The hardest to stomach of all, to accept as something human.

"He was alone when you went down?"

She nodded, her face still pressed against the corridor wall. Fighting death and the fading of hope. I fought my stomach. The dead Johnny Agnew wore a tan windbreaker over a blue wool shirt and chino pants. They were all red now, massive blood from at least two wounds in his chest, probably three. Close range, but not pointblank. Only the black hole in his forehead had been pointblank. The *coup de grâce.* I went behind the chair, moved the body forward to look at the exit wounds. They weren't all that big. A small-caliber, high-powered weapon.

"No telephone?"

"In . . ." She swallowed. "In the lobby." She breathed. Breathed again. Turned from the wall. "Is he—?"

"Yes. Did anyone come down while you were watching?"

"A man. I didn't see his face. He had a hat on, a blue topcoat. A dark hat."

I had seen his face—coarse, cold, barbered, bad teeth.

"Is there anything missing?"

"Missing?" She looked past me into the room. She walked in, looked around. She didn't look at Agnew in the chair, his mouth open, eyes staring, the blood dripping to the shabby carpet under the chair. Slow, thick drops. She shook her head.

"No. I don't know what . . . Johnny had on him."

Neither did I, and there was no point in searching him. The killer in the topcoat and homburg would have taken anything important. "You want to stay here or come down to the lobby."

"I'll stay."

The killer wouldn't be back. He had come for Agnew, could have had Angie Regan or me if he'd wanted us. I went down to call Lieutenant Marx. Then I went back up. She sat in the other armchair now, facing the staring eyes and gaping mouth of Johnny Agnew. The blood had stopped dripping.

"They'll let Kevin go now," she said. "I mean, he can't help Johnny now."

She'd found her way to face it, see the hope. We sat with the corpse like three people waiting for an important appointment. I've never found a way to deal with it, envy all those who can believe, see the dead in another, better world.

22.

THE BODY OF JOHNNY AGNEW had gone to the morgue. Lieutenant Marx had sent Mrs. Regan to the precinct to sign a statement that said she knew nothing, ordered Rosa moved to a safer room, had his men chase off the curious. Now we sat in the silent room of the old hotel. The hotel itself was a long way from silent, muffled voices behind all the closed doors like the undercurrent of drums at some remote jungle outpost.

"It's something else," Marx said. "Something heavier."

"It always was," I said. "You just didn't want to know."

"I still don't."

Marx is a rare cop, a rare person. He says what he thinks, good or bad. When he was a young patrolman on traffic duty he was knocked down by a car and refused to press charges, insisted it had been his fault. I've heard he refuses his share of the weekly book. That won't make him popular or get him fast promotions. No one really likes or trusts the different.

"You make the guy in the topcoat and homburg?"

"Not yet, if we ever do." Marx shook his head. "What, Dan? Something she knows, heard, saw? Something she did or has?"

Marx stared at the stain of blood still under the chair. We listened to the hum of voices through the dim corridors.

"It doesn't sound like family," I said.

"Anyone can hire a gun," Marx said. "I want everything you have, Dan. Right now."

I told him what I'd learned so far. It didn't take long. "Abraham Roth is scared shitless about something, and someone doesn't want me talking to Roth."

"Guys who throw bricks with notes on them don't carry guns," Marx said. "I'll take a look at Roth. What else?"

"Isaiah Monroe? That's big enough."

"And mean enough," Marx agreed. "Monroe's dangerous as all hell, and the trials stink. The only hard evidence they have is the empty shells in Monroe's car, and they weren't found until two months after the first arrest. Evidence like that I couldn't get past a third assistant D.A. But how could the old lady be a problem for Monroe or the cops over there? The Wind's buried for life, the good guys won both trials."

"A third trial? His people are pushing for it, and Lenny Gruenfeld's helping."

"You think Rosa could know something against Monroe that didn't come out in two trials?"

"Or something for Monroe that blows the whole case. There's always the chance of a judge with guts to look at the facts again, and Monroe gets off. Then they have to investigate what really happened, and all hell breaks loose for someone."

"Christ, they've been through two trials already, the second one a public circus not even Rosa could have missed. If she knows something, why didn't she tell it already?"

"Maybe she doesn't know what she knows."

Marx shook his head. "We'll dig into it on the quiet, those North Paterson cops are touchy about Monroe, but the family still looks good to me. Especially that sweetheart son of hers."

"What does the family gain, Lieutenant? Grenfell, his wife, the two brothers have hated her guts for fifty years, so why now? And what's Lenny Gruenfeld's motive? She's the only one in the family ever liked the old lady except maybe her three husbands, and they're all dead."

"The nuts in the hotel?"

"Which one and why?"

"How the hell do I know? What damn excuse do some of them need? They just don't like the way she talks. She makes noise when she sleeps. She's got the evil eye. Whatever."

"How do they get a gun? How do they think clear enough to get rid of a gun where you couldn't find it? Even Ederer."

"Who knows what nuts can do?"

"You can't have it both ways, Lieutenant. If they're crazy enough to kill for nothing, they're too crazy to handle it. And how does one of them hire a professional killer?"

"What if that isn't really connected? The family or one of the nuts in the hotel shot her, and Johnny A was blown away for something has nothing to do with old Rosa."

"You believe that?"

"No," Marx said. "Could be, but that much coincidence the odds say no. Politics? She knew something bad for the Commies?"

"I haven't spotted anything yet."

The undercurrent of voices from behind the closed doors of the dingy hotel rooms had quieted now, the cheap clock on the table where Kevin Regan had done his schoolwork read 3:00 A.M. The distant early morning sounds of the city reached into the room. Rumbling garbage trucks, drunken voices, the steady pounding of produce trucks on the avenues. Marx stared at the dried pool of blood under the armchair.

Marx got up. "Let's talk to Rosa again."

"At three A.M.?"

"Time doesn't mean anything to her," Marx said, headed for the open door, "and the hospital won't try to stop me."

Doors opened inches all along the corridors as we went down. Mrs. Regan was being brought back when we reached the lobby.

"You got somewhere to stay tonight?" Marx asked her.

"Our room," the thin woman said.

"Somewhere else."

"Kevin could come home tomorrow. Johnny's dead, they could let Kevin go tomorrow. I have to clean the room."

Marx stared at her for a time, then shrugged. I followed him out to his car. We drove downtown to St. Vincent's. They didn't give Marx any trouble. There were two patrolmen outside the door to the single room on a different floor where Rosa Gruenfeld had been moved, another at the nurses' station.

"One down watching the window," Marx said, "one of my squad in the room with her."

Nothing is airtight, but this looked close enough. The detective in the room had his gun out before we got through the door. Marx nodded. The detective faded back into the shadows. Rosa lay with her eyes open, the bird-like emptiness in the eyes.

"You can make your stand here." She turned her head to look at my duffel coat and black beret. "The mountains are close and the railroad. The ships aren't far."

"Rosa?" I said. "Tell us about Flaco? About Ben

Douglas?"

Her bony hand reached, held my arm. "You have to stop them running! They're running away!"

Marx bent over. "Tell us about Isaiah Monroe, Rosa."

"Stop them running or they'll run all the way home!"

"Are the Tcheka after Hans or Flaco or Ben?" I said.

Rosa whispered, her nails digging into my lone arm. "It'll be dark soon, then we can hold them. But you must stop them running away or we'll lose them all in the dark."

"Is it Hans, Rosa?" I said. "The Gestapo is going to arrest Hans?"

Her bird eyes looked quickly right and left. "We can hold this street. Set the barricades here, pull up the cobblestones! The cobblestones will stop the horses!"

"Flaco Cabrera worked for the Sheriff. Did he tell you something?"

"They have horses! Horses, Hans! Set the barricades high! Pull them off their horses! Pull them off, Hans! Pull Flaco down! Flaco you bastard! He's a traitor, Ben, a Judas. Oh, I know him! I know you! The Good Gestapo. I know him!"

She gripped me with both clawlike hands, dug blood from my wrist, pulled herself up from the hospital bed. The empty bird eyes stared into my face. Cunning and frantic eyes. Lost eyes in the dimness of the shadowed room. Then she fell back, and her eyes closed. Her withered hands crossed on her chest.

"No use," Marx said.

It wasn't and maybe never would be. I walked out the door into the glare of the corridor, lit a cigarette. Marx stopped to talk with his detective. I smoke less each year, but I haven't quit yet. There are too many times I still need a cigarette. I smoked it so hard I was down to a butt by the time Marx came out.

"Like that she's no danger to anyone," he said.

"Some people don't take chances."

We waited for the elevator, rode down in silence. The hour or so before dawn is the quietest time in New York. A moment of peace before the explosion of the day. Clear and cool on a March morning. Marx drove me to my loft. He probably lived out in Nassau County, had an hour or more before he got home. I asked him to get me in to see Kevin Regan again. He said he would.

Kay was asleep down under the covers. I didn't want to wake her, but she woke up, and I needed her. Death and solitude create a need stronger than beauty or desire. They tell me women sense that need, maybe they do. I know she came to me as hard and tight and furious as I went to her, and dawn came before I told her about Johnny Agnew and the soft, bloated face of the killer in the topcoat and homburg. I had started to shiver.

"She can't tell you anything, Dan?"

"I don't even know what world she's living in. A real world or a dream world or no world at all. A private padded cell."

"She has to come out of it sometime," Kay said.

"Sometime could be too late."

23.

I MADE BREAKFAST. Kay lay in bed and read the Sunday funnies. An American ritual. I don't read the Sunday funnies or lie in bed on Sunday morning.

"You're un-American."

"That's what they said in the merchant marine when I never took sack time."

"What did you do?"

"Read. I had more books in my sea chest than food."

"Definitely weird. How come you ended up a detective?"

"What else do you do with a good memory, useless knowledge, a lot of outrage, some hope and one arm? The NYPD owed me a favor, other people's troubles are easier to handle than my own."

"And you'll go on solving other people's troubles here."

"How many eggs do you want?"

"Two. People have troubles in California."

"Toast or an English muffin?"

"Go to hell."

I made her an English muffin to go with my special scrambled eggs, had the same myself. I served it in bed with the funnies and the *Times Book Review* for a tablecloth. We talked about her work while we ate, the job that had brought her to the city, her prospects for acting work in L.A. When we got to the fine life in Santa Barbara, only ninety miles north of Hollywood, I finished eating, washed the dishes and dressed. She watched me.

"A detective's work is never done."

"Dinner at Le Monaco tonight?" I said.

She nodded, settled back against the pillows to go through the *Times.* That would keep her until lunch, probably longer, and she had her own work to do. I went out into the cool sun of the Sunday streets, took the subway down to the Tombs. Marx had arranged my visit to Kevin Regan, there was no lawyer this time. Even on Sunday, Walt Eimold would be chasing every judge in town to get the charges dropped now that Johnny Agnew was dead.

"What happened to Johnny, Fortune?"

He listened, neither angry nor sad. His pale Irish face impassive, his blue eyes fixed on me as if he could see the murder room and the death of his brother. Only his scarred hands moved, opening and closing with the rage held inside.

"You know the man in the topcoat, homburg?"

"No, do you? The cops?"

"Zero on both. Out of town, the police think."

"And out of Johnny's league," Regan said.

"You're sure?"

"I'm sure."

"You think he really knew something about Rosa's shooting?"

"Has to be, doesn't it? Trying to help me. It shows you, eh? Keep your nose clean and cover your own ass." The Irish lilt shook in his voice. "Try to help your brother, and you get fucked all the way."

"Did he know who shot Rosa?"

Regan held his hand out. I gave him a cigarette, lit it. A faint color on his stark white face now as the rage and the shock turned into the plain anger we can all deal with.

"He was there that morning."

"Where?"

"In our room overnight. He was my brother. We talked. He wouldn't give himself up. He was going to get his share as long as he could, prison or damn. He left in the morning."

"What time?"

"Just before eight o'clock."

"So he could have seen the shooting."

"Or heard." Regan smoked. "My wife visited me yesterday. She said Johnny told her the old woman knew who shot her. He said the cops would pay for that and more."

It wasn't a surprise, but to suspect and to be certain are different things. Rosa Gruenfeld had known her attacker.

"How could someone have found out he was going to blow the whistle? Besides me and your wife?" I said. "Unless he was selling to both sides."

Regan smoked the last inch of his cigarette.

"Angie said he was feeling smart, sharp old Uncle Slick selling the snake oil. He was just dumb enough to do that."

He stubbed out the cigarette, stood up. I handed him the rest of my pack. He held the cigarettes, looked down at them as if there was something important about them.

"Maybe they'll let you off the hook," I said.

"You're dumber than Johnny, Fortune."

"You can't help him now."

"Hell, I don't get any brownie points on that, right? I didn't kill him, did I?"

24.

AT THE ONEIDA HOTEL they were all out on the street. Sunday is special in this country, even for those without beliefs and nothing to do on Monday. Except for Abraham Roth.

"Mr. Roth works Sundays, yessir," Don said. "My little honey says he's a hardworking old man. She was here already, give me a new watch. My birthday." A new Timex glistened on the wrist of the dark-haired, smooth-faced man who'd lost his past with his brain tumor. "Threw away my old watch."

"Fucking old Jew'd work Judgment Day for a extra buck," one of the Dover brothers said, drank his beer.

"Got the first fucking nickel he ever made," the other Dover said, taking the can from his brother. It looked like a long day for the Dovers if they were sharing one beer already.

"I don't hold with working on Sunday," George the

janitor said. "But it's okay for a Jew. Mr. Roth a good man."

"Where's his store?"

"Up the avenue," Barney Ederer said. He got up from where he sat against the hotel wall. "I'll show you."

We walked east, turned onto Ninth Avenue. Everyone was out in the sun in their Sunday finery. The affluent gentrifiers who owned the brownstones re-renovated into the town houses they had been at the turn of the century, the tenement dwellers and the derelicts. Not talking to each other, but not attacking each other either. There's always hope.

"Rosa tell you anything yet?" Ederer asked.

"You worried?"

"Nothing worries me any more, Dan. Except maybe some people like Rosa. She gonna make it?"

"I don't know."

"Nothing on who done it?"

"Only that Kevin Regan's brother said he knew something about it. Now he's dead."

"I'm glad I don't know nothin' about it," Ederer said. "I heard it was a pro took out Regan's brother. What's a pro doing worrying about a bag lady?"

"You tell me."

Ederer seemed to think. "Someone with money's worried."

"You should be a detective, Barney."

"No shoulds, no woulds. Here's Roth's store. Stay cool, Dan, I'm gonna go sit by the river."

He padded off in his thong sandals, smiled at the other Sunday walkers. I studied Abraham Roth's shop. The only store open on the block, it had two display windows with a center door. One of the plate glass windows looked new. Sweaters, dresses, shirts were piled in the windows with no attempt at enticing display, just low prices. Inside, the old man sat far in the back behind a small counter with a cash register.

"Get out! Get out!" He came at me waving his arms like a school principal clearing the playground of disorderly children. "Leave me alone! I do not want you! No police!"

"You want someone who throws bricks through windows, Mr. Roth? Sends threatening notes?"

"You will go away! You will leave me alone!" He was gray-faced, his haunted eyes like photos of Auschwitz. "Please . . ."

"Did he shoot Rosa, Mr. Roth? Did you see him?"

"No, no!"

"Who is he? Tell the police. They'll protect you."

"The police protect criminals, thieves, murderers!"

"Tell me about Rosa Gruenfeld."

I thought the old man was going to tear his hair out, wail into the mustiness of the shop. "I know nothing! Go to that terrible *gross*daughter! She was there! I hear her there when the old woman is shot!"

"You heard Rosa shot? You were there?"

"Yes! Yes! The *verdammt* old woman comes to put her nose in my business. Always she is crazy. I tell her go. Go! I hear the girl in lobby. She calls to her *grossmutter* she will be upstairs in the room. The old woman leaves, I hear shots."

"How long after Rosa left you? The shots?"

The old man shrugged desperately, wanted to answer, to get rid of me, his eyes looking at the open door. "How can I know? Perhaps five *minuten,* perhaps not so long. Go now, please?"

"You heard the shots? You didn't go out and look?"

"A man who looks is a fool!"

"Then why are you so afraid? Just hearing the shots?"

"Please." He begged, his hands twisting, twisting. "You go to the *gross*daughter. I see her this morning. In the hotel. In her *grossmutter's* room. She talks to those people. Go to her!"

He was terrified. Of what? That someone would see me with him, his eyes constantly toward the open door.

"Mr. Roth? Go to the police. Lieutenant Marx at the precinct. He'll help you."

He only shook his head, went on wringing his pale hands as I left, still stared at the open door. At the Oneida the Dover brothers had gone somewhere in search of stimulants or money to buy them, and old George the ex-janitor swept the sidewalk, cleaned up the neighborhood. I went up to Rosa's room. The door was closed, and there was no answer to my knocks. The door to the next room opened, and a head poked out.

"You lookin' for Rosa, mister? She—"

"I'm looking for her granddaughter."

Lenny Gruenfeld appeared behind the young woman.

"I'm in here, Dan."

It was the usual single shabby room, but cluttered with old furniture covered by gaudy handmade slipcovers. A four–or five–year–old child played on the floor.

"I've been telling everyone about that man who killed Kevin Regan's brother," Lenny said. "It's more than just Rosa now, and if they don't tell what they know they could be in danger."

The young woman said, "Rosa she was good to me, I'd sure help if'n I could, on'y I don't know nothin'. I mean, I got my kid to take care of, I goes to work 'fore six A.M. in the mornin'." She looked all of twenty, grinned at Lenny and me. "Ooooeee, I remembers how mad Rosa was when I come here. I was sixteen 'n seven months gone, you know? Old Rosa she takes right over, you know, asks me how I got pregnant. So I tells her I sees all the guys 'n girls carryin' on 'roun' my street 'n I wanted to have me a baby real bad. I just got to have me a baby, you know? On'y when I got pregnant, I din't even know. I mean, my mother she never did tell me nothin'. All I knowed was I was sick, 'n went to the clinic, you know, 'n the doc he says, 'I'm gonna call your momma to come get you 'cause you is havin' a baby!' My momma says, 'Keep her right there, Doc, I don't want no part o' her!' So I come here 'n Rosa she got so mad she went uptown 'n got in a fight with my momma 'n her fancy man, but it din't do no good. Rosa got me real good welfare, 'n I'd sure help out if'n I could, but I don't see nothin'."

She grinned at us. The child played silently on the floor behind her. It wore unisex coveralls of some material that looked like it would go up in flames at the touch of a match, silently pushed a battered truck with three wheels. It didn't even look up as Lenny Gruenfeld and I closed the door.

"She was the last one who'd even talk to me," Lenny said as we walked down to the lobby. "None of them knows anything."

"They can't afford to."

"That man last night. The police said he was killed because he knew who shot my grandmother."

"They don't know what he knew. He thought it was important enough to trade to the the police for his brother, and it looks like it was important enough to get him killed."

"He tried to sell what he knew to the person who shot Rosa too, didn't he?"

"That's what I think."

"Who? What is Rosa involved in?"

"That's what I'm asking you."

She shook her head. "Nothing. It just isn't possible."

"How about something you're involved in?"

We'd reached the street in front of the hotel. She turned east, strode in long, angry strides. Dressed for walking on a Sunday morning—denim jeans, yellow sweatshirt with the Monkey Preps logo, ankle-high black canvas and suede hiking boots, her short blonde hair brushed carelessly. The jeans on her perfect body could make a man's knees weak.

"Nothing I do could have any connection to Rosa, Dan."

"You were there that morning, went up to Rosa's room maybe five minutes before she was shot."

She walked so fast it was almost a run, anger behind the wall she kept between her and the world. "How do you know I went up five minutes before she was shot?"

"Old Roth told me."

"He was there? Then—?"

"He says he saw nothing. Rosa was talking to him, he won't say about what, but I think he's got trouble with someone. He heard you call out you were going up to her room. She left a few minutes later, and maybe five minutes after that he heard the shots. He closed his door and hid his head."

Lenny's long stride had taken us south toward the Village. The Sunday people watched us—the beautiful young body and the middle-aged roustabout with one arm.

"One of those Dover brothers told me she was talking to old Roth. I called I'd be up in her room and went up. I waited an hour, it wasn't unusual. Read a book, had a cup of coffee, heard the sirens but there's always sirens somewhere. When I went down finally to look for her they told me. I went to the hospital."

"Nothing the two of you were doing that could be dangerous?"

"We aren't doing anything together."

"How about the past?"

"Hers or mine?"

"Both."

"I don't know that much about her past, and there's nothing in mine except an ex-father, an ex-husband who never even knew Rosa and an ex-world with nothing I want now."

We reached the renovated brownstone on Perry.

25.

THE APARTMENT WAS THE ENTIRE GROUND FLOOR. Walls had been torn down to make one giant living room, bedrooms and offices and TV rooms front and back, a single large kitchen and French doors out into a patio with a high fence and a fountain. A drum set, guitars and keyboard stood beside a piano in the center of the room, amplifiers and controls ranged among the chrome and leather couches, the plastic and leather chairs, the teak and mahogany tables and bookcases and sideboards and oriental rugs.

"Drink?" she said. "Tea or blow?"

"A beer?"

Pop, op, abstract expressionist, post-pop and post-op paintings hung on the walls mixed in with rock posters for the Monkey Preps and fifty other bands. Steel and stone sculptures weathered on the patio. A stereo played somewhere, and someone was tinkering with a tune on a piano in another room. The child from the East Village club, Margo, came into the living room.

"Hello," I said. "You're Margo. Do you remember me?"

She sat down, watched me.

"At your mother's club, right? Do you like her music?"

"Sometimes."

"Are you going to be a musician?"

"I don't know."

"What else do you like to do?"

"Read, I guess. Are you going to catch who shot Rosa?"

"You know Rosa?"

"Sure. Mom used to leave me with her. We talk to people, carry signs. Rosa's always someplace with a sign. I like Rosa."

The skinny black bass guitarist, Matt, came out of a front room, made a pistol of his fingers, aimed it at the girl.

"Got you, pardner. We gonna string you up you don't come eat your lunch. What Cap feed you for breakfast, girl?"

"Pizza," Margo giggled.

"I'll string *him* up. Milk, yogurt and vegetable time."

He hoisted the girl up on his shoulder, carried her off into the kitchen. I could hear them giggling behind the door as Lenny returned with two Beck's and a glass. They had a second kitchen or a wet bar.

"I had to make a phone call."

"How long were you married?"

"Long enough and too long."

"Was he a musician, too?"

"No." She lay down on one of the long leather and chrome couches, drank from the bottle. "He was normal, like my father. I met him at one of the offices I worked in to pay for going to school. He was older, I was a kid. I was lonely, he seemed to find me exciting. Dazzling, he said." She drank, didn't notice a dribble on her sweatshirt. "That's pretty heady stuff for a twenty-one-year-old girl. My father and mother didn't want me, Rosa was always marching, protesting. He couldn't live without me, so we got married."

The beer dripped again. That's the trouble with lying down and drinking. "He seemed interested in my music, my studies. He helped with the housework and the cooking. When Margo was born he did more than his share. If I did well in school he bought flowers, took me out to dinner. Whenever we had a gig he took care of Margo, or got a sitter and came to listen." She noticed the beer on her sweatshirt this time, wiped it away. "One night, when I had about six months to graduate and the Preps had started to make a name, he came home excited. He'd gotten a promotion, was being sent to Europe. We were going to live in Europe. Him, me and Margo. He already had the tickets and a place over there. He'd wanted to surprise me with the wonderful news."

The bottle was empty. She rolled it on her stomach, over the mound that showed in the tight jeans. "He'd never taken me seriously. I was a child playing a game. My music couldn't be really important, to me or anyone else. Not as if I were a man with real work to do. So I left him and moved in with Cap and Matt. We've lived together ever since."

"The three of you?"

"Most of the time. Once in a while we need to be alone, have someone else."

"Who does what?"

"Everyone, everything."

"What about Margo?"

"Matt's better with her than I am. Cap's rotten, but he takes his turn."

The piano went on tinkering in another room. Someone writing a song, probably the blond keyboard man, Cap. Matt and Margo continued to giggle behind the closed kitchen door.

"Where's your husband now? Does he have a name?"

"He lives in California, he remarried, he was as glad to get out of the marriage as I was, and he never even met Rosa."

"You're paying me to do a job."

She let the bottle roll off her belly to the couch. "His

name's Pursell. Jeff Pursell. He lives in Westlake Village, I'll get you the address." She rolled to her feet in a single fluid motion. Her body was more than something to show off.

She was gone too long again. I finished my Beck's, looked into the kitchen. Matt and the little girl were eating popcorn, sharing a thin cigarette that wasn't tobacco and studying what looked like a photo report of the troubles in Central America. I walked out onto the patio. Various pieces of exercise equipment were scattered around among the tables and plants. Rock music was a demanding art. I was still standing on the patio, looking at the anonymous windows of all the buildings, when she returned.

"Here it is, but it won't do any good." She handed me the address, smoked a thin grass cigarette, held herself with her folded arms. "You'll never find out who shot her. No one will. She'll never be able to tell us, and it doesn't matter. Just blind chance without any reason. That's all life is."

"Maybe that's what life is," I said, "but it's not what got Rosa shot."

She stood in the living room in a kind of trance as I left, the pungent odor of her marijuana blending with that from the kitchen. But it wasn't pot that had her in a trance. Outside I found a doorway. She had something on her mind, had been gone from the living room a long time twice. One had been for a telephone call. Probably the other had been, too.

She came out in less than ten minutes carrying her acoustic guitar and wearing a blue down jacket over her sweatshirt. She walked to Hudson Street and a parking garage. I looked for a taxi. No taxi came, and I watched her drive a red Ford wagon out of the garage with me on the sidewalk staring after her.

I went back to the apartment. Cap answered the door.

"She's gone."

I pushed in. "Let's talk about her."

He remained in the doorway as I sat down on the same leather couch. Matt came out of the kitchen with Margo. The child had sullen eyes, as if she wanted to be alone with them.

"You know where she went?" I said.

"We don't keep tabs on each other," Cap said.

"No hassle, man," Matt said.

Onstage in their costumes they were wild, youthful. Offstage they both wore army fatigue pants, sweatshirts and running shoes, looked ten years older. They were in their thirties and tired looking. I thought again of the soldiers silent with their invisible scars in the pubs and cafés of World War Two.

"Which one of you is the main man?"

Cap closed the door, walked to Matt and the girl. They stood on either side of Margo, the skinny black and the stocky, sandy-haired Cap. I got the picture. It explained a lot about their sense of isolation. A unit against the outside. Communal in an individualistic world. Idealistic. But few are raised for it, and fewer women. A delicate balance.

"How did Rosa like it?"

They both stared at me, at each other.

"Man thinks we wasted the old lady, Cap'n," Matt said.

"For our lady love, Sarge."

"We's bad, Cap'n. Real cool killers."

Little Margo giggled, held one hand of each of them, looked up into their faces.

"Search and destroy, Sarge. They're all Commies."

"We got to save 'em from theirselves."

"Give democracy a chance to flower."

Foot soldier humor doesn't change. The bitter humor that tells the outsider he can never know what they know, can never feel what they feel. That covers the fear, the isolation, the detachment from a normal world that has become irrelevant. It hadn't been Vietnam. They were too young. Not as young as they looked and acted onstage, but not old enough for Vietnam.

"Honduras?" I said. "Colombia? El Salvador?"

They held Margo's hands, the three of them silent like some strange statue—the sandy-haired Caucasian, the scrawny black, the small girl between them.

"The man knows something, Sarge," Cap said.

"Man knows shit," Matt said.

I said, "I know that Rosa Gruenfeld's shooting is bigger than one bag lady, maybe dangerous to everyone, including Lenny."

I told them about Johnny Agnew. Their faces told me they hadn't heard about Agnew. The way they held the child between them, closed ranks, told me something else—that the most important thing in the world to both of them was Lenny and the band.

Or maybe it was only Lenny. For one of them, or both.

"She got real trouble, Fortune?" Matt asked.

"I don't know what she's got," I said. "That's what I'm trying to find out. I hope I find out in time."

"What do you want to know?" Cap said.

"Is she mixed up in anything with Rosa?"

"No. She's been busy. Missing practice, out of town. But she hadn't seen Rosa for months."

"Busy doing what?"

Matt said, "Ain't our business, ain't yours."

"Over in Jersey working for Monroe," Cap said. "What else I don't know. We don't ask questions about what we do."

"Where is she now?"

"Man's shittin' us, Cap," Matt said. "She in trouble, she tell us."

"You have to trust someone in the outside world," I said.

Matt made a noise. "Hell we does."

"She went to BLF headquarters in North Paterson," Cap said. "Four-twenty Wyandanch Street. You need help, you tell us. We were down in Salvador. Two years. We know all the dirty ways."

"Thanks," I said. "You both like the way it is?"

"The way what is?"

"With Lenny and the two of you."

Matt walked away with Margo. Cap just stared at me.

26.

I CALLED MY LOFT from Fugazy's to tell Kay I was going to Jersey, got no answer. In the rental Ford I took the Lincoln Tunnel, and it was midafternoon when I got to North Paterson.

Wyandanch Street was on the south edge of town near the black water of a tributary of the Passaic River. The debris-littered street had grimy apartments and boarded-up storefronts on both sides. Number 420 was in the middle of a block that had ruins and rubble on the south side, looked like Le Havre after the invasion of World War Two. It was a storefront, the only one I'd seen in five blocks not boarded up.

There is always more burglary, robbery and vandalism in the ghettos. The poor are vulnerable—everyone afraid, little police protection, and it's easier to steal, escape and hide among the familiar than the alien, easier to vent rage against the nearest target. A violent need to destroy the cage that imprisons.

So there were ruins, and the scars of fires, and boarded-up windows. Except number 420. An expanse of plate glass where "Black Liberation Force" was emblazoned arrogantly and defiantly. A challenge to both vandal and policeman. The woman who sat at a desk inside the door had her own challenge in her eyes when she saw my white face.

"Can I help you?" A flat voice so well spoken and finely modulated it had nothing human in it at all. I was not welcome. She wanted to be sure I knew that.

"I'm looking for Lenny Gruenfeld."

Neither her eyes nor her voice reacted.

I said, "Arlene Gruenfeld?"

"I'm sorry, I don't know the name."

I smiled. "No you're not, and yes you do."

"What?" Some of the modulation corroded.

"You're not sorry, and you do know Lenny Gruenfeld. You want to call out someone who doesn't go catatonic at a white face? Maybe Smoke or Loren O? You do know their names?"

"Cop?"

"It's not a raid, Miss, I'm not trouble. Just a working man on private business."

I would probably still be in that bare store trying to get past the desk if the skinny young black who called himself Loren O hadn't come out of the door behind the guardian woman. He wore the same Black Liberation Force uniform: black turtleneck, black jeans, black boots, pale green beret with yellow hat flash. But not exactly the same—the boots higher, the turtleneck a heavier material. I wondered how many of the outfits he had.

"She ain't here," he said. "What your name again?"

"Dan Fortune. Where is she?"

"How the fuck I know, man?"

"Her bassist, Matt, said she was coming here today. You know him? A friend of Isaiah Monroe?"

He hesitated, studied me. "Walk on back."

I followed him while the guardian of the portals

watched us in silence but not in neutrality. She didn't like me. I was white, and I was pushy. I was the enemy no matter what I said or thought or even did. She didn't trust me. She didn't, couldn't, trust anyone white. We had never given her any reason to.

Through the door was a single large room partitioned into a kind of public area and three small offices. In the public room there was a ping pong table, two pool tables, a poker table, a long sidetable with an automatic coffee machine and boxes of doughnuts. It looked like any YMCA or community center. Even revolution is part of its time and place. A busy young woman occupied one office, and the short muscular featherweight who called himself Smoke sat in the corner office.

"What's he want?"

"Lookin' for the Gruenfeld broad."

Loren O sat, stared me down. I smiled at him. He looked away. Cool arrogance takes practice. He was working on it, but he had a way to go. Smoke was older, watched me unblinking.

"She hasn't been here?" I said.

"Not today," Smoke said.

"Anywhere else she'd go for Monroe, for the organization?"

"She doesn't work for us, Fortune. I don't know what else she does for the Isaiah Monroe Justice Committee."

Loren O said, "Monroe ain't the BLF, mister. Never was."

"Sorry we can't help you," Smoke said.

Loren O said, "She just sing for The Wind, she ain't into the struggle, you know? Bleedin' heart liberal type. Into love 'n peace 'n brotherhood. She got a case for The Wind, too. Her bleedin' heart in her pussy. Don't do her no good with him inside, but she can dream 'bout it, sing to get him out, right?"

"Isaiah Monroe isn't that important to you?"

Loren O said, "Organization's bigger 'n any one guy."

Smoke said, "We all work for a new trial, and then another new trial, and another, until we get a fair trial and they let The Wind out. But we've got a lot of other fights, too, most of them bigger, more important for the people."

"What about Rosa Gruenfeld?" I asked. "She work for you or Monroe?"

They both looked as if they wondered what I was up to now.

"Who?" Smoke said.

I told them about Rosa Gruenfeld. All except her shooting.

"I never heard of the old woman," Smoke said.

"Shit," Loren O said, slouched in his chair, "what we need no old lady for, man?"

I didn't trust them, but sometimes you can tell when even liars are telling the truth. The quickness, the off-hand response without thinking. I didn't necessarily believe what they'd told me about Lenny Gruenfeld, but I believed they didn't know Rosa.

"How does it look for Monroe? A new trial?"

Loren O said, "How you think it look, man? It look bad. Ain't no way he gonna get a fair trial in this here country."

"There's a good chance for a trial," Smoke said. "All the trials in the world as long as they don't have to let The Wind out, you understand? He's buried, silenced, dead. And they're not going to let anyone dig him up. Why not another trial, as many as you want, as long as he's guilty?"

"Who are *they*?" I said.

Under the swagger, the rhetoric, Smoke was an educated man. It was there in his speech, in his manner, and he stared at me now as if I were either a fool or a knave, stupid or sneering at him. "You think it's a coincidence the Panthers all ended up dead, in jail or out of the country on the run? Carmichael? The Weathermen? Any real militants?"

I didn't think it was a coincidence. Power protects its interests, always has and always will.

"If you're black or brown or poor or female, and all you want is your share of the pie, that's okay. They won't make it easy, they won't give you nothing you don't take, but they don't mind too much if you try. But if you get militant, preach real change, stand up and say it's not just the rules're wrong it's the whole system, wham! That's it, the end. You're gone."

I said, "So you go underground. No rules, no holds barred."

"No one ever made revolution legal."

"Is Monroe guilty?"

Smoke leaned forward, opened a drawer in his desk. He took out a thin xeroxed and hand-bound manuscript, tossed it to me.

"First trial transcript, newspaper pieces, the whole story. Second trial looked at nothing except procedure. Take it home. I got lots of copies."

I got up. "If Lenny shows up, tell her I was here."

"Shit," Loren O said. He had a lot to learn, even about revolution.

"We'll tell her," Smoke said.

The guardian lady didn't look up as I went out. On the street some ragged youths stood around the rental car. It wasn't expensive enough to bother ripping off, but any white man's car could be worth smashing up a bit. A police patrol car appeared on the street, and the youths vanished like smoke into the rubble. I drove out of the area, found a McDonald's. While I ate my Big Mac, I read the story of Isaiah Monroe's crime.

27.

THE CROWD IN THE WHITE AMERICA CLUB of North Paterson on April 23, 1971, is laughing, watching the Mets in a night game at Shea, shooting shuffleboard against the right wall and pool in the back where two tables stand green under cones of light. Cigarette smoke is thick in the windowless room, couples are at the ten tables in the bar area, groups of men in shirtsleeves argue politics at the longer tables in the rear near the pool shooters. A typical Saturday night—crowded, busy, all white.

By midnight everyone is a little drunk, most a lot drunk. The political arguments have become heated. The pool games have become loud, the shuffleboard sloppy. At the bar and the small tables, voices are thick, and couples are nose to nose. At the door the two men who check membership credentials are relaxed. One has his sixth beer, the other whispers into the ear of his girlfriend. They don't see the door open, are unaware of the two masked men until the guns are in their ribs.

A long-barreled .357 Magnum revolver, maybe Smith & Wesson, maybe Colt, and a heavy 12-gauge automatic shotgun, maybe Remington, maybe Savage, maybe J.C. Higgins.

Women scream. Men duck. The bartender stares. The two guardians of the door back into the room, their hands up.

One of the masked men points at the bartender. "The take!"

The bartender is frozen. The man with the shotgun jumps over the bar, opens the register, scoops out the money. His hand is black. Or a light brown. Or a yellow-brown. Or deep black. Or not so dark black.

The bartender seems to bend toward something behind the bar. The man with the .357 Magnum, maybe Colt, maybe Smith & Wesson, maybe Luger, shoots the bartender. Shoots another man who comes drunkenly at him.

Bag of money in hand, the man with the shotgun pumps three times as drunken men lurch toward him, shoots three of them.

Screams drown the shots. A melee of falling, hiding, yelling. The two gunmen are gone.

Three men stumble out of the club to see a yellow, late-model, American-made, four-door sedan with an out-of-state license, maybe New York, maybe California, drive away into the night.

When the police arrive, the bartender and two other men are dead. An ambulance takes two badly wounded men away before they regain consciousness. The forty-seven witnesses describe the robbery and shootings and gunmen.

Everyone agrees on the entry, the masks, the theft, the number of shots. Forty don't know what make the guns were, the rest can't agree even on the number of shotgun barrels. Forty-five say it was two masked black men. They know they were niggers from their hands and their jigaboo way of walking and the spook voice on the one who spoke two words. Two of the three who went outside say the killers removed their masks as they got into the car and both were tall and light-colored, one sort of sambo tan and one a high-yaller. The third says both were big black bucks.

The police put out an immediate call for "two black males in a late-model, yellow, four-door, American-made sedan, armed and dangerous."

Half an hour after the killings, a sergeant and patrolman of the North Paterson Police, cruising at the edge of the black ghetto, see a late-model, four-door, yellow Oldsmobile sedan with New Jersey plates driving fast from the direction of Paterson and screeching to a stop at a red light. The sergeant turns on the siren and lights, pulls the Olds over. In the car he finds Isaiah Monroe and an eighteen-year-old member of the BLF named Sam Johnson. The sergeant recognizes Monroe at once, knows The Wind's reputation, involvements and inflammatory speeches.

Monroe is dressed in a gray flannel three-piece suit, white shirt, regimental striped tie, black loafers with tassles. Johnson has on brown slacks, a brown shirt and yellow tie, a tan corduroy jacket and brown suede shoes. The two men say they have been to an anti-Vietnam dance and rally in Paterson, have just taken two ladies home, are heading to BLF headquarters to do some protest work. The sergeant finds no guns in the car, no money, no other clothes, no masks. He asks Monroe and Johnson to drive to the club. They protest, but they see no reason to make an issue of it and unnecessarily antagonize the police.

At the club no one identifies the yellow Olds, none of those who see Monroe and Johnson point to them as the killers. The captain in charge thanks and releases them. Next day, having found no suspects, no yellow car, no guns anywhere in the area, no trace of the stolen money, the police pick up Monroe and Johnson again. They have checked the two men's story, found it to be true, but have also found a possible half hour unaccounted for between leaving the dance-protest rally, taking the two ladies home and being at the stop light in North Paterson. The various times given by the various people do not jibe precisely. So they formally question Monroe and Johnson, take them to the hospital to confront the two survivors.

Both wounded men are in intensive care, have just

been operated on. One is only semi-conscious. Neither identifies Monroe or Johnson. Both say the killers were tall, agree that the killers were the same size. Two of the witnesses who ran out and saw the killers flee repeat in writing their identification of two tall, thin, light-skinned blacks. The third is no longer sure of his big black bucks identification. Isaiah Monroe is a trim, powerful, muscular athlete six-feet-one inches tall, two-hundred five pounds, very black. Sam Johnson is six-feet-four, skinny as a rail and light brown.

One of the survivors dies after two days. The guns are never found. No money is ever found. Isaiah Monroe never goes anywhere without BLF bodyguards except for some casual moment to take two ladies home from a dance. He is already rich, has the certainty of making millions in pro sports. Sam Johnson has never been arrested, has never been in trouble.

One of the three witnesses who saw the car drive away dies in a fall from a bridge over the Passaic. The other two turn out to have long records of petty theft, assault, burglary and armed robbery, both have served time. Both were under indictment at the time of the killings in the club.

Two months after the killings, Isaiah Monroe and Sam Johnson are arrested again. The two witnesses now positively identify them, agree they had been mistaken about the two men being the same height and skinny, about both being light-colored.

A .357 Magnum casing and two 12-gauge shotgun shells are now found in the trunk of the yellow Oldsmobile. The mother of one of the women taken home by Monroe and Johnson testifies that her girl had come home half an hour earlier than Monroe and Johnson said. The one survivor now says they were the two who shot him, he had been in shock when he said they weren't.

Both men are tried in North Paterson, convicted by an

all-white jury, sentenced to two consecutive terms of life imprisonment. The two criminal witnesses are both acquitted of their crimes and never go to prison. The survivor moves to Florida. Ten years later a second trial in North Paterson affirms that all was done correctly in the first trial, confirms the sentences.

28.

THEY WERE WAITING when I left the McDonald's, their black-and-white parked behind my rented car to prevent any escape.

"May we see your driver's license, sir?"

He was a sergeant. The other was a patrolman. The patrolman stared at the empty sleeve of my duffel coat, at my black English Armored Corps beret. The sergeant stared only at my New York driver's license and my New York investigator's license. He drew his gun, stepped back, held the gun on me with both hands.

"On the car! Lean!"

I leaned. The patrolman patted me down.

"He's clean," the patrolman said.

The sergeant made a noise. It wasn't a pleased noise. He would have preferred to find me armed. I wasn't any more welcome to the NPPD than I'd been to the BLF. Nobody likes the unknown.

"Stand up."

I stood, turned. He still held the gun on me.

"What'd you want with those guys?"

"On a case, looking for someone who works with them."

"Who works with them?"

"Arlene Gruenfeld. She's—"

"We know who she is. What case?"

"Someone shot her grandmother in Manhattan. She hired me to find out who and why."

"What the hell's that got to do with the BLF?"

"That's what I asked them," I said. "You tailing me, or do you just roust and hassle everyone who talks to the BLF?"

"They're a dangerous pack o' thugs, buddy," the patrolman said. "We watch anyone goes near 'em."

"Shut up, Guardino," the sergeant said.

"What makes them thugs?" I said.

"Get in your car, Fortune," the sergeant said. "Follow us."

"What do they do?" I said. "Protest poverty and ghettos? Picket exploiters? Oppose governments, yell for change?"

"They carry guns, buddy." I was too much for Patrolman Guardino. "Right on the street, down to city hall, even to Trenton! They tell the blacks to kill cops!"

"I thought all Americans had the right to own guns."

"Not punks like them!" Patrolman Guardino would either be off the force in a year or go a long way.

"Get in the fucking car, Guardino!" The sergeant would have to talk to Guardino. "You follow us, Fortune. You got that?"

"What's the charge?"

"A goddamned big mouth! You want to argue about it?"

I followed them to the square where the rally for Isaiah Monroe had been held yesterday. The stands, seats and banners were gone. Only the bums, Sunday strollers and pigeons were left. North Paterson is a small town, police headquarters was in half of the ground floor of the old City Hall. The floors and corridors were all dark carved oak and heavy beveled glass, hushed and cool, echoing solidly as I was walked to a corner office. Small gold lettering announced it was the office of Chief Ezra F. Reynolds.

"Sit down, Fortune."

He had the voice and appearance to go with the office and the building. A deep voice of quiet authority, paternal and reassuring. Neat gray hair, but not short. His own man. A tweed suit, white button-down oxford shirt and striped tie. The suit was old and comfortable, and the tie was loose. A jaunty checked vest with watch chain to show the individualist.

"Chief Reynolds, in case you missed it on the door. Now tell me exactly what your business is in North Paterson."

I told him what I had told the sergeant. He watched me. I told him the rest of the case, including that I had no clues as to why Rosa had been shot except that the assailant seemed to have been waiting in the hotel lobby for her, and I was looking into the possibility of a connection to Lenny Gruenfeld.

"I see," Reynolds said. "You came to North Paterson to find a suspect, but neglected to report to us. You know you check in before you work. You're not even licensed in this state."

"I didn't consider I was actually working, Chief. Just trying to find Lenny Gruenfeld."

He had me cold if he wanted me. I hoped he didn't. Kay would be mad about the missed dinner, and I'd be chewing nails.

"Those BLF people are thugs. They believe in nothing. They have no respect for law and no sense of order. They only harm the legitimate aspirations of the black people. We take a strong view of anyone who works with them, legitimizes their violence."

"We just talked about Lenny Gruenfeld."

I was starting to sweat. He had the manner of a college professor, the appearance of a Victorian gentleman, the voice of an antebellum minister, but under it I sensed something else—the fire-and-brimstone conviction of a fanatic.

"Fortune, do you think I'm a fool?" He flicked his intercom. "Bring them in, Marian."

A uniformed female sergeant herded in Smoke and Loren O. The skinny black youth was sullen and holding back. Smoke was curious and wary. They saw me. Smoke laughed.

"I should have known he was one of your tricks, Reynolds."

"Fuckin' fink," Loren O said.

The Chief was not amused. "*Chief* Reynolds, I've told you before. I like to be called Chief."

Smoke bowed. "One of your tricks, *Chief* Reynolds."

Loren O sneered. The Chief considered him for a time. The Chief would remember. I wouldn't want to be someone the Chief remembered. He still looked at Loren O as he spoke.

"Mr. Smoke, will you please repeat what you told us?"

The leader of the Black Liberation Force said I had come to find Lenny Gruenfeld, had questioned them about Isaiah Monroe and the murders at the White America Club and had taken a transcript of the trial.

"I didn't come to ask any of that," I protested. "Smoke gave me the transcript."

"We can't know what you came to do, Fortune, only what you did," the Chief said. "You're a licensed investigator from New York, you questioned witnesses in a case under the jurisdiction of the North Paterson Police Department. You failed to report that you were doing any of this, and that is a crime."

My plans for the night were going up in smoke. Not to mention Kay's plans.

"Careless," the Chief continued, "sloppiness overlooked by too many police departments. It creates bad habits and poor judgment. I don't think you seriously intended to try to operate in secret, so this time—"

The man walked past the Chief's office door. All I had was a quick glimpse through the old-fashioned glass of the door, but his short thick body and swarthy face above an unbuttoned collar and loosened tie brought back St. Vincent's. The "friend" of Rosa's I'd lost on the stairs, and maybe seen once more outside the hospital dressed like a doctor. I went after him.

Up the corridor he turned into a room. Chief Reynolds shouted in disbelief behind me. Inside the large office of desks and men my swarthy quarry was removing his jacket. I saw the shoulder harness and the gun, saw him sit down at a desk. He saw me. Whether it was recognition, or the intuition of a policeman, I couldn't tell, but he knew I had come to talk to him.

"You want something?" he said. "Mr.—?"

"Tell me about Rosa Gruenfeld," I said.

Close, he was a smaller man. Stocky and muscular with his jacket off, but shorter, perhaps five-feet-eight, and younger. Late twenties or early thirties. A dark Italian face of the narrow type with heavy eyes and a thin nose over full lips.

"I know a singer," he said, "Lenny Gruenfeld, but no Rosa. Who are you, Mr.—?"

The Chief arrived with his female sergeant and two patrolmen with guns drawn and aimed. From his purple face and incredulous eyes I guessed the Chief wasn't used to people running out of his office while he was talking to them.

"Sergeant!"

She had her cuffs out, stared at me and my one arm.

"Cuff him to yourself, damn it!"

She did, the Chief walked out. The uniformed trio paraded me back to his office, and the swarthy detective I'd chased brought up the rear. The Chief sat and steamed for a time while I stood cuffed to the sergeant. But when his voice finally came it was reasonable. Too reasonable.

"Would you care to explain?"

I explained. The Chief and everyone else looked at the short swarthy man I thought I'd seen at St. Vincent's.

He shrugged. "I haven't been in New York in six months, Chief. You can check the sheet. Who is this guy?"

Chief Reynolds told him who I was, then told me who the swarthy man was as he got to the point without pussyfooting.

"You're accusing Sergeant Giannini of being involved in the shooting of this old woman?"

"Of being at St. Vincent's," I said. "Of asking about Rosa Gruenfeld, looking in on her, not mentioning he was a cop."

"Why, Fortune?"

"That's what I want to know, Chief."

"Giannini?"

Detective Sergeant Giannini shook his head. "I never heard of a Rosa Gruenfeld, Chief. Last time I was in New York was on the Diabelli killing, remember? I made the pickup."

Chief Reynolds nodded. "That was six months ago, Fortune."

"Then he's got a twin brother."

"Or you made it all up," Reynolds said.

Giannini said, "What kind of look did you get at this guy, Fortune? I mean up close, head on, not moving?"

"That's a good guess. Or you know it was all on the move because it was you."

"It wasn't," Giannini said. "Give me a reason. Anything."

"A lot of Italians look alike, Fortune," the Chief said. "If that's ethnic prejudice, Giannini, I'm sorry. There are many truths they call prejudices today."

Giannini said, "What dates, Fortune? The times?"

I told them. Giannini laughed, looked toward the two BLF men still standing in the office out of the way.

"You picked some great days. Tell him, Smoke. I can get the files."

Smoke said, "That first night the Sergeant had me right here until past six, Fortune. Bad luck."

Loren O was sullen. "That other time him and his goons was roustin' a meet down at HQ."

I couldn't think of better alibis.

"Sorry," I said.

Giannini smiled. He had a soft face, a peasant turned middle-class in a new life. "That's okay, the Chief's sort of half right. I got a pretty common Italian face."

"You finished with us, Chief?" Smoke said.

The Chief nodded. Sergeant Giannini took the two BLF men out of the office, the two patrolmen holstered their pistols and went with them. I turned to follow.

"Where do you think you're going?" the Chief said. "Working without reporting, accusing one of my officers. You need a night to think of the wisdom of playing by the book or staying in New York. Toss him into the tank, Sergeant."

29.

I USED MY CALL to reach Kay. She was furious. At me for going to Jersey, at them for keeping me.

"It wouldn't be any better in California," I said.

"You made your point. Do I call a lawyer?"

"Tomorrow. You'll find his name in my desk file. I've got a hunch this is a one-nighter. They want to teach me a lesson, but they won't want me to take up space too long."

"Will you be all right?"

"Probably," I said. "I'll make it up to you."

"You bet you will."

They put me through the full treatment: forms and rights, empty pockets, fingerprints, no shoelaces or belt. If you've never been through it before it can scare the hell out of you. You don't exist as an individual, you don't really exist at all. Only the first few days in the army is anything like it, and there you have lots of company. When they throw you into the tank, you're not really human, and you're alone.

Alone with twenty eyes, a hundred different stinks and a thick hostility. An amorphous hostility, undirected and directed everywhere, that comes from suspicion and anger and fear. It fills holding cells like the steaming vapor of a swamp waiting for the last arrival. That was me, and the ten others in the tank all stared at me. Ten bunks and ten men and no one moved.

They looked at my missing arm.

I looked for the weakest. In jail or in life, if you want a simple existence without conflict or confrontation do what everyone else does, what is expected. If this had been the joint, any big slammer where the really tough were, the deadly and crazy and dangerous, I'd have had to play it differently. But here anyone bad would be in another cell, isolated or already shipped out to stronger security.

These were just the drunk and desperate, the poor and petty. Illiterate and malnourished, disorderly and mean, but dangerous only to their own kind except in gangs in dark alleys, or when cornered in fear. All they needed to know to leave me alone was that I was the same as them, wouldn't rock the boat. So I picked an old man, drunk, all but senile, and scared. He had the top bunk near the only window. In March none of the others wanted it, too cold. I shoved the old man off, climbed up among the fleas, lice, roaches and God knows what other forms of life and sat staring out the window.

"Fucking no-good one-armed son of a bitch mother-fucker," the old man screamed at me.

He scuttled to a warm spot against the wall on the floor. The others all turned back to thinking about themselves, muttering to themselves, playing with themselves, while they waited for morning and maybe another bottle, shot, snort, dose or smoke. I'd acted small-time mean, was neither the weakest nor out to be the strongest, they could forget me.

That was the theory, but it was a long night.

With the bugs and cold and not quite trusting my own theory, I didn't sleep much, and when the turnkey came to get me before breakfast I didn't complain. The sergeant who had me sign my paperwork and gave me back my belongings told me Chief Reynolds wanted to say good-bye.

"I hope you slept well, Mr. Fortune," the Chief smiled.

"I've slept better."

"A long night? Perhaps it won't be wasted then. It could have been longer. Think about it."

"No chance," I said. "You weren't going to feed me."

The Chief stopped smiling. "I suggest you remain far from North Paterson."

"As far as I can," I said. "Believe me."

I sensed I was pushing it too far. You have to know when to back off when dealing with the police or anyone else who has the power to hurt you without much you can do about it. I made my voice serious, sincere.

"I'll report first from now on, Chief."

He wasn't sure, but he nodded. "I hope so."

On my way down the halls I looked for the swarthy detective, Giannini, but he wasn't visible. Maybe it was just as well. I asked the sergeant who had cuffed me if I could use a telephone. She directed me to a pay phone inside the back door. I called Kay, told her to forget the lawyer.

"I'll get some breakfast, then I'll be home. Say an hour and a half."

"I'll give you two hours, then I go find consolation."

"After me, what is there?"

"I'll make do."

I went to another sergeant for my car keys. He had me sign a form saying my car had been returned in the same condition it had been when they impounded it. I reminded him I hadn't seen it yet. He smiled. I signed. It wasn't my car, after all. If anything was wrong, Fugazy could sue.

Nothing seemed wrong with the car when I got to it in the parking lot, or when I started it. Nothing except the man who opened the passenger door and slid into the front seat beside me. Average-to-tall, a hair overweight, in a dark blue three-piece suit with a white shirt, blue tie, shined black shoes, short dark blond hair. Well-dressed, neat, the big revolver he had to carry only vaguely visible under the suit coat even to a trained eye. Without his briefcase this time.

"What did he look like?" I said. "The guy who jumped me in the Oneida Hotel. The one you chased, made him drop his knife."

"A kid. After loose change and your wallet. Turn left out of the lot. I'll tell you where after that."

"You didn't follow up on the kid?"

"Not my problem, Fortune."

I followed the one-way signs around the square until he directed me into a broad avenue that looked like the main street of North Paterson.

"Rosa is your problem? That's why you watched me?"

"Anyone in contact with her," he said. "Take a right."

I took a right.

"You people are insane," I said. "The whole Bureau."

"She's been a Communist all her life, Fortune."

"So has Mikhail Gorbachev."

"Left next corner. What the fuck does that mean? He's a Russian, for Christ's sake. She's supposed to be an American."

"You have to believe in capitalism to be an American?"

"You have to believe in freedom. Free enterprise. Angle left and go straight."

There's no point in arguing color with the colorblind. I angled left.

"She's never hidden what she believes, never done anything except try to change our minds. She's no danger to the country. Worry about those who sell us for money like good capitalists."

"We worry about them all," the FBI man said. "Even you."

"How'd I come out?"

"Soft, a bleeding heart, probably not reliable when the chips go down, but clean right now."

"Thanks," I said. "Where the hell are we going?"

"A man wants to talk to you."

"What man?"

"You'll find out soon enough, right?"

Secrecy becomes a part of their lives. A reflex. Tell nothing to all those faceless people outside the privileged few who need to know. The people, the mass of citizens, can't be trusted, must be protected from themselves.

We were out of town now, in an area of broad estates and great houses.

"In that gate."

It was a large iron gate open in a high brick wall around wooded grounds and a long blacktop drive with a massive white antebellum plantation house at the end.

30. THE TALL, THICK-CHESTED North Paterson Democratic Party chairman I'd met at the Isaiah Monroe rally, F.X. Keene, sat behind the green felt of a poker table, the cards in his soft hands. There was a pool table behind the politician, two pinball machines in a far corner, a wet bar, ping-pong table, chess/checkers table and two slot machines. The game room.

"Moonlighting?" I said to the FBI man who sat down at the poker table. "Or does Mr. Keene work for the FBI on the side?"

"Community of interest," Keene said. "A situation that involves both of us and you, Dan."

Keene dealt hold-em, two cards for each of the three of us. The FBI man looked at his. Keene nodded me to a seat at the table where the other two cards lay.

"Agent Cardenas is concerned about Lenny Gruenfeld and her grandmother, the possible involvement of Communists with Isaiah Monroe. Under the circumstances that concerns me too, especially with you in North Paterson talking to Smoke and his people. Is there a connection between Rosa Gruenfeld and the BLF?"

I looked at my cards. A pair of kings. If we'd bet, I'd have had to raise before the flop.

"You've got good contacts in the police," I said.

Keene burned a card, turned over the three-card flop. "What have you got about Lenny Gruenfeld and her grandmother?"

The flop was king and four of hearts, ten of clubs.

"They liked each other. Lenny was there when Rosa was shot, but I can't even think of a motive. What's the

FBI found?"

"*Nada*, nothing, zilch," the FBI man, Cardenas, said. "They hadn't even seen that much of each other lately."

"Since Lenny started singing for Monroe?"

Cardenas said, "All I know is it doesn't look like the girl had any part in the shooting. It's something else."

Keene burned and turned a queen of diamonds.

"Like what?" I asked.

"Regan and his brother. Old man Roth. The weirdos in the hotel. The Party faithful. Her family. Some nut off the street in that neighborhood. You name it, Fortune. The way she lived you got more possibilities than God made little fishes."

"And you don't care much which."

"Not much," Cardenas said.

Keene said, "But Dan does, that's why he's come to North Paterson." He burned, flopped a six of hearts. "Is there anything to connect North Paterson with Rosa Gruenfeld, Dan?"

If we'd been playing for money there was a flush out there now as well as a high straight, and it was time for my three kings to fold and go. I wondered if it was an omen.

"No," I said. "I haven't found any evidence against Kevin Regan, old Roth, the family or the people in the hotel, and no real motive for anyone."

Keene said, "Cardenas tells me a small-time criminal was killed because of involvement with Rosa."

"Kevin Regan's brother. He saw the attacker, or knew something else about the shooting, and was killed for it. Nothing more as far as we know now, except it pretty well shoots down any idea of a random nut from the street."

Keene turned over his ace-nine of hearts for the winning flush, gathered up the cards. "Neither of you has uncovered a connection between Monroe and Rosa

Gruenfeld?"

"Not a damn thing," Cardenas said. He'd had the nine-jack for the straight. It wasn't my day for cards. "And we've looked hard. When it's politics, we look real hard." He stood. "I got work. If I come up with anything on Rosa, Fortune, I'll call."

I hadn't seen a signal, but I had a hunch Keene wanted to talk alone. He'd dealt me a ten-eight of spades, flopped a six of spades, a king of clubs and a nine of diamonds. He studied his two hole cards. Indoors, his smooth face was pale, the blue–gray eyes and small mouth serious.

"I need to know everything that happens in North Paterson, is that clear, Dan? Everything."

"Looks to me like you do okay," I said.

He burned and turned a seven of clubs. Maybe my luck was changing.

"I'm way out on a limb for Monroe and another new trial. I'm getting plenty of flack as it is, and I'm vulnerable. If it turns out there is, or even was, Communist involvement, I could be crucified along with the whole Democratic Party. I'd have to do a fast dance and get the hell out, *muy pronto*."

"I can't really see Rosa and Monroe tied, I think you're safe." I watched him start to deal again. "Somehow, I don't see you as a Democrat. How'd it happen?"

He sat back, still held the deck. "I got an appointment to an unexpired term. The guy who died was a Democrat. They were in power. It's easier if you get appointed the first time, not elected. I wanted to be in, they wanted to stay in, we both found out I know how to keep us in."

"By becoming the Republican Party?"

"If that's what it takes right now, sure. Give the people what they think they want, and they'll let you have what you want."

"Make us think we want what you want us to want?"

Keene laughed. "You can fool all of the people some of the time, and some of the people all of the time, and that'll win most elections, get you a majority nine times out of ten."

He turned the last card. King of hearts. My luck hadn't changed. A full house could be there now against my straight. I tossed my cards in. Keene grinned, showed his king-nine.

He lit a cigarette. "Give the voters their basic needs, and they won't much care what else you do. The thing you have to watch is exactly what is important to them, what they really care about. On what they don't care all that much about you can do anything you want. Use their greeds, fears, prejudices and hates." He gathered the cards and shuffled. "This is North Jersey. We get them jobs, fix the streets, let them have their guns, keep the beer flowing and the blacks out of the white neighborhoods. Keep welfare low, but spend most of it on the blacks. Foreigners and Commies are on the border, anything government-run takes their right of choice away. Keep the Latins in New York. Speak Italian on Columbus Day, talk brotherhood on Christmas and America first on July Fourth, tell ethnic jokes on Passover and praise the Cardinal on Easter. Tell them Castro and Khadafy are undermining the country, and no damned Arabs are going to buy New Jersey."

I watched him work the cards, his hands almost as slick as a magician's. He would be all nerves and plans, never relaxing for an instant. Life and work identical twenty-four hours a day, the only real need success and power here and now.

"I don't think you've got much to worry about even if Rosa was mixed up with Monroe," I said.

He shook his head. "If the Communists are using him I'm in more trouble than you could imagine."

"It's starting to look to me like he's innocent."

"That's why it would be so tragic for him to be involved with Communists."

"Would it make a difference?"

"You know it would."

He looked at his watch and stood up. I remembered Kay. I was in real trouble now.

"The police going to let me out of town this time?"

He smiled. "I have nothing to do with the police."

"Yeah," I said.

31.

WHEN I REACHED MY LOFT it was long past noon, and Kay was gone. Sooner or later she'd give up on me permanently. People who don't see anything beyond a brief passage through a sorry world get fanatic about their work, or art, or whatever the hell they do from one day to the next, and fanatics make lousy playmates.

I turned in my rental car, walked among the afternoon people of the Village to Lenny Gruenfeld's Perry Street apartment. I couldn't see Rosa a threat to anyone in the Isaiah Monroe battle, but so far it was all that seemed big enough—assuming there was any sense at all to the killing and shooting, which assumed a lot in twentieth-century America. I needed a connection between Rosa and the pro- or anti-Monroe forces besides Lenny, or something or someone else with a big enough stake to kill people.

Cap opened the door. In the same sweatshirt and camouflage fatigues. He leaned on the doorframe.

"She here?"

"Tied down on the bed," he said. "Matt got her in a

closet with a booby trap that blows if anyone except him touches her."

He had not liked my earlier question about possible sexual trouble in their *ménage à trois*.

"I'm looking for a killer, Cap."

"Old Rosa didn't like our morals so we wasted her."

"Okay, you don't like me. I still have to talk."

"I don't."

"Yes you do," I said. "If you give a shit about Lenny."

He leaned there blocking the doorway, then stepped back. In the big double living room their instruments and amplifiers were strewn and wired among the chrome and leather and plastic furniture. Matt sat on a red plastic straight chair picking a series of runs on his yellow bass. As gaudy as the colors of the paintings on the walls, and as silent. He didn't even look up, sat alone with his music like a distant motionless cowboy I had passed once on the vast prairie of the Montana High Line.

"Where is she now?"

"Out with Margo."

"Doesn't Margo ever go to school?"

"Off and on."

Matt stood up, put his bass into a guitar stand and left the living room. I watched him walk to the front door and out.

"Lenny has her in a private school for show business kids," Cap said. "They're flexible about putting in class time."

"Kind of haphazard, isn't it?"

"We don't figure they've got much we want her to learn."

I nodded to the door. "Where was he going?"

"Ask him."

"When did Lenny get back from New Jersey?"

"We don't keep tabs on each other, Fortune. We don't

need any part of all the shit and hang-ups."

I sat down. "What happened to you two down in El Salvador?"

"We had a ball. We were the bigshot Yanks showing those spic soldiers how to do it right. How to move in on a village fast and hard. How to wham in on a rebel column in choppers before they could get out of a village and into the jungle. How to lay a bomb pattern, how to burn out an area so it couldn't support the rebels. How to kill neat and fast and thorough so the civilians would get the point about helping rebels."

He walked around among the instruments in the big room, bent and played a chorus of "Yankee Doodle" on his keyboard. "Nothing happened to us, it happened to everyone else. The rebels they chucked into a mass grave or the river. The eighteen-year-old conscripts got a couple of Hail Marys and a medal for the family back in the slum. The villagers got their crops burned, their huts bombed, their water polluted and their relatives kidnapped. Mostly it all happened to the villagers. Drafted by the rebels, killed by the soldiers and the death squads."

I watched him walk the room. It was an old story, but he was too young to know that. Troy to Vietnam. Probably a lot earlier and certainly a lot later. Force, the worship and the revulsion. The worshippers are always the same, only the reactions of the nonbelievers change.

"What did you do?"

"Do?" He stood among the musical instruments, the walls of color behind him, and almost smiled. "We quit. Flipped out, wigged, fragged the brains. That's what they said anyway. The official verdict: get 'em out, they been down too long, jungle got 'em." Now he laughed, but it was a laugh without humor. He sat, leaned forward with his hands clasped. "We sent a bomb run in ten miles short on a village search and destroy, blew the hell out of the soldiers waiting to secure the place. We dropped supplies over rebel lines. We went early on a village raid, warned the *campesinos*, pinned our own guys until everyone got safe away. We told the CO why, what we thought of what we were doing, and he had us out of there and in psychiatric stateside in six hours. Jungle fever, combat fatigue, whatever. We got desk jobs in Kansas and the fast track to honorables and out."

If he'd squeezed his hands any harder he'd have drawn blood. He was out of it, maybe, but he hadn't escaped. Not yet, maybe not ever, and the backlash of communal guilt and private rage can create a crazy logic with unexpected actions.

"You came to identify with the rebels down there?" I said.

"We came to identify with the poor bastards who want to do nothing except plant their beans, harvest them, eat enough to stay alive and have a little fun with their women and kids."

"When you see your country doing wrong, it can turn you radical pretty fast."

He was up again, walked the room with a combination of anger and contempt on his face. "What about when you see damn near every country doing wrong? The Soviet in Afghanistan, Indonesia in Timor, Vietnam in Cambodia. South Africa, Uganda, Chile. When we walked out of the army we walked right out of everything."

"Nothing counts?"

"Just us. Back to the cave. Start over."

"That goes for Matt too?"

"For all of us."

"Did Rosa like that?"

He stood over me. "You know, Fortune, you're really something. You twist and turn everything. Accuse with every question, see dirt everywhere, look for the worst in everyone."

"You don't find a lot of good yourself."

He watched me. "No, I guess we don't. But we're out, gone. Out of it all. Wars, politics, causes, debates, any involvement. We make music, the rest is shit."

"Even for Lenny?" I said. "Working for Isaiah Monroe?"

He sat down again, slowly shook his head. "Maybe she's not as far outside as me and Matt, she wasn't down there. Maybe she still sees some hope, but she didn't shoot Rosa."

"You're sure?"

"That day was the first she'd gone to see Rosa in months."

"Why did she go that day?"

"She'd been over in Jersey a lot, rehearsing when she wasn't over there. She just realized she hadn't seen Rosa."

"What did Rosa do for Monroe?"

"I never heard Rosa even knew about Monroe."

"Matt knew about him."

"Matt walked away from all that, too."

"You're sure? About Matt?"

"I'm sure."

"None of you has any connection to Monroe except Lenny?"

"Not me or Matt, and I'm pretty sure about Rosa."

I stood up. "Okay, tell Lenny to call me."

He nodded, and as I closed the outside door I saw him get up again, walk to his keyboard and start to play.

I went up to Hudson Street and on across to St. Vincent's. It was getting late, the sun low and the wind rising from the river. There was a change of weather in the air, April rain moving toward New York on the west wind.

The patrolman outside Rosa's room nodded me in. A doctor and Nicholas Grenfell stood beside the bed where Rosa lay with her eyes closed, no more than a wrinkle in the covers. Marx's detective was a shadow in a corner. The doctor looked at me, then looked back at Rosa in the bed.

"She won't talk to anyone today, Mr. Fortune."

"Worse?"

"About the same, just tired. I've been telling Mr. Grenfell there's no medical reason to keep her here now."

"You can't toss her out the way she is!" Grenfell fumed. "Look at her. She's an infant, a vegetable. She's a victim of public violence. The city is responsible."

The doctor sighed. "I'm simply telling you she no longer needs hospital-level medical care, and we can't keep her. The board will review her case tomorrow."

"I want a second opinion," Grenfell insisted.

"You'll get six opinions, Mr. Grenfell. The entire board," the doctor said, his voice curt. "Now I have other work to do."

Alone except for the silent detective, Grenfell and I stood over the high hospital bed and looked down at the motionless old woman with her eyes closed and a faint smile on her face. Maybe from some dream she was living among her delusions.

"They'll take her money," Grenfell said. "Every nickel."

"I didn't know she had any."

"Of course she does. She has medical insurance too, but they don't pay for a nursing home."

"How much does she have?"

"I don't know, but why should some nursing home get it?"

"You can probably get the state to pay the tab."

"Not until she uses up every penny of her own."

"That sounds like a law you'd vote for."

He glared at me, at the old woman silent in the bed, at the room, maybe at the world. Then he walked out. I stood for a time, maybe hoping she would open her eyes, wink, laugh at her son caught up by his own rules and then tell me all about everything. She only lay there, an enigma wrapped in a riddle.

It was dark by the time I came out of St. Vincent's and walked uptown to my loft. If Kay wasn't there, I'd go on to Bogie's, unwind with some Beck's and dinner. I was thinking about the good beer when I saw the movement.

He came out of an alley, grabbed my lone arm and threw me down in the darkness of the alley.

32.

HIS FIRST MISTAKE was standing between me and the light of the street.

A scrawny kid maybe five-feet-six wearing cheap black rayon pants that shined even in the dark at the mouth of the alley and a cheaper imitation leather jacket. If he had on a shirt it was open to his navel to show the silver cross on a sunken chest. The knife in his hand shined in the light, too.

His second mistake was *machismo*.

"Hey, cripple man, what you do wit' that arm? You gon' hurt real bad, cripple man. You stay 'way old man Roth."

He stood laughing at me, lightly tossing the switchblade from one skinny hand to the other. I got up, grabbed an ashcan cover, walked right at him. His laugh faded, his mean eyes widened, he hesitated. For an instant, frozen. I smashed the ashcan cover into his face, switched to the edge as he staggered back bleeding from the nose and slammed it against the side of his scrawny skull.

He went down sprawled at the mouth of the alley, I

kicked him in the belly. Again. He vomited whatever he'd had for dinner. It looked like pizza. I grabbed his head, smashed his face into stone of the alley, dragged him up by the collar of the imitation leather jacket, rammed his face into the building wall.

By now he was half blood and whimpering. Something about no-good bastard dirty fighter.

"You want a fair fight, join the Y."

I clamped his arm in a break hold and shoved him along the street to a telephone booth. On the avenue people stared. I looked mean and official, spread him on the ground with my foot on the back of his neck, dialed the precinct, told them to send Lieutenant Marx and lit a cigarette. I was smoking too much.

Marx and his men got there in ten minutes. Two of them picked up the kid, Marx talked to me.

"Give it to me, Dan."

I gave it to him. We all went back to the alley. Marx had a videotaper fix the scene in evidence, found the Latino kid's knife on the ground. It was a mate to the knife in the Oneida Hotel after I'd been attacked outside Abraham Roth's apartment.

"What's your business with Mr. Roth?" Marx asked the kid.

The kid said nothing, still bleeding from the nose and mouth. He could barely stand, no real strength in his skinny body, no stamina, and that was his biggest mistake—being born dirt poor in a slum where there wasn't much food and less hope and nothing to do to get out except steal.

"Take him to the hospital, then take him in," Marx told his men. To me he said, "Let's talk to Roth."

The shadows on the night street outside the Oneida Hotel scattered and vanished as Marx parked. The narrow lobby was emptier than the street. When old Roth opened the door and saw me, he tried to close it.

"Police, Mr. Roth," Marx said.

Roth seemed to hold to the door as he looked at me with wide, accusing eyes. "You say if I talk to you—"

"I said I'd try," I said. "Your little friend didn't give me any help."

"Friend? What is friend? I have no—"

Don't try verbal sarcasm on someone who doesn't speak the language too well.

"Can we come in, Mr. Roth?" Marx said.

The old man knew when he was beaten. Maybe that was his trouble. The apartment was as musty as ever. This time the bed in the second room was made, and Beethoven played quietly on the stereo. The Seventh, much too low for dancing. Marx sat down on the straight chair. Roth stood. I leaned against a wall.

"What did the kid threaten to do if you didn't pay him off," Marx said. "You know his name, maybe?"

"I know nothing. I do not want police."

"We've got him, Mr. Roth. He made a mistake, attacked Fortune here. He's in pretty bad shape and in jail. You don't have to worry about him any more."

I thought the old man was going to faint. He held onto the back of a dusty old couch. He looked at me, his voice a croak.

"You have hurt him? *Mein Gott!*" His legs gave out, and he sat heavily on the floor, held his face in his shaking hands. "I am ruined. He will break my windows, destroy my stock, beat me. I cannot stand being beaten."

I said, "He won't do anything, Mr. Roth. Not now. He's going to be too busy trying to save himself. He's just a loner, no gang, and the police know him now."

"It's over," Marx said. "Tell us the whole story."

The old man looked up. "Over? What is over? It is never over. They will be back. I know. I see."

"Who'll be back?" I said.

"The thieves, robbers, murderers! The ones who never

work, do not earn, do not build, have no substance or order."

"He stole from you?" Marx said. "Murdered someone?"

"Did he shoot Rosa Gruenfeld?" I said.

"*Nein.* No!"

"Mr. Roth," Marx said, "if we don't get it out of you, we'll get it out of him. One way or another."

On the floor the old man sat hunched into a ball, his head down, his arms wrapped tight around himself. He shook with something more than fear. The terror of his whole life. Marx's words seemed to echo in the bare room—it would all come out now. The old man's voice was almost not in the room.

"He has done nothing. I pay him, he does nothing."

"What did he threaten to do?"

Roth looked down. "He will break my windows, burn my shop, kill me. But he does nothing. One window. No more."

"How much did you pay him?"

"I do not know."

"We can find out from your bank."

"It is five, six years. Maybe fifty thousand dollar."

"Fifty thousand dollars?"

"What I have. I have not much more left."

"What were you going to do when you ran out of money?"

Roth shrugged. "I die."

"What about Rosa?" I said. "Did she try to stop him?"

"*Nein!* She does not know." He glared up at us, looked from me to Marx. "*Verdammt yenta!* She ask, but I do not tell her who he is. She is troublemaker. She does not understand what is real, *ja*? She say I must fight. She does not know you do not fight these people. They have no morals, no order. Inside them there is only death, the chaos, *ja*?"

"Rosa didn't know who the kid was?" I said.

Marx said, "We have to fight them, Mr. Roth."

"The police?" The old man's voice was scornful. "The police do nothing. Hitler did something. Hitler brought order, safety, morality. Hitler he stopped the punks, thieves, goons. Now no one stop them, for peace you can only die."

Marx sighed. "Get your coat, Mr. Roth. We have to take your statement, have you identify the kid."

"No!"

"He won't see you. Can you give me his name?"

Abraham Roth stood slowly, went for his overcoat on an old-fashioned hatstand near the door. "Carlos."

Marx nodded to me. "You want to come too, talk to the kid?"

"No, I think the old man's right. The kid had no reason to attack Rosa. He's been worried about me, not Rosa."

We went out through the dingy lobby to Marx's car. His radio was calling urgently. Marx leaned in while we waited on the sidewalk. He turned.

"The killer just tried again."

33.

MARX LEFT ROTH at the precinct on the way to St. Vincent's. At the hospital the corridor outside Rosa's room was crammed with cops. There was blood on the floor, blood on the wall.

Captain Pearce was there, saw me. "I should have known."

"The granddaughter hired me."

"You know where she is?"

"No." I didn't tell him Lenny hadn't been home less than two hours ago. "Is Rosa—?"

"Never got to the old woman," Pearce said. "He was dressed up like an orderly, pushed a specimen cart right up to Merkel outside her door. It's a tough job, sitting guard on a door. Nothing happens for so long. Merkel never got his gun out." He looked at the pool of blood on the shiny hospital floor, the red-splattered plaster next to the open doorway. "After he shot Merkel he jumped into the room. He had the gun silenced, but Albano inside the room knows the sound of a silenced gun, heard Merkel grunt, make a sound. Albano got between the bed and the door, opened fire before the guy was a foot into the room. He doesn't know if he hit him or not."

"The gunman didn't make a fight?" Marx said.

"Took a fast dive back out the door, sprayed the corridor, shot a nurse and made it down the stairs."

"Albano stayed with Rosa?" Marx asked.

Pearce nodded. "A good man you have there. Nothing was going to pull him out of that room."

"How'd the guy get away?"

"We don't know yet."

I said, "He went down, or more likely up, one flight, pulled off the orderly outfit, had different clothes under it and just blended into the staff. He could still be around, but you won't find him. I'd bet he's out by now and long gone."

Marx nodded. "A pro."

"The way he didn't fight," Pearce said. "We take him, it's more trouble for his clients than missing Rosa."

"Any description?" I asked.

"Some," Pearce said. "He was short and heavy—"

"A bloated face, manicured nails, bad teeth?"

"How the hell—?" Pearce said.

Marx filled the Captain in on the case and the gunman

who had probably killed Johnny Agnew.

"We didn't get much description, but short and heavy with bad teeth fits what we did get," Pearce said. "Damn! What the hell's so important about an old bag lady radical?"

"Yeah," Marx said, "what?"

I said, "Maybe you better keep her in the hospital a while."

"Keep her?" Pearce said.

"The doctors say she has to be moved to a nursing home," Marx said. "It'd be harder to protect her there."

Pearce was grim. "I'll take care of it."

They kicked it around, Marx going over the case in detail, and his and Pearce's men working over the corridor and room for any evidence against the gunman. They didn't include me in their deliberations, and there was nothing I could do. I told them I was going. They didn't stop me.

A gunman in my vicinity makes me nervous. Especially one who knows what I look like close up by the light of a match. I watched everyone as I rode down and walked out into the early night. A colder night, people bent into a sharp west wind from the river. Every short stocky man looked like the gunman. I was glad to reach my dark vestibule and find it empty.

My office wasn't empty. Kay sat behind the desk, smiled at me as I came in. A tight, not-exactly-warm-and-friendly smile. Lenny Gruenfeld was across from Kay in a straight chair, her back to me. I sensed they hadn't struck up an instant rapport. There was more tension in the office than between two grizzlies bumping heads on a narrow trail. The fastest way to get people's minds off each other and their egos is to give them a bigger crisis. I told them about the new try to shoot Rosa.

"The same man who killed Kevin Regan's brother?" Kay said.

Lenny said, "They know who shot Rosa?"

"Yes and no." I sat on the edge of my desk between them. "Yes, they think it's the same gunman who shot Johnny Agnew. No, they don't know if he was the one who shot Rosa, and we still don't know the why of any of it." I leaned closer to Lenny, tried to put an intensity in my voice that might find chinks in her wall. "There's got to be something in her life important enough for someone to want her dead, something we haven't found yet. Something she knows, or did, or saw."

Lenny shook her head slowly as if searching through her mind but finding nothing. Kay watched her with an expression that said: I don't believe you, lady. You may be fooling Dan, but you don't fool me. You know a lot more than you're telling us.

"Dan's right, Miss Gruenfeld," Kay said. "No one hires a murderer without a strong reason. You know your grandmother better than anyone, you must have some idea."

Lenny's cold face said that she'd hired me, not Kay, and would like to suggest Kay go somewhere and make a pot of coffee or some brownies. She didn't even look at Kay.

"Rosa went her own way, lived her own life," she said. "I told you I hadn't seen much of her the last six months."

"It doesn't have to be the last six months or the last six years," I said. "It could be twenty years ago, maybe forty."

Lenny hesitated. "That's why I came. There's something I remembered. I don't know if it means anything or not."

"About Rosa?"

She thought for a moment how to tell it. "It was over a year ago. We were out on the Coast playing a gig in L.A. Four bands in a stadium, and the promoter papered flyers from San Diego to San Luis Obispo. After the show an old man came back to our dressing room. He told the stagedoorman he wanted to talk to Nikolai Gruenfeld's daughter." She looked up at me. "No one calls my father Nikolai except me and Rosa. So I went out and met him. He was an old Mexican—big mustache, *charro* sombrero, decorated vest and shirt, white pants and boots. He looked eighty with that thick, wrinkled, almost black leather skin old *vaqueros* get, but he didn't act seventy."

"I've seen them," Kay said. "They live their life outdoors, and if they survive they stay active into their eighties."

"Old Mexicans I've seen are fat and senile," Lenny said.

"If you say so, dear," Kay said.

Lenny said, "This one was tall, over six feet. Rings on every finger, a gold crucifix around his neck."

I said, "What did he want to talk about?"

"He said he'd known Rosa and Flaco in the old days up in Santa Maria. Things had been going bad the last few years, he couldn't work. He'd seen my name on the flyer, had come to sell me some things of Rosa's he'd kept all these years. He wanted me to have them, was sorry he couldn't just give them to me, but he really needed the money. He almost cried, gave me his business card, squeezed my hand: *Muy desolato, senorita.* The old fraud."

The card was a cheap copyshop job bent and dirty: Porfirio Sabado, Instructor, with an address in Santa Maria, California.

"Fraud?" I said.

"What he wanted to sell me could have belonged to anyone—cheap rings, a pocket watch that didn't work, a felt hat with the initials R.G. scrawled on the band, all kinds of old postcards, some books with Rosa's name in them in the same ink as the hatband initials, old Communist Party pamphlets. All junk and all fake. He probably hadn't known Rosa or Cabrera at all, just heard about them, saw my name, connected it and decided to try to con me. He looked like a con man to me anyway. I told him he should write to Rosa, she'd pay him a lot more than I could to get her stuff back."

She laughed. It was so unusual for her it seemed to shake the loft. "You should have seen his face when I told him Rosa was still alive. He barely stayed long enough to mumble he'd write to her, then split like coyotes were chewing on his pants."

"Because he was trying to con you with the fake keepsakes," I said, "or some other reason?"

"Other reason?"

"Did he act like he ran because his bluff had been called, or because Rosa was still alive?"

Lenny shook her head. "I don't know."

"Any marks, scars, features that stood out?"

"A big nose, curved like a hawk. The rings. One finger was crooked. On his left hand. The middle finger. I remember because it didn't have a ring on it."

"Can we go and talk to your father again tomorrow?"

She stood up. "You can. I'm going to be busy. I've left a check in that envelope on the desk for a couple of weeks. I want you to keep working." She nodded to Kay. "Glad to have met you, Miss . . . is it Michaels?"

"Kay Michaels," Kay said. "I'll call you Arlene."

Kay smiled. Lenny didn't. They both held the pose for a few seconds before Lenny walked out and closed the door.

"Spoiled bitch," Kay said, and smiled at me.

"Because she has different values doesn't make her spoiled."

"I'm not sure I want you to come to California."

"Do I have to give up female clients if I do?"

"Only those who hate any woman around you, want you all to themselves."

"She's young enough to be my granddaughter."

"That must be one of her different values. She took one look at me when I opened the door and turned to stone."

"She does that for everyone. Lives inside a wall."

Kay shook her head. "If she's not up tight over you, she is over something. Very tight."

Sometimes you can get too close to a case, too comfortable with a client without even realizing it.

"You're sure, Kay?"

"I'm sure. That's a woman with something on her mind."

Did Lenny have the same thing on her mind I did? She'd come specifically to tell me about the old Mexican in California.

"You want to take a drive to New Jersey tomorrow?"

"I'm not going to let you go there alone again. This time you might never come back."

"I thought you came to New York for business."

"That too."

There are advantages to having an office and bedroom all in one.

34.

A DAMP CHILL WAS IN THE AIR as I drove through Jersey to Nicholas Grenfell's big house. Kay stared at the cliffs of the Palisades, at the dumps and mud and black water and high refinery flares of the Jersey Flats. At the endless tract houses of northern New Jersey as if she'd never seen any of it before. I sometimes forget how little we see when we travel only by air.

Only the small Honda was inside the four-car garage of the big Colonial. An older woman answered the door. Mr. Grenfell was out, we could talk to Mrs. Grenfell if we wanted. I said we wanted, and Alette Grenfell met us in the antique living room with its elegant furniture. She wore black slacks and a black silk turtleneck on what had once been a slender face and figure turned bony and drawn now under the short silver-blonde hair. In the dining room the older woman ran a vacuum cleaner.

I introduced Kay. Alette Grenfell smiled graciously, waved us to sit and apologized for the vacuum cleaner noise.

"Mrs. Broberg only works for us three days a week."

"Money troubles?"

"Businesses have ups and downs, Mr. Fortune. Nicholas is spending long hours at his office. Perhaps I can help you?"

"If you know a lot about Francisco Cabrera you can."

She shook her head. "Long before my time. You will have to talk to Nicholas."

"When do you expect him home?"

"I never know. Sometimes lunchtime, sometimes midnight." She sat. "You don't like Nicholas, do you, Mr. Fortune?"

"He's not a particularly likable man."

"No, I expect he's not to most people. He's angry, and he has strong views. But he's hardworking and honest."

"So was Hitler," I said.

I heard Kay make a noise behind me. It wasn't the way to win friends and influence people. But friends and influence weren't what I was after. Alette Grenfell looked at me for some time before she took the bait.

"Did you ever want to do anything, Mr. Fortune? Succeed, be important?"

"I thought I had."

She shook her head. "I mean really succeed, not just work. It's easy for those who never had any ambition, for those who had help from the start. Nicholas had to begin with less than nothing. When he got out of the army he had no money, no family, not even a real name. He'd made his own name, and he had to make his own way. He came to New York, went to Fordham on the GI Bill, worked at two jobs to pay his rent and build up some capital. When he graduated in 1950 he was immediately hired by Union Carbide in their New York executive-training program. He was the best young executive they had, won quick promotions. We were married in 1955 when he was assistant marketing manager for plastics. We bought this house, invested in other land, Arlene was born, and it became clear Carbide didn't realize Nicholas's potential. We decided to leave Carbide to become marketing vice president at Paulson Chemical. But they didn't really appreciate his abilities either, turned out to have no imagination. They were going to stay a small insignificant company, and when we were still only a vice president after our son Richard was born we decided it was time to strike out on our own. We sold our investments for what we'd put in or even took a loss, pooled and borrowed, and Nicholas finally opened his own marketing consultant firm. He'd done it from zero through long hard work, not by taking help and handouts or pleasing other people."

She believed every word of it, and so did I, but each of us heard a different story. What I heard was that Nicholas Grenfell hadn't been much of an executive or investor, would probably have been a third-line manager except for self-delusion and a pushing wife and had spent a life of small privileges and advantages defending the enormous privileges and advantages of the rich and powerful as if he were one of them.

"But business isn't so good right now?"

"It takes time and struggle to succeed with original ideas," Alette Grenfell said. "Many of his concepts are too advanced for the old women who run the big companies. There's too much backing of weak business practices, support for losers, evading hard economic truths. Nicholas tells the truth, and the soft people don't like that. But the real businessmen understand, and sooner or later will give Nicholas his due."

She was spinning the same old web, defending her beliefs and illusions against reality. What I saw in the unpolished brass, half-empty garage, part-time housekeeper and general air of anger and neglect was a man in over his head, barely getting by each year and blaming everything except himself and his values. A man and a woman who would go under before they gave up their beliefs. A lot like his hated mother.

"It's so easy for Arlene, and all those who never had to fight, to condemn him," Alette Grenfell said. "She never lived as he did, knows nothing about reality. She never had to wonder how she would survive, even exist. She can be so noble, so admiring of old Rosa, who never faced reality either."

"They're both wrong?" I said. "Rosa and Lenny? I would've thought Rosa had a harder life than your husband, and—"

Nicholas Grenfell stood in the archway from the central hall of the big old house. "Both wrong, Fortune, yes. Rosa never saw the truth, and Arlene rejected it. Our way of life has produced more good for more people than any other system. More freedom and more enjoyment."

"In how much of the world, Mr. Grenfell?" Kay said.

"In all of it eventually!" Grenfell snapped. "Who the hell are you?"

I introduced Kay, told him she was a successful actress. He snorted at the profession but warmed up to the success.

"If do-gooders would let us alone," he said to her, "we'd solve all the problems eventually."

"I don't know," Kay said. "Sometimes I think that for us to be winners there have to be an awful lot of losers."

His wife came to the rescue once again. "Mr. Fortune came to ask you about your stepfather, Nicholas."

"Which one?" Grenfell said, still frowning at Kay.

"Flaco Cabrera," I said. "Did Lenny tell you she met an old Mexican who had known Cabrera and Rosa before Flaco was killed and Rosa went to prison?"

"I talk to my daughter as little as possible, Fortune."

I told him what Lenny had told me. When I described the old *vaquero,* he looked startled. When I got to the crooked middle finger on the left hand it became shock.

"Middle finger left hand? You're sure?"

"She noticed because it was the only finger without a ring."

Grenfell sat down on the green brocade love seat. It clashed with his blue suit. I expected Arlette Grenfell to say something, but she was too intent on him, the shock on his face.

"Christ," he said, "I wouldn't put it past Flaco."

"Cabrera?" I said.

"He broke that finger in two places in a brawl with some deputies. Broke it again, I forget how. It was crooked as long as I can remember."

"You think Rosa knew Cabrera might be alive?"

He looked at me. "If she did—"

He didn't finish. He didn't have to. There was no statute of limitations on murder.

"When Lenny told him Rosa was alive," I said, "he ran fast. He could have come to New York."

"No telling what else he's done over the years either," Grenfell said, suddenly laughed. "God, old Flaco! It would be exactly like him to have skinned out with a deal back then. And if he thought Rosa was a danger now, he'd do something about it."

It was my thought, too. "You had no idea? He didn't try to contact you? Sell you keepsakes?"

He smiled grimly. "Even Flaco'd know better than that."

"Mrs. Grenfell?"

She shook her head.

They were still shaking their heads in the vast living room when Kay and I left. We drove back toward New York in the noon traffic.

"When will you fly out?" Kay asked.

"As soon as I can pack a bag."

"My car's parked at LAX. Take the keys."

"You stay in the loft. Save money and answer the phone. I'll call in wherever I am."

She watched the scenery pass. "You think he was afraid Rosa would blow the whistle on him after all these years?"

"She would have," I said.

35.

THE 747 CAME DOWN into LAX through the late afternoon haze over the San Bernardino and San Gabriel Mountains, with the sea to the left and the great sprawl of Los Angeles on all sides.

I got my bag, found Kay's new Subaru in the long-term lot and crawled along Century Boulevard in unseasonal ninety-degree heat to the 405 Freeway. It was the usual stop-and-go early rush-hour traffic on the 405 through Sepulveda Pass, smoothed into a steady flow as I merged into 101.

It was too late to reach Santa Maria in time to do any

good, and I wanted to stop in Westlake Village. Jeff Pursell, Lenny's ex-husband, was a long shot, but I had to rule him out. Westlake Village is a cardboard community around a manmade lake that makes me think of a rich kid's doll-house village. Everything was built at the same instant—houses, streets, lake, community club, shopping center, marina, golf course—without history or a reason to exist except as bedrooms for Los Angeles.

The woman who answered the door at Jeff Pursell's house looked like she had been created with the house, the lake and the country club. Everything was in place: neat dark hair, pastel green knit dress, stockings, medium-high-heeled green pumps, lipstick, eye shadow, wedding ring, smile and highball glass.

"If you want Jeff, I'm afraid he's away."

There was a faint invitation in her voice, in her slightly anesthetized eyes. An invitation to a drink, a hint of more but without much possibility. Even the hint vanished along with her smile when I told her I was there for Lenny. Everything closed up. Lenny would always be the cloud, the woman who hadn't wanted the man she'd settled for.

"Jeff's been in Japan for two months," she said coldly. "I talk to him every day. You can talk to his company."

She gave me a telephone number. I checked into the plastic motel built with all the rest of the ersatz village, called the company. They confirmed that Jeff Pursell was in Japan, had not left even for a day in two months. I showered, shaved, watched basketball on television and went to bed. In the morning I ate a good breakfast in the coffee shop with a fine view of the hot and dusty brown hills that were the real countryside. It was up to ninety as I got back on the road north.

The temperature drops ten degrees down the Conejo Grade into Camarillo, another ten with the ocean at Ventura. Into Santa Barbara the highway follows a long series of curves in the coastline. Mountains are close to the right. They come down to the water itself at Gaviota, where the highway turns inland through Gaviota Pass and the hot, dry, brown and dusty green back country all the way to Santa Maria.

Santa Maria is a bus-stop town on a brown plain at the edge of a large dry riverbed. A developer's town, with new tracts going up all along the edges, flags and bunting flying to lure the blue-collar dreamer looking for a home. An Anglo town, beer and baseball, but with a Latino population to the west close to the farmed fields.

The address on Porfiro Sabado's card was out in the Latino farm area. Six unpainted plywood shacks around an open yard of hard-baked adobe dirt. A California bungalow court for farm workers, pickers, transients, migrant workers. Mostly Mexican, the rich man was a single Anglo with a pickup. The manager, who was probably the owner but didn't want any of his tenants to know that, was a fat Latino in brown slacks and an undershirt.

"Hey, the Anglo wants that fucker Sabado," the manager said in Spanish to the men who lounged around. They stared at me, at my missing arm, at Kay's car.

"*Migra*?" someone said. "Cop?"

I had no license in California, and this wasn't somewhere a private detective would impress anyone.

"Hey, he got no arm."

"That's some car."

It's a mistake people make, assuming a "foreigner" doesn't speak their language. Especially about English-speaking people. I didn't speak Spanish, but I'd picked up enough over the years around New York to understand a lot.

"Is he here?" I asked in English. When you had an advantage, you used it.

"Not here," the manager said.

"How long ago did he leave?"

"I don' know. Maybe year, two year."

"Did he leave a forwarding address?"

He shook his head and said in Spanish to the audience, "Hey, the Anglo wants to know if old Sabado he leaves address."

They all laughed, looked at me with a mixture of scorn, pity and just plain amusement.

"He's lucky the old thief has the same name this year," one said to the manager.

"Or the same face," another said.

They didn't think a lot of Porfiro Sabado, but they wouldn't help an Anglo give him trouble. I needed an inducement. One that sounded real, made them think Sabado would want me to find him. The inheritance line wouldn't work, not here, and not the lost bank account. I decided on the truth, or close to it.

"A year ago he wanted to sell me some stuff belonged to my grandmother when she lived in Orcutt. I didn't have the money then, now I'd like to buy if I could find him."

They all grinned at each other. Talked in Spanish.

"Mother of God, that old scam," one said.

"Hey, the old man can use the money. Didn't he wait table over in Guadalupe a while ago? Maybe they know where he is."

The manager said to me, "Maybe you ask over Far Western Hotel in Guadalupe. He used to be waiter there, okay?"

I thanked them all and got out of there. Kay's car and my lack of an arm would tempt them sooner or later.

Guadalupe was a Latino town down a long straight two-lane state highway west of Santa Maria. It had the most Mexican restaurants and the lowest public school test scores in the county. High unemployment and local gambling. The Far Western was a big steak-and-salsa palace on the main street across from a legal draw poker parlor. The hotel's redneck barroom and large barnlike dining room were crowded with tourists from all over the state. I hadn't eaten, and it never hurts to get goodwill from someone you hope will help you, so I had the special rib-eye steak and a beer before I got to business.

Over pecan pie I asked the waitress if she knew Porfiro Sabado. She was twenty years too old for her Old West dancehall dress, but the ribbon bow was jaunty in her too-red hair.

"He someone famous, honey?"

"He worked here as a waiter."

"Tell you true, honey, I never could keep them Latino names straight. They come they go around here."

"Maybe you could ask back in the kitchen?"

"Sure will. You like more coffee?"

I had more coffee. When the overage dancehall girl brought the check, she seemed to have forgotten all about Porfiro Sabado.

"No luck on Sabado?" I said.

"Story of my life, honey." She scooped up my credit card.

When the credit card returned it was in different hands. Younger, less jaunty and male. A big man—suit, tie, blond western mustache and neutral eyes.

"You want to sign your tab in the office, sir?"

I followed him out of the big room, across a dark corner of the L-shaped barroom, into a small cluttered office with western regalia all over the walls. There was nothing wrong with my credit card or the bill, so I didn't have to ask why I was there. The big young man, manager or whatever he was, put the saucer with my card on the desk, sat down, nodded me to a chair.

"Cops or immigration don't usually have one arm."

"Sabado seems to have quite a reputation around here."

The improvisation that had worked at the farm shacks wasn't going to hold up here. It was for friends of Sabado. I didn't think this man was a friend. I decided on the real truth, or some of it, told him I had a shooting in New York that might be of Sabado's wife from fifty years ago, and if Sabado was the man I thought he was he could be involved.

"Who do you think he is?"

"Francisco Cabrera, an old labor organizer in the Thirties."

He shook his head. "Sabado uses other names, but that's not one I know. Who's paying you?"

"The granddaughter."

"The old lady going to make it?"

"They don't know."

He pushed the saucer with the bill and my card across the desk to me.

"The restaurant got nothing to do with any of it?"

"Nothing."

I signed the charge slip, pushed the saucer back.

"He was a lousy waiter," he said as he gave me the customer copy. "Late, slow, drunk and a thief. Last time I heard he was going under the name Frank Castro, working around Lompoc with a phony fortuneteller."

"You have an address?"

"No, but the fortuneteller works as Star-Reader Vargas."

The sun was low as I drove south on Highway One through farm fields and the dusty back country along the edge of Vandenberg Air Force Base. It was dark when I reached Lompoc, a drab little city that had all the vices and virtues of a farming town, an Air Force town, a tract and shopping mall town.

I found a rundown area where the farm trucks were parked at feed stores, stopped at a saloon with neon signs for *burritos* and Tecate beer. The four men in work clothes at the bar and the five in finery at the two pool tables all stopped to look at me as I reached the bar.

The bartender was a young Latino who moved quickly to me.

"Can I get somethin' for you, mister?"

"A Tecate," I said, "and where I can find Star-Reader Vargas."

He popped the Tecate, put a thin slice of lemon on top of the opened can. "What do you want with the Advisor?"

"Advice."

"You believe that shit?"

"I believe she can tell me what I need to know."

He almost smiled. "Last I heard she's set up shop in a store over on Jalisco Street around Mercer Avenue."

"Thanks."

There was light behind the white-painted storefront window on Jalisco Street lettered in red with *Star-Reader Vargas* and crude occult symbols. What looked like dried grass, some bones and a hank of hair hung over the entrance. Inside, the light was dim in a room formed by brown drapes hanging floor to ceiling. A silent woman sat as if in a trance at the far end behind a small bare table. A straight chair was set in the middle of the floor.

"Sit. I must feel your aura. Silence."

She raised her arms, turned her closed eyes up to the ceiling where the only aura I saw was cracked plaster and two cockroaches. I sat. The silence was so thick I felt it getting to me. The whole draped fakery seemed to throb, expand. Then I realized there was a very low pulse playing from some kind of tape recorder beyond the drapes, an almost subliminal weight of sound. The woman abruptly lowered her arms, opened her eyes.

"You are not here to learn. What do you want?"

Her voice was hoarse but not unpleasant. A whisky voice. Her swarthy skin looked as smooth as velvet. She was stout and fifty, but her heavy black hair shined with youth. Her hands were soft and supple. Quick hands that seemed to have a life of their own, separate from her thick body. If she wasn't in league with the devil, she took good care of herself.

"You're wrong," I said. "I *am* here to learn."

Her transcendental manner dropped away. "Learn what?"

"Where I can find Frank Castro, or Porfiro Sabado, or whatever his real name is."

"What for?"

I went back to my original lie. "I've got a client wants to buy some keepsakes of her grandmother's Sabado wants to sell."

"Client?"

"I'm a private investigator."

The soft hands tapped lightly on the table. "Show me."

I showed her my license. Her fingers went on doing their dance on the bare table. "Your client got a name?"

I'd been sure it would come, but not certain how I'd answer it. If the old Mexican was Cabrera, the truth might send him running. If he was Cabrera and had shot Rosa, it could make me the next target. But it could be my only way of getting to him.

"Arlene Gruenfeld."

The hands stopped moving. She closed the eyes again as if in a trance, or communing with her spirits for guidance.

"Wait here."

She vanished behind the heavy drapes that hid the rear of the storefront room. What would come back out I had no way of knowing. This was one of the bad times. Exposed and vulnerable. It's when a gun makes you feel more comfortable. But it's a false comfort. If there was someone behind the drapes who wanted me dead, a gun wouldn't protect me. My best protection was his need to know why I was there. I needed to talk, not fight, and a gun keeps talk away, can make someone decide to shoot first.

Star-Reader Vargas and a skinny youth came through the curtains.

"Gregorio will take you to Frank Castro," the woman said.

I got up to go back out to Kay's car.

"No," the woman said. "That way."

The youth, Gregorio, led me through the bare room behind the curtains to the back door and out. If I had someone watching the car or the front door, they would have no way of following me.

36.

THE NIGHT WAS DARK but not silent in the back alleys. Traffic passed out on the streets as if we walked in some kind of tunnel. Radios and TVs sang and talked and laughed in Spanish. Portable stereos—ghetto blasters—moved through the darkness of the alleys and out on the lighted streets. Voluble voices from the distant lands to the south, most here for so many generations they knew less about those lands than I did.

Over it all a silence—the bottomless silence of waiting. Of staring at nothing in dark rooms. A silence of solitude. Out of time, even out of space. The silence of the long, empty days, of those who live outside an invisible wall as Lenny Gruenfeld lived inside an invisible wall.

"In here."

It was a three-story Victorian with cupolas, bay windows, a shadowed porch. Gray in the night, its yard was silvery, bare dirt littered with trash and rusted debris. The windows were broken or boarded over, and the doors were torn away.

"You're sure?"

Gregorio walked up onto the rickety porch and into the black rectangle where the door had been. Inside, I saw an empty room of bare walls. Everything not part of the walls or floors had been stripped away, even the bannister of the stairs up to the second floor. Cavernous, like some prehistoric cave, an ancient tomb looted by grave robbers.

Gregorio went up the stairs. There were voices on the third floor.

Six small, dark, nervous men stood in the corridor. As we came up two went into a room. The other four waited, whispered to each other. Old and young, the faces of Indians from Aztec ruins. Words in Spanish, but not a Spanish I knew. Words and sounds that made no sense to my ears. Ancient faces and *patois* Spanish. From south of the Rio Grande, but not Mexico.

They heard us. Dark, frightened eyes stared along the dingy corridor. Frightened eyes, but violent too, determined. The way a starving animal is determined. When need is greater than fear, animals and men become dangerous.

"Who are they?" I said, turned.

The corridor behind me was empty. A different man stood on the floor below looking up the stairs. Heavy, a thick mustache, black eyes fixed up at me without expression. Someone else came from the room the two small men had gone into.

"Tell your friends, *amigos*. The paper makes 'em legal. Amnesty, *si?*"

He was old, with a wrinkled face the color of leather. Tall and hawk-nosed. Quick eyes and a strong voice. He wore rings on every finger but the crooked one, a dirty black stetson, jeans and a western shirt, a silver buckle. He spoke to the two small men who had gone into the room. Each clutched a blue paper in front of him like a shield, a prize. They mumbled something in their unintelligible Spanish, hurried past me down the stairs.

The old man motioned to the next two in the line. They followed him into the room jabbering in the *patois* Spanish the old man seemed to have as hard a time understanding as I did.

"Slow it the fuck down, okay?" And in Spanish. "Slow, slow, amigos." Motioning with the palms of his hands flat down.

In the room the old man and a young man sat behind a table. On the table were stacks of the blue forms, a battered stapler, a revolving rack of worn rubber stamps and two small American flags in weighted desk stands. One of the men from the corridor handed the old man money. The old man counted it, stamped two different rubber stamps down on each of two blue forms, stapled them together and handed them to the waiting man.

"Gracias," the man said, bobbed his head. *"Muy gracias."*

That much I understood. So did the old man.

"De nada." He smiled at the man who clutched the forms, spoke sideways to the younger man going through the ritual with the other customer. "An' *nada* is what they got, right, Nacho?"

The younger one, Nacho, grinned, handed over his stapled blue forms to his eager supplicant. The old man called out in Spanish for the next pair. They went in, went through the same ritual and left hurrying past me.

Then I was alone.

The man from the floor below leaned against the wall behind me. In the room the old man had a pistol. So did the younger man. The old man smiled over broken teeth, spoke in English.

"You looking for me, *amigo?*"

"If you're who wanted to sell Rosa's keepsakes to Arlene."

The young one with the gun said, "He's a fuckin' Anglo!"

The man behind me swore in Spanish. "What the fuck's he talkin' about, Flaco?"

"He's a cop," the young one said in Spanish.

"On'y a private," the old man said in Spanish, and then in English to me. "Arlene figure me out?"

They moved in and out of English and Spanish as they moved in and out of the two worlds, at home in both and neither. Bilingual, but more. Bicultural and even binational, the two countries too close together and too far apart at the same time.

"I figured you out," I said. "Nikolai helped. And Arlene didn't send me, Rosa did."

"Rosa?"

"Someone shot her."

He licked his mustache, rubbed his nose with the pistol.

"A lot of people know I'm here," I said. "She isn't dead."

The young one said, "What the fuck's he talkin' about?"

"He talkin' about nothin'," Flaco Cabrera said.

"Shit," the one behind me said. "He say shootin'. Say people know he here. Maybe he don't come alone."

The young one stood and walked to the window. He looked out, motioned to the old man. The old man looked out and down. They both turned to me.

"What do you want?" Cabrera said.

"Some talk."

The young one with the gun said, "So talk to him, Flaco."

"He got no way out," the man behind me said.

Cabrera looked at both of them, shrugged. They walked out and left us alone. They wouldn't go far, or would they? Something told me they weren't happy with the talk of shooting, the interest in Cabrera. The old labor organizer, Communist, labor spy, informer, employer's agent, murderer, etc., sat down behind the table with its forms and tiny American flags.

"Jesus," he said, "how old she gotta be now? Ninety?"

"Eighty-eight," I said. I sat facing him across the blue forms on the table. "You're selling those forms to illegals."

"That's what I'm doing." Except for the broken teeth and wrinkled leathery skin, he could have been sixty.

"Those forms are nothing," I said. "They get those forms at any INS office for the asking. Those forms don't mean a thing."

"Not a fucking thing."

"You're cheating your own people."

"You live how you got to, Anglo. I tell Rosa that. Her an' her goddamned Party, her theories."

"They trust you. You cheat them."

"No way you cheat someone don't trust you."

He sat there behind the pathetic little American flags, the worn rubber stamps, the battered stapler, that all looked so official to the refugees from the poverty and persecution and killing of their tiny feudal lands to the south. He had lived almost eighty years, and that was all he had learned, all he had found. How to live at the expense of others.

"What happened back there in the Thirties?"

He shrugged. "The old bastard tries to cheat me, we get into a fight. He's dead, but I'm a big problem. I know too much, an' they need me, so we make a deal. No one wants no trial, only the family got to save face. So I 'die', right? The family an' the Sheriff look good, there ain't no trial, I got money in my pants, a new name, stay out of the county a couple o' years. Then I come back. We all looks the same. The Anglos don't know the difference an' the Latinos don't talk. Only trouble is Rosa and the kids, so they get 'em out of the way."

"They sent her to prison, and you didn't give a damn?"

"Me an' Rosa was finished anyway."

"Just like that?"

His eyes sank deeper into the leathery wrinkles of seventy years in the sun. "I got to be dead, she got to go. She want no more part of me anyway, eh? I'm a fink, a traitor, a *cabron*. She got always too many crazy ideas, Rosa." He leaned across the table toward me, the little flag fluttering as he moved. "I say, hey, Rosarita, do what you want, have some fun. She say when she do what she want she feel bad. There got to be somethin' she oughta do, somethin' she got to be workin' for. I say, fuck that shit. You my wife, you work for yourself an' me. She say she got duties. I tell her she's crazy."

"And now?"

"Hey, she too old for me, eh?"

"Not too old to be trouble. You ran fast when Lenny told you she was still alive."

"Sure, Rosa know what I sell the kid is crap." He grinned through the white mustache. "I get new wife after, eh? I don' know where she is, but she find out about Rosa, *ay Chihuahua*. Maybe she track me down. That trouble who needs?"

"What about murder trouble? There's no statute of limitations on murder, and you were never tried."

I saw in his eyes a flash of the killer he had been and probably still was if he had to be, but it was there and gone. "Almost fifty years, *amigo*. Ain't nobody know what happened to even make no trial. They never even charge me, who gonna figure what happened now?"

"They say she's got some money," I said. "You're still

married to her. You don't miss a chance like that."

In the silent room of the abandoned house he idly spun the rack of worn rubber stamps, fingered the dime-store flag as if thinking about the lifetime of chances to steal and con and cheat he hadn't missed, or maybe those he had. "Okay, I grab a bus, go east take a look. Shit, she ain't changed a goddamn. Lives in a dump, got rags on her fuckin' back, walks aroun' makin' speeches, carryin' signs. Still fightin' cops, takin' care of ever'thing 'cept herself. Ain't learned nothin' in eighty years. A hundred years she never learn. I take the bus back, that's it. She don' give me no trouble, I don' give her no trouble."

"You didn't talk to her? Not even for old time's sake?"

He spun the rubber stamp rack. "I think, you know? We got good times, me an' Rosarita. I watch, go 'roun' after her a while." Somewhere behind the dark old eyes, the wrinkled leather of his *vaquero* face, I saw for the first time something that could have been doubt, regret, even loss. A sense of having lost something better than he had. Or maybe it was only the loss of his youth, the regret of having grown old, the doubt of death closing in on him. "It ain't no good, you know? She don' be no different. What I got to say? What she got to say?"

"So you don't know why anyone would shoot her? Or who?"

He shook his head, shrugged again.

"She was no danger to you," I said. "You're not worried about the past, so you're not worried about me."

I stood, walked to the door. His eyes watched me all the way, but his hand with the gun did nothing.

"Maybe you better tell your friends not to worry about me."

He tucked the pistol into his belt, picked up a blue Dodgers baseball jacket. "They long gone, Anglo. You think they gonna risk to help me? You an' Rosa both crazy. Okay, I walk down first, you stay right here maybe five minutes. You got that?"

"I won't tell about your little INS scam."

"Don' make no difference you do."

He walked past me out of the room and down the stairs. I waited, I didn't know why. When I followed five minutes later I found out.

37.

THE SHERIFF'S CAR WAS PARKED in the shadows across the alley. It was visible from the windows of the room, was what the younger man, Nacho, had seen and shown to Cabrera. It could also be why I had gotten out untouched. Not my intelligence or toughness, just some help I hadn't even known about. It happens that way a lot of the time.

I walked to the patrol car through the loud ghetto night. Poverty, long hours at low pay, and hopelessness, don't make for contemplative pleasures. The uniformed man behind the wheel of the cruiser opened the door.

"Wondered if you were going to get out of there."

"You want me, Sheriff?"

"Lieutenant Holley," he said. "Get in."

I got in. "The manager of the Far Western?"

"Among others," the Lieutenant said. "You knew he was Flaco Cabrera?"

"I was pretty sure."

"If you'd reported, we could have told you for certain."

I had visions of another night in jail, maybe more than a night. But if I'd reported I might never have reached Cabrera.

"I didn't know what his status was out here."

"You mean you didn't know what our status was," Holley said.

"That too."

He drove out of the darkness of the back alleys into the streets that were wider but no less noisy, his eyes slowly scanning both sides of the street. He drove easily, in no hurry to take his official presence out of where it was not wanted.

"The Sheriff could give you a lot of trouble, Fortune, but he won't. He just wants me to send you home. Understand?"

I watched the night of the rural ghetto. They're better than urban ghettos, but bad enough and still outside. It's not being poor, it's knowing you'll always be poor. You, and your children after you, and their children. Being outside, knowing that to those inside you don't count.

"You don't want the past to rise and make waves," I said.

"Old Sheriff David's been dead twenty years, retired ten years before that. His deputies are all dead. The wetbacks, the union leaders and the Communists are all dead or gone. It's history, Fortune. Mythology. From another age."

"Rosa Gruenfeld's not dead," I said.

"Rosa Gruenfeld never knew anything about the killing." He turned a dark corner into the sudden glare of a lighted main thoroughfare full of neon and open shops. He shook his head with a kind of wonder. "Some of those old radicals really live long. Maybe it's keeping busy, never giving up chasing crazy ideas. Old Sheriff David told me about her and Cabrera when I first joined the department. About those days and the trick he had to pull with Cabrera. He never did know what happened when she got out, where she went."

"Jailed her and forgot her."

"They were bad times, the unions and radicals were

scaring the hell out of people like the Bannisters. The county needed jobs, and the Bannisters and other big ranchers had the jobs, the work. So Sheriff David came up with the trick."

"In the end," I said, "what was good for the Bannisters."

"What was good for everyone. The wetbacks, the foremen, the towns, even the Sheriff. Everybody kept their jobs, got paid."

We were in the center of the town, the bright streets crowded with evening shoppers, young people out for a good time, and cruising cars with radios blaring. It was too late to get back to Los Angeles in time to catch a flight to New York.

"You have a good motel in town?"

"Some of the best. V.I.P.s visit Vandenberg all the time." We were in front of the Sheriff's substation. "Maybe you better take a cell for the night. You never know what old Flaco and his buddies could decide to do. You spotted their little scam."

"Why don't you stop them? Don't the Bannisters, or whoever has the money and jobs in the county now, want that?"

He leaned back in the front seat of the cruiser. "We arrest them all the time. Trouble is we can't catch them in the act of taking money, the victims are all undocumented aliens and won't testify or even sign a complaint, and there aren't any outside witnesses. We have to let them go every time."

"Besides," I said, "Cabrera keeps the illegals poor, so they have to go on working for the Bannisters or whoever. Without cheap labor the Bannisters couldn't make enough profit on their ranches, would put their money somewhere else out of the county, and your job is protecting the county and its interests."

"Is that so bad, Fortune?"

"It is when the county and the Bannisters become the same thing. You better take me back to my car."

"You're sure? You're an outside witness against old Flaco."

"You going to use me against him?"

He swung back behind the wheel, started the engine. Flaco Cabrera didn't have to worry about me in this county, or probably about much of anything as long as he kept his scams small and his mouth shut. The Bannisters were probably just as important now as in the Thirties, and the old scandal would stay under the rug.

And I didn't want to spend another night in jail even with the door unlocked, no matter what Cabrera might do. A motel out of the county, and a jet home in the morning.

38.

I OVERSLEPT, and the 747 didn't deposit me at JFK until 7:30 P.M. By the time I reached my loft it was 9:30. Kay wasn't there. A note was: *Sherlock, Gone to the theater and dinner with Jeffrey. In case you've forgotten, Jeff is the producer who thinks I can act. Eat your heart out. California Kay.*

I opened a Beck's, sat in front of the television set and thought of when Marty left me for her producer. Kay was older, a lot steadier and in her way more successful. At least less hungry for the success with a capital "S" so many of us seem to need in end-of-the-twentieth-century America, content with her smaller success.

I went out to the diner on Seventh Avenue that featured veal cutlet on a Wednesday. The cutlet was good, so were the home fries and the pecan pie, and after coffee I walked down to St. Vincent's. Rosa was still in her room. The police had insisted, and the doctors were not happy. They wanted the bed. She greeted me with her bright, empty eyes and grasping claw-like hand, did not know who I was and fell asleep when I tried to ask about her third husband, Ben Douglas. She was a bird, an infant, and they would have their bed soon. Not even the police could fight the Medicare/Welfare watchdogs forever.

Bogie's for some more Beck's kept me away from the loft until pushing midnight, but there was still no Kay. She was a big girl, she probably wouldn't show before noon tomorrow. We were grownups, we had no strings, no claims on each other. I was tired, had jet lag. Intelligence said go to bed. Intelligence, common sense and maturity. I turned on the television, sat in front of it with my shoes off but nothing else. So much for intelligence, common sense and maturity. She'd be tired if she did come home, but I would be waiting. Call it need. Call it love. Call it Rosa Gruenfeld's bright, empty bird eyes. I had a beer, watched a talk show.

When I was a boy we had the last of the pulp magazines, B movies and radio—adventure and superheros with no connection to the world any of us really lived in. That, of course, was the point. Reality was the last thing anyone wanted. Next we had comic books, then paperback originals and finally television, and still no connection to reality. Except one reality—the projection of our prejudices and our fantasies. From the menace of the Black Apes and the Yellow Peril in the pulps, to very much the same thing in TV today with a bit more tinge of Red.

I had another Beck's.

We no longer live in a world of words but a world of images. In a way, Hitler won. The Third Reich was an image, the projection of a fantasy. The trouble isn't that

TV gives us nothing but mindless entertainment instead of solid subject matter, but that it turns all solid subject matter into mindless entertainment. The news becomes a sit-drama. All serious public concerns become junk. Wars and toxic wastes are the same as "Dallas" and "Dynasty," a summit meeting no more important than a superbowl. A summit meeting *is* a superbowl.

I smelled the smoke.

And saw the flames.

Maybe it was the beer. Or the jet lag. Or too much heavy thinking. But I should have smelled the smoke long before I could see the flames. When you see the flames it's too late. That's what half my mind told me. Cool and dispassionate, in a matter of milliseconds, as the other half, the automatic part, had me on my feet and across my office to the front window and the fire escape.

The cool part of my brain heard the screams above and below. The breaking glass and shouts on the avenue. Sirens somewhere. Car horns. A kind of wind, sibilant, and crackling like logs in a fireplace. The odor of wood, a hot wind and the fire escape invisible below behind sheets of flame. Distant white faces, and the sirens close and the screams.

The automatic brain—that worked and didn't think or listen to the cool brain that thought about such abstractions as if the flames already blocked the fire escape and the fire engines were not here yet my chances were slim and none—had me back at the rear windows. Something fell past and lay dark on the concrete of the rear yard. Jumping, the cool brain analyzed, was a poor choice, but if I did not get out very soon the smoke would kill me before the flames.

The best chance was to . . . to . . . automatic brain tore sheets . . . knotted . . . tied . . . the back window . . . down and down . . . burned sheets and falling . . . turn to the left so I don't hit on my good arm . . . turned and turned and hands clutched, grabbed . . . concrete is cold even when the sky is a hot flame, but Kay is beautiful even when she is crying . . .

Kay is crying. Kay did not stay the night with the producer who thinks she can act. Maybe California's not so bad. Kay is looking down. Kay's hands touch.

39.

KAY SAID, "THE FIREMEN SAY that after the sheets burned through when you were passing the first floor, you turned in midair so you'd land on your left side."

It's branded into my subconscious—protect my lone arm no matter what. I wish reality were that automatic in all of us.

"How much did I break?"

"Two ribs, dislocated your left shoulder. The firemen caught you, but your ribs hit a helmet and your shoulder got twisted. The burns on your legs and back are pretty minor."

We were in a hospital room, I'd realized that the first time I woke up. The second time I knew I hurt, but not that much, and knew my arm was safe. The third time, now, I was aware of the dressings on my legs and back, the pain in my ribs and shoulder. Kay sat beside the bed feeding me ice cream.

"Only a day and a half?"

"That's all. Seems like years, doesn't it."

"I was waiting for you," I said.

"I came home."

"Asleep, I wouldn't have made it."

"You don't know that, but I'm glad you waited. I'm glad you're foolish and stubborn."

"Too foolish and too stubborn."

"We'll talk."

"How long will I be here?"

"Until you're better."

"It's good ice cream."

The fourth time the ribs hurt more and the shoulder less, and Lieutenant Marx was there with Kay. One old man, two jumpers and three cats had died, five were burned severely, two critical, almost everyone in the building had been injured.

"It happened fast," I said. "Anything of mine saved?"

"Only clothes and your gun," Kay said.

"Too fast, Dan," Marx said.

"Arson?"

"The fire department investigators say one hundred percent."

"They let me look this morning," Kay said. "Your duffel was on the floor in the living room where the fire didn't reach, wet but not burned. Some other clothes."

"An old building like that?" I said to Marx. "Low rents and a hardware store?"

"It started in the hardware store right under you," Marx said, "spread fast with a 'whooshing' sound witnesses on the street heard. The fire people say both mean some flammable fluid, probably gasoline. Every electrical and gas outlet, every heater duct, every appliance connection was okay. The store was empty, all keys and personnel accounted for, but they found picklock scratches on both rear door locks. The place was full of gasoline cans, but one was way across the room against a wall where they're sure the fire was torched."

"I'll look for more," Kay said. "I've got the clothes and gun in my hotel room."

"Me," I said to Marx. "Someone wanted me dead."

"That's what I think," Marx said. "It wasn't a real professional, but no amateur. Especially those picklocks. No one in the building has big insurance. Witnesses saw a guy around the building as if waiting for someone, others saw the same guy walk off fast right before the flames whooshed up inside."

"Well dressed," I said. "Topcoat, tie, maybe a homburg. Short and thick, heavy face pale and pink, bad teeth."

Marx nodded. "Built like a fireplug, but expensive clothes with gloves. Gray gloves. They'll smell like gas."

So he was after me now. No orders that first time, but now he had his orders. Johnny Agnew had been a con, a crook, a bum, but I was a kind of cop. For me it would be an accident.

"I must be a problem," I said.

"How?"

I told him all I'd done. Had I gotten in Grenfell's way? Offended someone in California? Talked to the wrong people in North Paterson? Beat up a Chicano kid? Nosed around the Oneida Hotel too much? Showed up in Great Neck? Become a threat to Cap or Matt or Lenny Gruenfeld? Spoiled some FBI scheme or scam?

"All I can do is go around again," I said.

"After you get out of here," Kay said. "Now you rest."

"I'm fine."

"The doctors will tell you when you're fine."

"I've got a man on your door," Marx said. "Take two days."

'How many men can you put on doors?"

"Rosa leaves tomorrow. Even Pearce can't fight Medicare any longer."

"Leaves for where?"

"Some nursing home."

"What does Grenfell say?"

"Nobody gives much of a shit what Grenfell says. He

isn't going to pay for the old lady so what's he got to say?"

Marx would have paid for his mother. The large family is gone, the hometown and the relatives, the old house where there was always an extra room. How do you care for a senile old lady in a two-room apartment? When you both work? When your brother lives in Los Angeles and your sister in Toronto, and Uncle Joe and Aunt Mabel are in Sun City, Arizona?

"One day," I said. "Nobody can do anything about the ribs, the burns are okay. I better find out what I'm close to before it's too late for Rosa and everyone else, including me."

"Maybe we'll find out first," Marx said.

They left me to the mercies of the nurses. I hoped Marx would solve it all first. I'm not proud. If they wanted me enough to burn down a building they would try again, and I didn't much care who stopped them.

Next morning the shoulder felt almost normal. The ribs hurt when I breathed, but the burns were under control. Kay arrived with her ice cream and ministrations in midmorning. We were going over what she'd found unburned at my loft, trying to guess why the clothes had come through, when Lieutenant Marx walked in.

"They tried again. Poison this time."

Kay and the nurse got me into a wheelchair. A head nurse, checking the medicine cart, had noticed the substituted pills.

"They were capsules and not even the right color."

The police laboratory crew said probably sodium cyanide. Not your run-of-the-mill pharmacy stock, not easy to procure except in a chemical supply shop or laboratory. There was none in the hospital pharmacy.

"Anyone could have switched them on the cart," Marx said. "The head nurse on that shift just happens to always check the pills. Rosa got lucky."

"We got lucky," I said. "I'm not so sure about Rosa."

Marx wasn't in the mood for ultimate questions.

"The cart was at the nurses' station half an hour," he said. "If it was our homburg and topcoat, he botched this one."

"And changed his M.O.," I said. "No one noticed anyone?"

"It's a big hospital. It could have been anyone except that gunman. He wouldn't have blown it that bad."

"He wouldn't have blown it the first time," I said.

"You think this was the original shooter trying again?"

"Unless we've got three killers."

"And not one good motive," Marx said.

"What about her money?"

"How'd you know about that?"

"Grenfell's yelling about a nursing home getting it all."

"He would." The Lieutenant had taken a strong dislike to Nicholas Grenfell. Policemen are human. "It's all of eighteen thousand in a money market savings account at Citibank. Started at forty-nine thousand and change sixteen years ago, she's taken out an average of two thousand a year ever since to supplement her social security or for whatever."

"Who gets what's left?"

"No one. We can't find a will or even a beneficiary."

"Which means Grenfell."

"The brothers and the granddaughter could try for a share."

"But they wouldn't."

"Grenfell's got a hundred times eighteen grand in his house, his company, stocks, you name it."

"Most of it mortgaged, business is bad, and he once worked for a chemical company."

"What good does peanuts do him? Besides, he's alibied all the way for the shooting."

"What about the Party? I'd have thought she'd leave it anything she had."

"They say no, but we're still digging. It looks like she just didn't believe in wills or lawyers."

I didn't remind him Rosa was still alive. If someone has no future, even if still breathing, what tense do you use when you talk about them? Marx got busy, Kay pushed me back to my room. Eighteen thousand isn't much to kill for these days, except maybe for someone around the Oneida Hotel, but how would any of them get their hands on it?

Marx came up with no leads on the poisoner, and the next morning I sent Kay to find a doctor to get me out.

"Miss Michaels says you want to leave. She'll nurse you, and I couldn't let you miss something that good." The doctor had on his best we're-all-in-it-together smile, examined my chart to look scientific. "The nurse will change your burn dressings, show Miss Michaels what to do. I want a last X ray of the ribs and shoulder, then I'll sign the discharge. Deal?"

Performance medicine. Everything's one big happy family, from White House to Wall Street. We're all equal, we just have different jobs, and some of us understand better what has to be done for the good of everyone. In the Soviet it's totalitarianism. For us it's just Daddy and the boys know best.

The nurse did my burns, an orderly wheeled me to X ray and back, Kay got me dressed in the cords, Viyella shirt, turtleneck, moccasin boots and duffel she'd salvaged. They all smelled of smoke. Everything was going to smell of smoke for a long time.

I filled out all the proper forms in the cashier's office, was wheeled to the waiting taxi. I gave him the address of my loft. Kay had to correct me, tell him to take us to her hotel. I suddenly smelled all the smoke in my clothes, in my mind.

"I'm so sorry, Dan," she said, sat close against me. "But now you'll have to start over. Why not California?"

"Give me a few days to get the smoke out of my mind."

The country had changed over the last forty years. The jet made everywhere next door. Even in my trade. I still had an edge in New York, but how much and for how long? When you get older, where you are and who you know changes too. It was a different city, New York, with different people. I was different. Why not sun and warm temperatures. Mountains and a bluer sea. Kay.

The taxi dropped us at the Gotham Hotel, the doorman helped me into the elevator. In her large room I sat on the bed and knew I wasn't going to do any work today. Maybe it was the smell of smoke in my clothes and my mind. The memory of the flames and falling. Maybe it was the fear of change. I wanted her.

"What about your burns, the ribs?"

"We'll manage."

40.

APRIL HAD COME while I was in the hospital, and rain fell thin and raw on the burned-out ruins of my loft across Eighth Avenue. It looked like a bombed building around some harbor of my war. The office section was gone, the bedroom, with my bed hanging on the edge, was open to the day. I could put up a canvas wall and live in it, but they wouldn't let me. They would tear down what was left, build a new apartment house where I couldn't afford the rent. I would have to make a move.

For now I walked up and around the corner on Twenty-third to Communist Party headquarters. My personal moves would have to wait, the work comes first in the detective business. Maybe that's why I like it. Joe Kennedy, the other one, was alone in his office pecking out a letter on an ancient typewriter. The big ex-longshoreman gave me his grin.

"Change your mind? Sign you up in five minutes."

He looked like he hadn't moved since my last visit. Action was slow in the radical business. Everyone was worried about taxes and three-piece suits, foreign competition, the trade deficit and a 2,500 Dow Jones. Times were good for the upper- and middle-middle class, and the sons of the poor weren't dying in Central America yet.

I said. "It's still Rosa Gruenfeld."

"How is the old battler?"

"A nursing home. Doesn't look like she'll come out of it."

His grin saddened. "That's a shame. But, hell, she had one damn good run. Went out kicking, right? She hurtin'?"

"No. She just doesn't know who she is. Or was."

He looked out at the gray city. All he had to hold onto were his memories of everything he had done and tried to do. He was what he had done. His big broken hands touched the bullet scar on his left cheek.

"You thought of anyone who could have wanted her dead?"

It took him a moment to bring his mind back. "You sayin' they don't know yet who shot her?"

"No." I told him about Kevin Regan and Johnny Agnew, the professional killer, Flaco Cabrera and Isaiah Monroe and the botched poisoning.

"Christ, maybe she did go out fightin'." His voice was as excited as shocked. "I figured some street bum, maybe a fanatic. This sounds like something big."

"What?"

"Beats me. Nothin' she done I know of the last ten years or more except spiel the crowd on a park bench, hassle the enemy P.R. men, jump in on any damn-all protest she could get to."

"What about her money?" I said. "Eighteen thousand might be a lot to the Party now."

"Anything's a lot to the Party now." He didn't grin. "But what do you think the FBI'd do if we was named in the will of someone got shot? How long you think whichever of us didn't have an alibi'd be out of jail? You think we'd get the money? Before hell freezes over?"

"Where'd she get the money in first place? Almost fifty thousand, the police say."

"I guess from Ben Douglas when he died."

"Where'd he get the money? I thought he was blacklisted."

"Don't know where he got his dough, or much else about him. He never was a member. Said he had to be independent. Everyone got to do it his own way."

"Where do I find out about Douglas?"

"His brother." He swung around in the chair, pawed through a ragged filing cabinet, came out with a yellowed scrap of paper. "Last address we got is Apartment Seven, Four-twelve East Eighty-fourth. Angus Douglas. He ain't paid his dues in twelve years."

"He's a member?"

"We got a small world and gettin' smaller. A good job of suppression, repression, co-optin' an' hoodwinking in this country. We got outplayed, outtoughed and whupped. Everyone thinks they wants what they got today, only more. We're history, Fortune. History no one even knows about."

"That sounds like giving up."

"Hell, no. This country ain't the world."

It was a view most Americans would find impossible to understand, his sense of a world beyond this country.

Americans who would leave us someday like one of those fenced and guarded enclaves of the rich. The Balboa Island of the world.

I left him pecking away on his ancient typewriter, walked across to the Lexington Avenue subway and rode up to Yorkville. The cold drizzle got under my collar as I walked to First Avenue. Number 412 was a typical six-story tenement as gray as the day. Apartment 7 was on the second floor. The man who answered my knocking was small, thin, white-haired and as alert and quick as a real estate agent at a new development.

"Ben and Rosa? Come on in."

Wrapped in layers of torn sweaters, a red British paratrooper beret, baggy corduroy pants tied at the ankle with rope over army boots, he perched on the arm of a ragged red couch and waved me to an even dirtier armchair. The apartment was a twin of Rosa's room. A shambles of stacked furniture, newspapers, books, old phonograph records, filing cabinets and so much assorted bric-a-brac it was obvious Angus Douglas never threw anything away. Dominating it all were thick volumes of stacked notebooks on a cleared table in front of the one visible window, one volume open and by itself on the table.

"Oral history of the world," Angus Douglas said, pointed at the stacked notebooks. "Everything I learned, saw, heard, smelled, felt, experienced, read about. The past. All gone now. TV, money, real estate, condominiums, suburbs, Sun Cities, golf, country clubs, fast food, trivia. History of a dying culture. A real world out there waiting to roll over us. All we've got is money and nothing to spend it on except guns and entertainment. Everything's entertainment. Watch a man die before your very eyes. See his head blown right off. How'd you find me?"

"Joe Kennedy at the CP sent me."

"They're all dead but don't know enough to lie down.

Rosa was right. The future belongs to the people, not the parties."

"When did you see her last, Mr. Douglas?"

"Couple of years ago. Used to travel around with her all over the city, Jersey, Connecticut, upstate. Gave it up. Got to write it all down before I go."

"Can you tell me about her and Ben? Their marriage, how they lived, where he got his money?"

He had a pink, smooth, peaceful face with the open innocence of a baby. Blue eyes that I sensed mirrored whatever he was thinking or feeling at any instant. The innocence of someone no longer concerned with anything but his own truth.

"That was real life, those two." He perched on the couch arm, smiled as if seeing Ben and Rosa in his mind. "They finally found each other after so many wrong roads. I used to just like to be with them. They loved and lived the same. That's a rare thing. She didn't even break down when he died. They'd had their years, she could go on alone because they'd had the best."

"And he left her a lot of money," I said. "Where did he get it? He was blackballed the last years."

"Not so much money. They worked hard, saved."

"Someone tried to kill Rosa, Mr. Douglas. Maybe what little money she had was enough, or maybe where the money came from."

"Kill Rosa?"

"Shot her, tried to poison her."

For a time he just sat there on the arm of the grotesque red couch. Then he stood and walked to the table full of notebooks, began to write in the open book. Continuing his oral history of the world with the attacks on Rosa. I waited. He finally put the pen back into his pocket, turned.

"You want to know how Ben and Rosa had money? I'll tell you a story, then you'll know."

41. "IT'S OUR MONEY," Ben says.

He grips Rosa's arm. His fingers are so thin they dig into her like knives. She bites her lip, brushes his strands of wispy hair back from his yellow, emaciated face.

"It doesn't matter, Ben. Let them keep their handout."

His grip tightens, pulls her closer to the bed. They are in their apartment, all his needs around him on small tables and chairs—books, newspapers, notepad, pencils, the dishes of ice cream that is all he will eat, the pain pills that do little good between the times for the doctor and the morphine. He has come back from the hospital because he does not want to die with strangers. Only with her. It is the end of the month, and he pulls her down to him.

"No! I won't let them cheat us, Rosie. This corrupt society isn't going to cheat me, beat me. Never."

"Ben, sweetheart, we don't need the money. You need to rest, not get excited. You—"

His grip loosens on her arm, falls away. He smiles. His breathing is shallow, an effort. "We're a crazy species, aren't we? I don't have two weeks, not even that long, and yet I have to rest, take it easy, conserve my strength. For what, Rosie girl? I'm going to have plenty of rest soon, and I won't let them cheat me out of what is mine."

His smile is a skeleton smile, and she says, "Ben—"

"I can rest in two weeks. Take it easy." His voice is a thick, hoarse whisper. "It's my right. I'm unemployed, they owe me my unemployment."

"You're not strong enough. You can't go in and sign."

He closes his eyes in the sudden pain. A whisper. "I can sign. You'll help me, Rosie. They won't beat us."

They wait until the doctor makes his visit, gives Ben his shot, and Ben sleeps a few hours. There will be perhaps an hour with less pain and more strength. He cannot dress himself, and she is not strong enough to dress him. They compromise on sweat pants, jogging shoes and his overcoat buttoned to the neck. His war correspondent's cap. She gently brushes his strands of hair before she puts on the cap, and they go out and flag a taxi.

At the unemployment office the line is short, but he cannot stand for more than a few minutes, so Rosa sits him on a bench and stands in the line herself. The clerk at the window sees them, sees Ben sit to wait and Rosa stand in the line, but does nothing, makes no move to help. The clerk looks annoyed that Rosa is in the line instead of Ben. It is not proper procedure. The unemployed person is supposed to stand in line. The other unemployed in the line speak to Rosa, insist that Ben go to the head of the line.

The clerk seems about to deny this arrangement, but he sees the faces of the other unemployed and takes Ben's papers. The clerk does not hurry as Ben stands and holds onto the counter. The clerk takes his time. Rosa is about to say something, but Ben stops her, and the clerk finishes and Ben signs and they leave.

Ben is very pale as they ride home. His breathing is labored, and he holds onto the straps inside the taxi. The taxi driver looks at them curiously but says nothing.

"This society won't use me without paying in full, Rosie. Not while I'm breathing. Not as long as I have one second."

"All right, dear," Rosa says. "Yes."

"You need money, Rosie. It's the only way to be free of the corruption, the manipulation. Until we can change it all."

"I know," Rosa says, holds him against her in the taxi.

"You'll be all right," Ben says. "No more Cabreras, no more prison, no more being ridden down in the streets. You can go on with the work. You'll have enough they can't break you down."

"Try to rest," Rosa says, holds his skeletal body against her in the taxi. "Angus will be at the apartment."

"I'm okay. Not even any pain. They won't use my money for their repressions."

The taxi stops, and she helps him up the steps into the small elevator. He is smiling.

42.

"THE TWO OF THEM," Angus Douglas said. "Ben always made good money, never needed much. Owning, buying, being rich—the Holy Trinity—meant nothing to Ben even before he met Rosa. After, they both made good money. Being blackballed only kept people from admitting they hired you. If you were good you worked, in or out of the country. Business is business."

"Rosa made money? Doing what?"

"You see? You really know nothing about her. Real no one knows. What do you think Rosa was doing all the years after she got out of that prison? Two husbands and her daughter dead, her son as good as, and she was still a young woman. She had work to do for the Party, the world, and what did she know? Husbands, soup kitchens for field hands. She wanted to do more."

His eyes looked past me as if reading Rosa's life from his own book. Or writing his next entry in his mind.

"She went to the New School and NYU and got her Ph.D. It made a lot of the old Bolshies in the Party suspicious. What was she learning? But she taught at the Jefferson School, wrote articles for *Masses and Mainstream*. That's when Ben met her. He worked for *The New Republic*, they got married. The miracle was all their lives they'd waited for each other. They believed together, nothing else mattered. Blackballing, Party infighting, persecution, what did they care? If you need little, have some money, know the law, what can they do to you except kill you, and they were never such a violent danger the FBI could get away with that."

"Where did they work?"

"Anywhere and everywhere. Under the table, overseas for *The Guardian*. Rosa wrote articles, pamphlets, sections of books and whole books. All under other people's names but her own ideas. One of the invisible in this country. The militant radicals. A tiny minority today, unseen and unknown by everyone except the police. If someone shot her, I'd look at the authorities."

"At eighty-eight, Mr. Douglas? Out of the Party, no longer writing, making speeches no one listens to, giving out obsolete pamphlets, marching in minor protests?"

"To some people no protest is too minor, no radical pamphlet obsolete." He stood up. "That's not so bad."

He hurried to the open notebook, sat down and began to write. I was forgotten. He had never even asked my name, or why I wanted to know about Rosa, or how I knew she'd been shot. Unconcerned with who I was or what I wanted. Unimportant to him. His work was all that was important.

"Thanks, Mr. Douglas."

He didn't hear me. I left him still writing. Out on the street the wind blew the drizzle like needles against my face. I leaned into it across to Lexington and the subway, rode down in relative warmth to the Shuttle and then to

Fourteenth. The wind was stronger as I bent away from it down to Lenny Gruenfeld's apartment. There was no answer.

The Oneida Hotel was too close and too far across town to make the subway worth taking, and a taxi was too expensive for so short a trip, so I walked. California looked better with every leak in my boots, every slosh in my collar.

A hard rain was a disaster for the denizens of the Oneida. They had nothing to wear and nowhere to go, so it was stay in their holes or get soaked and frozen. The dingy lobby was attractive then, and they sat around it now, huddled or expansive depending on their supply of warming liquid. Even Barney Ederer had a shirt on and a bottle of white port. He offered me a seat on the floor beside him and a pull. I took the seat.

"Who around the Oneida knew Rosa had some money?"

"Did she?" He took a swallow of the cheap wine.

"Eighteen thousand," I said. "As good as a million here."

"And just as crazy. Even if we could of got it out of her some damn way, how long you think before the cops come down in a search and destroy as soon as anyone spends a dime?"

I took a swallow of the sweet wine. At least it warmed your belly. "If logic had anything to do with crime there wouldn't be much. Need, and stupid hope, and you've been too interested from the start. You've had something on your mind. Maybe eighteen thousand dollars."

He drank.

"Asking questions," I said. " 'How is Rosa? Is she going to make it? Has she said anything?' "

"So I like her."

"That's not enough around here."

He sat silent against the wall, the others sleeping or

drunk around us in the shadows. He drank his cheap booze, shivered in his one flannel shirt and torn corduroy pants. But it wasn't the cold that made him shiver.

"When you first come to a place like this you still got some fight." He looked around the dim lobby with its figures as silent as stone statues set to watch the ancient graves of kings. "Then it gets to you. You're in your room and outside someone yells they're being beaten. Help, call the cops. You want to, but you can't move. It's like you're paralyzed. So you don't move, you don't even go to the phone." He drank. "That morning I'm in the lobby. One of my nightmares. So I'm there and I see Rosa go back to talk to old Roth. I see that granddaughter come in, go on up to her room. I see this guy come in. I don't like the look of this guy, so I walk out, sit on the curb. I wonder about a stranger in the place that early. But I just sit. Then I hear shots. I don't move maybe five minutes. Nothing happens, so I go look. I don't see nothing. Then I hear her behind the counter. I call the paramedics. I should tell about that guy, but I don't. I keep quiet, do nothing."

"What did he look like?"

It was hard for him. The conditioning of his whole adult life said say nothing. First Nam, then the Oneida. "Kind of short, stocky. Dark like a spic or a dago. We had a sergeant, Costa, looked a lot like that, only taller. A son of a bitch, Costa, but a hell of a fucking soldier."

"What was he wearing? Any mannerisms? Something special?"

"Suit and tie. No one wears a suit and tie around here except social workers, cops and the landlord's lawyers. He was no lawyer or social worker I seen before."

"You're saying he was a cop?"

"Who else comes around here acts like that?"

"Acts like what?"

"Like he owned the place. Like he's watching us all."

You can know what you don't know you know. Your body knows, your reflexes. Your hand can tell you something is hot before your mind does. And someone who lives his life under the shadow of the police can know a cop without knowing how he knows.

I gave Ederer a ten. "Get something worth drinking."

He held the bill, but he didn't look at it. I had made him think of Vietnam. I hoped I hadn't triggered an episode. It's a hazard of my job. I make waves, bring up what people don't want brought up, leave damage in my wake.

I barely noticed the rain as I walked east to my loft. If Giannini was lying, then Smoke and Loren O were lying too. Was Chief Reynolds in on it, whatever it was? If it was anything. I had no real reason to think Giannini was lying, that Smoke and Loren O would do anything for a cop. I was on Eighth Avenue looking across at the ruins before I remembered I had no loft.

I walked on up to Bogie's, called Ed Green's office. He had an extra desk I could use for a minimal price. Green's office is on Thirty-eighth Street off Park, the high-rent district. He was on his way out when I got there, but he stopped to give me a key.

"You got to move into a better neighborhood, Dan."

"I'm thinking of California."

"Montana. I can't take heat or palm trees. Fishing, clean water, snow and cheap real estate. This ain't my city anymore. We had it, now it's someone else's turn. Time to move on. No one has roots anymore."

I got the number of the Santa Barbara County Sheriff's office from information, asked for Lieutenant Holley. I told him what I needed. He was reluctant at first.

"Just ask Cabrera where he followed Rosa Gruenfeld when she marched, protested, fought with the police."

"Listen, Fortune—"

"Do it, Lieutenant. I don't want to cause trouble for your department or the Bannisters. It's old history, and no one can do anything, but it still carries a stink."

There were voices. Angry voices. Then Holley came back on.

"I'll get back to you."

I went down to Fugazy's for my Ford and drove to New Jersey.

43.

THE RAIN HAD STOPPED, and the same sullen youths lounged in front of the same boarded buildings on Wyandanch Street. What else did they have to do? I parked in front of the Black Liberation Force storefront, made sure all eyes saw me go into the headquarters. The guardian of the temple remembered me. Not fondly.

"She's still not here."

"Smoke will do."

"You have an appointment?"

I sat down in a straight chair. "You know, Miss, after the revolution you're going to have to get over this prejudice of yours. I mean, the new order's going to have to live with the surviving whites, browns and yellows. Ever think about that?"

"No," she said, unblinking. "There won't be any whites."

What do you say? Whatever we have in this world today, we made. It doesn't really matter that she'll feel differently then, when the world is a more just place. I know that, but she doesn't, and there is no more way to reach her or her opposites than there is to reach Lenny Gruenfeld and her men behind their invisible wall.

"I'm sorry," I said. "But he'll want to see me, so—?"

"He's not here."

"Who is here?"

"No one."

She sat as rigid as a stone statue or a jungle cat.

"When will someone be here?"

"I wouldn't know." She didn't exactly smile, but her face relaxed a millimeter. "It could be all day."

She'd gotten the deep anger out, could almost deal with me. That's one answer, but it's the hard way. I didn't want to wait all day, and I didn't think she'd mellowed enough to tell me where Smoke was. Not voluntarily, anyway.

"How about Sergeant Giannini? You expect him soon?"

"Who?"

"Giannini. Your boss spends a lot of time with him."

"I wouldn't know."

"Well," I smiled. "Tell him I'll be back."

"I'll tell him."

She got busy with some papers as I left, but it was an act. I'd gotten to her, she was waiting until I was gone. Outside, my car was untouched. The power of the BLF in the neighborhood. I drove to the corner, turned toward the Passaic and parked on the next block where I could see the storefront over the rubble and through the gaps. I hoped she would come out soon, it was no place for a one-armed honky with New York plates to stake out.

She did. She came out, locked up, stood on the sidewalk. A sleek orange Continental with more exterior chrome than a Fifties hot rod pulled up in front of BLF headquarters, and she got in. They couldn't see the color of my skin at the distance, and she hadn't left her post to notice the car I was driving.

The gaudy Continental led me to a back street a block from the main square and the courthouse. The lady guardian of the BLF gate got out and opened the door for a tall black man who walked into a magazine and paperback bookstore with the slow, exaggerated, undulating walk of an athlete affected by half the young males of America. Careless and provocative at the same time— Like, I'm a millionaire never finished high school, man. I'm *big*, man, don't give me none of your shit. The woman followed him inside.

For a bookstore on a backstreet it did good business. A stream of customers went in, most of them studying worn paperbacks or slim pamphlets. They came out in just as steady a stream, carrying nothing they hadn't gone in with. It wasn't books this store was selling, it was dreams. I knew a numbers drop when I saw one. This one looked like a combination of a "writer" for direct bets and an "office" for runners to drop their collections. Someone was getting paid off big.

New Jersey has legal betting from casino gambling to lottery tickets, but the numbers racket keeps growing. Better odds, tax-free winnings, easy times and places for poor people who work long and odd hours. A ghetto dream for the small people who feel nervous out of the ghetto. The safety of the familiar and the lure of the illegal. It's hard to beat 600–1 odds in your neighborhood candy store, and people who live on illusions that are never going to come true don't much care who gets rich on their hope, the state or the Mafia or the Black Liberation Force.

Smoke and Loren O came out with the lady guardian. The tall imitation athlete with the orange Continental didn't appear. He would be the lady's private life, giving her a lift in a crisis. The three revolutionaries hurried to a battered Buick painted defiantly in the BLF green and yellow with the flash. It was easy to follow, advertising doesn't always pay. They went straight back to their headquarters. I looked for a public telephone booth, but they had all been vandalized. I was out of the ghetto before I found a working one at a gas station.

The BLF was listed in the phone book. Everybody is

public relations-conscious these days. The woman answered, recognized my voice before I gave my name.

"He's back, you can see him."

"Put him on," I said

"He'd like to see you."

"Sure," I said. "I tailed you to that numbers drop. The orange Continental's cute. You better put him on."

There was some silence, some distant voices, some clicks on the line as more than one receiver was picked up.

"What's going on, Fortune?"

"Yeah, what's going on? What else you into besides the numbers?"

"You get funds how you can," Smoke said. "People are going to gamble. It's better than stealing."

"It is stealing. From your own people."

"For something more important than today."

"Is that what Rosa Gruenfeld knew? You pay off Giannini? That's why he tried to kill her?"

The answer came too fast. "We don't pay off Giannini, payoffs are handled a lot higher up, and you know it. We didn't know anything about the old lady before Lenny Gruenfeld told us. She had no connection to us. If you can find one, go ahead."

He was too sure. The numbers operation was too open for one old lady to have worried them in North Paterson.

"The Mafia runs the numbers," I said. "That where the hired gun came from?"

"What are you on, Fortune? What hired gun?" Smoke almost laughed. "Look, come on back, we'll straighten all this out."

"Maybe later."

I hung up. I hadn't asked the right question. It was the first smell of a real connection to people who hired professional killers, and Smoke and Loren O had left the numbers shop in a hurry when the lady gatekeeper had told them I'd been around talking about Giannini. I didn't think they wanted me back for some more polite conversation.

I drove to the same stakeout on the next street where I could watch the BLF store through the gaps in the buildings. It was as bad a stakeout as it could be. On an empty street with open spaces of rubble all around and no good reason to be there. Word would be passing already about a cop or enforcer in the area. Who else would park there in broad daylight?

And who would drive past BLF headquarters twice, slowing each time but then not stopping? It was a dark blue Ford sedan, and the third time it appeared I knew: someone who had spotted me and didn't want me to spot him.

I drove away as far as the first building that hid me and pulled off the street into the rubble between two buildings. I stood at the corner of the building. The Ford cruised past on the cross street to be sure I had gone on. I slipped back on foot to where I could see the BLF store. The Ford was nowhere in sight. A man came along Wyandanch Street in the distance. Unobtrusive, average-to-tall, a little overweight, short dark blond hair, wearing a windbreaker and cords now instead of his dark three-piece suit, but out of place anyway. Too Anglo, too neat. The FBI man, Cardenas.

He went into BLF headquarters.

I drove for New York. There were many reasons for an FBI man to go to Black Liberation Front headquarters. Even to not want to be seen. But to show up at this exact moment, and to not want to be seen by *me*, was something else.

44.

IT WAS DARK when I reached Perry Street, the wet April haze cold and windless as I stood and rang at Lenny Gruenfeld's door. Rang again. After the fourth ring her voice spoke through the door.

"Yes?"

"Dan Fortune."

There was a silence.

"Just a minute."

When she opened the door she wore a thick white robe that looked as soft as fur, had bare feet.

"Come in, Dan."

She walked ahead of me into the mammoth living room with its instruments, speakers, music stands, wires and gaudy paintings.

"You caught me just getting dressed."

She sat on the couch, made room for me to sit beside her, pulled the thick robe closer over her breasts in that gesture women have that seems intended to hide their nakedness under the robe but only emphasizes it.

"Where're Cap and Matt?"

"They took Margo to the movies. The club's dark tonight."

She was telling me she was home alone, but there were cigarettes in the ashtrays on the coffee table. People had been with her. How long ago, I couldn't tell. There was a cold draft from the partly open French doors out onto the patio. She got up and slid the doors closed all the way.

"I hate it when it gets stuffy in here."

She sat close to me, tucked her legs up under her and

the robe in that perennial female pose of smallness and warmth that asks to be enfolded, held. I felt her tension like an open wound in the room, a gap in her invisible wall. The plastic bubble gone, leaving her as naked as she was under the robe.

"Did you just come to visit, Dan?"

I told her about California, the fire that had burned me out and the poison try.

"Alive? It was all a trick back then. Prison, everything?"

"They had an economic problem."

"Do you believe them now?"

"I believe they'd all rather it didn't get brought up, but not enough to kill Rosa after almost fifty years. To keep on trying to kill her and burn me out."

"It seems to make as much sense as anything we know."

"How about eighteen thousand dollars for a reason?"

I told her about my talk with Angus Douglas, and with Barney Ederer and the Black Liberation Force people.

"She has a Ph.D.?" She seemed to see something through the walls. "All that work for nothing. Even before she was shot."

"Would eighteen thousand be important to your father?"

"He could probably use it, but not enough to shoot her."

"What about that FBI man, Lenny? With Mr. F.X. Keene, and now with your Black Liberation Force people?"

"They're always hassling the BLF," she said.

"Cardenas wasn't hassling Keene. Working with him."

"Isaiah says you don't trust the Keenes, but you use them. As long as they have something to gain, you can use them."

"Why would the FBI be worried about me seeing them go into BLF headquarters?"

"They're always sniffing around. Maybe he was harassing them. Maybe he wants a payoff. How do I know?"

She was answering, even staying on the subject, but she wasn't saying anything. On the couch in the thick white robe, her blonde hair catching the light, her legs curled up and toes just visible under the edge of the robe, she was enough to take a man's mind off any subject. The ring of the telephone somewhere in the back of the apartment finished the job.

When she went to answer it, I found her bathroom. There was no steam, and the shower floor was dry. Jeans, a T-shirt and sneakers lay on the floor as if taken off in a hurry so she could answer the door in her robe and look like she'd been alone.

When she returned she had two Beck's and two glasses.

"Lenny, is something going on about Isaiah Monroe?"

"Always," she said, poured the beers into the glasses. "A new trial, parole, a pardon, fund-raising."

"You weren't alone when I rang, why go to so much trouble to pretend you were."

She drank her beer. "All right, yes. Some of the Monroe committee were here. They don't trust easily, Dan. Not even me. Do you blame them? All their lives scared by the majority, the good people, the authorities. Black, brown, yellow and even white if they don't think like the majority. For some of them to be known to be trying to help Isaiah would cost them their jobs, or their clients. They don't know you. So they told me to act like I'd been alone and went out the back."

"Who was here?"

"BLF people, social workers, community activists."

"Smoke and Loren O?"

"Not tonight."

"Keene?"

"He sent someone."

It made sense. Smoke and Loren O couldn't have beaten me in, and the meeting sounded too low-level for F.X. Keene.

"Do you meet often here? Could Rosa have stumbled over something? Something you don't even remember?"

"We don't meet here often. Mostly I sing at the rallies and the prisons. Usually they work in New Jersey. There just can't be any connection to Rosa."

Her blonde hair moved like gold silk, the thick white robe gapping open over her breasts. She had never been so animated, and for someone who made her living at least half with the allure of her body she had a less obvious sense of her own sexuality than any woman I'd ever met. As if she never thought about it. A shell within the shell. Tonight there was a difference.

"Matt and Cap don't approve of Monroe, of what you're doing for him? That's why they go out?"

"They didn't know about the meeting. They just took Margo to the movies." She pulled the robe over her breasts again. "They don't like me doing anything except with the band and them. They always take Margo for ice cream after the movie."

"Does that take them long? The movies and the ice cream?"

"Long enough."

She let the robe fall open over her breasts. They were everything her tight clothes said they were.

"It's not a good idea," I said.

"It's been there almost from the start. For you, too."

"For me especially," I said. "That still doesn't make it a good idea. We live in different eras, Lenny."

"Let's find out what the difference is."

Sex, business, politics, it's all in sensing the moment when you can make a move and know that even if something outside stops it, no one will get hurt. That instant when you know it's okay because you both want it. So she smiled and moved close and touched me with her body under the thick white robe. Put her arms around my neck and looked at my face.

"There's something different about you, Dan. You don't let other people do your thinking, you don't care about power. You know that because you've got power and money and status doesn't mean you're right or know what's good for everyone."

Out of the robe, her body was even more than it had seemed in clothes that first time I saw her standing over Rosa's bed in Intensive Care. It made me feel not so much old as crude, hacked out, made from common clay while she was made of the smoothest marble by the greatest sculptor.

"You don't buy all the lies they tell us, all the grubbing for a big bank account. You're like us."

She wasn't marble. I thought about Kay. Would I do it because I didn't want to go to California? Didn't want to commit to Kay or to anyone? Was I going to make myself lose Kay the way I had lost Marty? All disguised behind the need to do my work, explore the unknown land? "Lenny," I said, "listen to—"

But she wasn't there. She had already pulled away from me, huddled at the end of the couch. "I can't. I just can't. I'm sorry. I thought I could. I like you, Dan, but . . . it's him."

"Monroe?"

"You know so much, but he knows more. You stay outside, but he fights."

I found my cigarettes. "I didn't know you'd been with him."

"I haven't. But I want to, and I will. Maybe a woman *is* different. Maybe a woman will always try to find herself in something else—a cat, a child, a man. I don't know. I just know that when I listen to him, see him, he's what I want, what I need. No one else, nothing else except my music. He's part of that too, the music. Part of the whole world, that's what Matt and Cap won't understand."

Her fantasy of Isaiah Monroe was like the rest of her isolated world. A fantasy and yet only too real. Behind her invisible wall, even with Cap and Matt and the child, she was too isolated, and Monroe had entered. The idea of Monroe. Until every man, Cap or Matt or me, was only a substitute for Monroe even if Cap and Matt had been there first. In a way, Monroe embodied all the good in Cap and Matt, all the outrage and frustration and denial, but Monroe added hope, a future. A man and much more than a man. Her salvation from a useless life, from a useless society as she saw it.

"I . . . I want to make love to other men, but I can't. I really did want you, Dan. It's just . . ."

"I know," I said. "Sometimes you just can't."

For her, sex and the world were too entwined. She was in love with a hope for the world. I didn't envy Matt or Cap or even Margo. And I didn't believe she had just suddenly wanted me. Not the way she felt about Monroe. There was something else behind it. Something she was hiding.

I gave her a kiss and left. She was my client, but I had a strong feeling that she wasn't on my side. Not all the way. She was holding back. If it had anything to do with the shooting of Rosa or not, I didn't know. As I walked east and north in the night it occurred to me that maybe she didn't know either. The way she didn't know that it wasn't Isaiah Monroe the man she was in love with, it was the symbol. The symbol of Monroe that was a way back into the world she had not quite given up on.

When I got back to Ed Green's office there was a message for me on the answering machine. It was from Lieutenant Holley out in Santa Barbara. "Cabrera says he tailed the old lady all over New York and across to Newark and Jersey City and some town called North Paterson. All she did was hand out stuff, make speeches, march around in demonstrations and get arrested a couple of times. That's it, Fortune, and take some advice. Stay out of Santa Barbara County."

I walked up to the Gotham Hotel. Kay was in the room. We went down to the lounge for a nightcap. I told her about Lenny.

"Was it California? Me? Or just the ribs?"

"The ribs hurt, but not that much."

"Then it was me? Us?"

I drank my Beck's. "Whatever it was it stopped me."

"I think that's good enough. Let's go up."

We went up to the room. It was too late to go to New Jersey now anyway.

45.

CLOUDS PILED DARK over the city the next morning as I walked to the precinct. Lieutenant Marx was busy, I cooled my heels in the squad room thinking about Flaco Cabrera following Rosa around like the ghost of the past until he realized she hadn't changed in almost fifty years, could do him no good and probably no harm.

"Nothing," Marx said behind his overloaded desk. "We can't find any connection between Regan, Johnny Agnew and Rosa. None between her and old man Roth and that Latino kid, Carlos Arriba. Except the Oneida Hotel. Grenfell's alibi for that morning checks out solid, and

Lenny Gruenfeld hasn't any motive. No one has a motive, and the gun hasn't shown up. If your Cabrera is out, that leaves no one and everyone." He shook his head. "Without a weapon, a witness, or a motive, someone comes in and tells us or we file it. Ninety-nine percent."

"Can you get me in to see Isaiah Monroe?"

He sat there and looked at me. "I'd rather get you in to see the Pope. You think Monroe's the connection?"

"Cabrera puts her in North Paterson."

"When? A year ago?"

"She could have gone back."

"Then your client's lying?"

"Maybe."

"It may take a while. Go do something."

I walked back through the gusting wind to Lenny Gruenfeld's apartment on Perry Street. I rang a long time before the door opened. It was Matt this time. He carried his bass as if I'd interrupted a practice session, didn't ask me in. There was no sound behind him, and no movement in the living room.

"Session?"

"Practice makes perfect. You want Lenny, she ain't here."

He didn't move from the doorway. All of them asked me in only reluctantly. As if the apartment were a sanctuary, a cave, a world in a different universe, and they wanted nothing from the outside to intrude. As much a part of them as the invisible plastic wall they carried with them.

"You know she meets with Isaiah Monroe's people here?"

"Sometimes."

"You went to school with him, didn't you?"

"Long time ago, 'nother country. The Wind got blown one ways, I got blown somewhere else."

"You don't believe in his ideas? What he wants to do?"

"Shit." He started to close the door.

"You know Lenny's in love with him."

He held the door half-closed. "She think she in love with what she think he is."

"Where does that leave you and Cap?"

"Waitin'."

"For how long, Matt?"

"Long as it takes. That one thing we got plenty of, time. We done dropped out, *adios,* so long. We goin' nowheres and ain't in no hurry to get there."

"Why don't you believe in what Monroe wants?"

"'Cause all he gonna do is change who on top, get a share of the pie."

"What do you want?"

"A whole damn new pie."

"Cap and Lenny too?"

"Cap knows. Lenny still got hope for the Monroes."

"What's that going to do to the three of you? The band?"

"Slow the band down."

"That's all? You're not afraid you'll break up?"

"Like I said, we got all the time. The Wind ain't going nowhere, Lenny wake up sometime."

"If Monroe's free? A new trial turns him loose?"

"That way she get over it faster."

"You're sure of that?"

He just looked at me. "That all, Fortune? I got to practice."

"Tell Lenny I was here, I'll be back."

I let him close the door this time, walked up to Bleecker and on across to Seventh Avenue and St. Vincent's. Rosa was unchanged, Lenny wasn't with her, and they told me at the nurses' station they were moving her out tomorrow to a nursing home. I sat down in the white and busy corridor and thought about that for a time. Then I called Marx. He was still waiting for an answer from Trenton. I thought about Rosa and the nursing home a while longer, then went down and back across Perry Street to see if Lenny was home yet.

When I crossed Bleecker Street I saw the car turn the corner at the far end of Lenny's block.

Sometimes I move fast enough to think that I'm not getting as old as I am. Call it reflex and the years of learning to survive as an average-sized one-armed man in a world of larger two-armed men. The doorway I found was recessed enough to hide me in the shadows of a dark day.

The dark blue Ford sedan cruised slowly up the block from Hudson Street, hesitated in front of Lenny's building before turning down Bleecker in front of me on its way to Charles, where it turned right. The FBI man, Cardenas, was behind the wheel.

When it appeared again it parked across from Lenny's apartment in a suddenly vacated spot. I hadn't seen anyone get into the car that left so conveniently. Its driver had to have been sitting in it. I know a stakeout when I see one.

I waited until a truck came along Bleecker big enough to hide me from the dark blue Ford until I was out of sight, then walked back to the precinct. Marx had my appointment arranged.

"I told them to tell Monroe you were a reporter, but you were really working for us on a special case involving radical activities in the city. We wanted to see if anything could be traced to Monroe." He shook his head. Half-angry, half-sad. "They jumped at it. They want anything they can get against Monroe in case there's a third trial."

I was on my way to Trenton before noon.

46.

THE FIRST THING YOU SAW was that he wasn't a large man. The next, how large he was. In his prime he'd been an inch over six feet, two hundred five pounds all in the chest and shoulders and thighs. No hips, a twenty-nine-inch waist, tight buttocks. A running back. A slugging third-baseman. A sprinter and long jumper. Not large, but solid, dense, like an impenetrable mass that seemed to fill the small visiting room.

"Sit down, Mr. Monroe."

He smiled. A thin, cold, mocking, weary smile, and I saw a man no longer young, with eyeglasses, scars on his tired face, a thickened waist, faint gray in his hair and a slower walk. The motion not as graceful, the balance not as perfect, the power diminished. The physical force drained and faded. The Wind blowing now, if it blew at all, on a different fuel.

"You don't like to be called Mister?" I said.

"Only by people I call Mister." He sat. "I'm writing a book, Fortune. I don't give interviews."

"I'm not here for an interview. I'm not a reporter."

Everything drained from his face except an alertness to danger that was automatic now, a suspicion that had become part of him early in life, and an anger he'd been born with.

"What the fuck you think—?" He was half out of the chair.

"I'm a private detective working for Lenny Gruenfeld. The New York police sent me to ask some questions."

The superb balance was still good enough that he could stop in midmotion. He sat again, but not all the way. A millimeter above the chair. The brain was still there too, maybe sharper. He understood instantly that whatever I was doing I didn't want New Jersey to know.

"What questions?"

I told him about Rosa and her shooting and the hired killer.

"I never heard of Rosa Gruenfeld. I don't know anything about an Agnew or a Regan or a hit man. I think you better—"

"What about Smoke and Loren O? Or Lenny Gruenfeld meeting people secretly in New York?"

The eyes behind the glasses fixed on me as if I were a specimen under a microscope. "I know Smoke. My people hold meetings."

"That include Francis X. Keene?"

"It includes anyone who wants to help me."

"How about Detective Sergeant Giannini of the North Paterson Police?"

"The NPPD doesn't like me very much."

"The FBI?"

"They like me less."

"Why would the FBI and F.X. Keene be working together at the same time he's on your third trial committee?"

He said nothing.

"Why would the FBI go to the BLF and not want to be seen?"

He said nothing.

"Why would Smoke and Loren O alibi Sergeant Giannini?"

"They wouldn't."

"Why would the FBI tail Lenny Gruenfeld?"

Shock can show in many ways. For Monroe it was an almost imperceptible shrinking as if he had in an instant become a smaller man. A psychological blow, there and gone. Replaced by a mask as if nothing had happened.

But I had seen it.

"Something's going to happen isn't it?"

"You're wasting your time."

"Rosa Gruenfeld's been shot. Johnny Agnew's dead. I think Lenny Gruenfeld's in danger, and it's all connected to you."

"You better get out of here before I call the guard."

"Look, I don't care about you, but I care about Lenny. She thinks you're genius, lover and savior, and she's going to get hurt because of you."

"Why don't you care about me?"

"Because you're going to hurt a lot of people."

"Is that my fault?"

"No, it's just you. You are what you are."

"What am I, Fortune?"

"A force. A walking wound. Anything and everything except just a man."

He sat there and seemed to study what I had said, examine it. I could hear the guard shift outside the door. "They can't ever let me out of here, but it doesn't really matter. They've already gotten me. All that's left is the hate. That's all they're going to leave the whole world eventually. Hate of the white man and this country. I'm gone, I don't count anymore."

"Is it some kind of attack? Guns, bombs?"

"Not in this country. That's outside, the third world. The Establishment is too strong. They've got a co-opted, traduced, moronized majority conned into living the way the corporate society wants them to. But there's a sickness, a confusion. People sense something wrong, are restless, uneasy, and the moral refusal will grow."

"I thought you believed in violence?"

"Not when there's no chance. Remember the Panthers, George Jackson, the Symbionese Army, the Weathermen? All we can do is refuse and wait, the fight is outside. We'll win the war outside, and then this country will be irrelevant."

"Who'll be relevant? The Soviet?"

"No. Not the USSR, not Cuba with Fidel the Castillian. All white men will be irrelevant."

He sat there without expression. Looked at me through the thick glasses. The scarred face and bent shoulders as rigid as stone. He said it all without emotion. A flat, quiet, steady voice, almost matter-of-fact.

"What are Lenny and the others doing, Isaiah?"

He held out his hand for the first time. I gave him a cigarette, took one myself, lit them both. He smoked awkwardly, like a man who had only started to smoke a few days ago.

"I didn't do what they put me in here for, but I could have. I didn't murder those men, but I *might* have, and from the point of view of those in power it's the same thing. Sooner or later I will kill some white men, maybe them, so I'm as good as guilty, have to be restrained for the good of society. For the good of *their* society."

"What's happening, Isaiah?"

He smoked until the cigarette burned his fingers, slowly stubbed the butt out in the ashtray on the table.

"They're going to break me out."

His face still showed no change of expression, but now I knew what the shock had been when I asked him why the FBI would be tailing Lenny. He had known then he was not going to be freed. Not now, not ever.

"When?" I said. "How?"

"I was supposed to hear in three days."

"From who?"

"Lenny Gruenfeld."

So there it was, what Lenny was hiding. Because she knew it had gotten Rosa shot? Or because she really couldn't see a connection to Rosa, didn't know it was a trap to get rid of Monroe once and for all? Shot in a jailbreak. The powerful don't have to be imaginative or original.

"Why would Smoke and Loren O set you up?"

"There are a hundred ways to corrupt people. Smoke could want me out of the way. Loren thinks it's best for the cause. They got paid. The police have a hold on them. It doesn't matter. They'll finish me off one way or the other. All I can do is try to take a few with me, hope my story helps the blacks and browns to take over the future."

He went to the door. "I'll survive this one, but you better be careful, they won't love you for blowing their scheme."

He knocked, the guard let him through, and I was alone in the small room.

47.

IT WAS LATE AFTERNOON when I reached the city, drove downtown to Lenny Gruenfeld's apartment. I had to park on Hudson.

The black sedan had been parked on Perry Street on the far side of Hudson, came across Hudson as I walked up to Perry. But the driver's timing was a hair off. The car passed me before I'd made the turn onto Perry, had to stop. Call it the sixth sense a detective develops, ESP, pure luck, but when the car stopped I looked at it. A black car motionless in the street. Another car came up behind the black sedan.

He got out of the sedan. Top coat, white shirt and tie, homburg, round pink face, hands in his pockets.

I ran south down Hudson and across the wide street through the screeching brakes and honking traffic, the contorted faces of the drivers open-mouthed at me. I heard no sound, saw nothing but twisted faces, looming cars, cobblestones. All in slow motion. Onto Charles Street and on toward the river.

Almost to Greenwich Street I heard the running behind me. The sharp, explosive pop of a silenced pistol. The sound of the firing, but no whine of bullets, no sudden impact to end my running and maybe me. The targets of hired killers are not supposed to be moving.

On Washington Street I reached Tenth and the abandoned garage. It used to have a ramp to parking on the second floor. The ramp is gone but the second floor is still there, and stairs through a half-hidden door at the rear go up. I went up.

It was some minutes before he appeared in the garage below. Slow and wary, not sure I was even in the garage. I stepped through a hole in the second floor wall that was hidden behind a mound of debris into the condemned tenement next door, found where the stairs had collapsed and a rope dangled, slid down to the street level and came out onto Washington Street.

No black sedans were in sight. I walked to Christopher, found a cab cruising outside the PATH station and rode up to Ed Green's office. I watched the entrance for fifteen minutes to be sure the killer hadn't beaten me there. With any luck they didn't know yet I'd moved in temporarily with Green.

I called Kay at the Gotham Hotel. She wasn't there. I left a message for her to check out and tell no one where she was going, call me at Green's number when she had another place.

"You're Mr. Dan Fortune?" the desk clerk asked.

"Just leave that message for—"

"I have a message for you, sir. A Lieutenant Marx called about ten minutes ago."

"Read it."

"The killer tried again in the hospital. They have the

killer. Hey, that's exciting, what—?"

I locked the office when I left, flagged a cab on Lexington. It took fifteen minutes to get across Fourteenth. I paid him off at Seventh Avenue and walked south to the precinct. The duty sergeant told me to wait, called Marx and sent me on up to the squad room. Marx sat on the edge of a desk looking down at Nicholas Grenfell. Two of Marx's detectives stood around him. Grenfell sat with his head down, his face half-turned away from Marx toward me. His hands were cuffed behind him, his face was bruised, blood oozed from the corner of his mouth.

"We've got you cold," Marx said as I pushed up. "You might as well tell us the rest. You hired that gun to kill her while you established an alibi. How'd you find him? Where is he now?"

"No." Grenfell shook his head. Back and forth as if he couldn't stop. "No. You've got it all wrong. She was dead anyway. We talked. Alette and I. It would be a mercy." He nodded now, up and down. "Yes. A mercy."

He sat in a long white physician's coat ripped off one shoulder, buttons torn away, and underneath his dark blue banker's three-piece pin-stripe suit with blood-stained white shirt and regimental striped tie. Marx saw me.

"If you want that gunman," I said, "he was a couple of blocks away about half an hour ago."

I told him about my chase and escape.

"Must have been around for backup," Marx said. He looked down at Grenfell. "We caught him in her room trying to give her the poison himself. Had the pills in his hand, a glass of water, was talking to her nice and quiet. Trying to make her take the pills. Two of my men grabbed him."

"For the money?"

"That's what it looks like."

Grenfell's head jerked up. "They're sending her to a

home! They'll take all her money. We need that money, and she'll die anyway. She's as good as dead. She *is* dead, and they'll take all her money and keep her alive a useless nothing. We *need* that money, don't you see? We discussed it. She was dead already—"

He talked on, more to himself than us now. The detectives and patrolmen began to drift away, go back to work. Marx sat on the desk, bent down close to Grenfell.

"The gunman, Grenfell. When did you contact him? How did you find him?"

I said, "I don't think he did, Lieutenant."

One of the other detectives said, "Crap, Fortune. We caught him redhanded. Don't be a hotshot."

"You don't think he had her shot?" Marx said.

"The money isn't enough for that," I said. "After she was shot, after they realized she'd go into a home and they'd lose what money she had, they couldn't resist helping her along so they'd get the cash. He's not a killer, just a weak, greedy man who never got over childhood hates."

Marx chewed a lip. "I don't know, Dan. He looks pretty good to me. A hired gun gave him his alibi."

"Chasing rainbows again, Fortune?" the other detective said.

"If you have anything, Dan, you better tell us," Marx said.

"Soon," I said.

I left them starting again on Nicholas Grenfell. They had an attempted murder, they would get all they could out of him.

48.

PERRY STREET WAS DARK as I stood again at the corner of Bleecker. I hadn't gone near my rental car still parked on Hudson, and I waited and watched for some time in the shadows of the doorway. The topcoated hit man would figure I would stay away from Lenny's apartment now. Or would he figure that's what I would assume he would do and so do the opposite? No matter what he or I decided, it remained a fifty-fifty chance. He was there somewhere on the dark street waiting for me, or he wasn't.

I walked across Bleecker and along Perry Street. I didn't hurry. What counted was seeing him first, and if not first, as soon as he made a move. I saw nothing. No one stepped out of a doorway, got out of a car, suddenly opened a window. He was not waiting at Lenny Gruenfeld's door. I rang.

Cap answered. He was in his black Viet Cong pajamas, white headband with red Chinese characters, cartridge belt, thick-soled sandals, ready for the night's gig over in the NoHo club.

"Not now, Fortune, okay? We're on warmup."

I bulled him inside, kicked the door closed. "There's a hired gun somewhere out there. Stay out of lighted doorways."

I pushed past him into the mammoth living room. Matt tuned his bright yellow bass dressed in the jungle camouflage fatigues, the yellow helmet liner, rhinestone belt and combat boots.

"What the fuck's he want?"

Lenny stood at the mike, eyes closed, swaying to

music conjured up inside her head. Her skintight black body suit had never looked tighter or thinner. The white boots and short leopard jacket seemed to be from some dream of mine, the French Army bush hat as jaunty as the first time I had seen her. She opened her eyes when she heard me, put on the oversize sunglasses that completed her stage uniform.

"I talked to Monroe," I said.

"Congratulations," Matt said.

"What was your job? Smuggling in the gun?"

She picked up her red guitar synthesizer, began to sway again behind the microphone in the center of the giant room.

"Gun?" Cap said behind me.

Lenny said, "He doesn't know what he's talking about."

"We ever gonna get to work?" Matt said.

I said, "Listen to me! There's a hired killer out there. There's FBI, the National Security Council for all I know. If they don't know I talked to Monroe they're going ahead with the plan and want me and anyone around me out of the way. If they know Monroe talked to me, they're going to have to cover up."

She picked the guitar, hot chords that reverberated from the amplifier through the big room. Both Cap and Matt had stopped playing now, watched her and watched me. The little girl, Margo, came out of an inner room, stood there silent and wide-eyed.

"All right," I said. "I'll tell you. Smoke and Loren O came to you. They said there was no way Monroe was going to get a third trial. He would die in prison. They maybe had proof an 'accident' was planned in prison. So they were going to break him out. It was all arranged, but they had to have someone to take the gun in, the keys, whatever. They had to bribe guards. He'd be out of the country in an hour after he broke out, safe in Cuba or Angola or maybe even Russia. All they needed was someone to be the contact. Someone clean, uninvolved."

"Don't listen to him," Lenny said to Matt and Cap.

I said, "What you didn't know, don't know, is that it's a setup. A trap. He'll be killed attempting to escape, just like George Jackson. Smoke and Loren O are part of it, maybe jealous, maybe something else, who knows, but you weren't part of it. So they had to watch you. You see?"

She said nothing. No one did. She held the guitar, stood in the skintight black and looked at me. They all looked at me.

"All along we thought the attacker had been waiting for Rosa, watching for her. He was watching all right, but not for Rosa. He was watching for you, Lenny. He was tailing you."

"You sayin' he was gonna shoot Lenny?" Matt said.

"Not Lenny, no. He was only tailing Lenny."

Lenny said, "Why, then? Why shoot Rosa if he was following me? It doesn't make sense. None of it makes any sense. You're wrong. You—"

I went closer to her. "He was watching you, but Rosa saw him—and Rosa *knew* him. Remember what she babbled from the beginning? 'the Good Gestapo.' 'I know you.' What was 'the Good Gestapo' doing there? She recognized the man tailing you, and if she told you it would blow the whole scheme."

The vast room was so silent the little girl, Margo, came closer to her mother, frightened. "Mommy?"

Lenny reached down, touched the child. "Who?"

"Did you ever see anyone who could have been following you?"

"No."

"Anything unusual. Someone staring at you, hiding when you looked up. A face you noticed more than once and wondered about. Someone outside the apartment when you went out. Someone who always seemed to be there? Maybe not the same man, but always someone? A car that seemed to pull out whenever you went out."

She shook her head each time, her hand still on the shoulder of the child who looked up at her. Cap and Matt had put their instruments aside now.

"Lenny?" Cap said. "That time I told you maybe someone was hanging around outside all weekend?"

Matt said, "Sometime I feel eyes, you know?"

"They're always staring," Lenny said. "The fans, the studs, the groupies. You learn to forget it. How would I notice?"

"Probably one of three men," I said. "Or even all three at different times." I described the killer in the topcoat.

"The man who murdered that Agnew at the Oneida," Lenny said. "I never saw anyone like him."

I described the FBI man, Cardenas. "Mostly he'd be in a suit, maybe blue."

She shook her head. I described Detective Sergeant Giannini of the North Paterson Police, "Short, dark, stocky. Could have been in a suit, or jeans and a leather jacket. Work clothes, a windbreaker. A baseball jacket and hat. A—"

She stood like a statue, one hand holding the gaudy red synthesizer guitar that hung around her neck on its cord, the other on the shoulder of Margo, who now looked at me accusingly. I was doing something bad to her mother. Lenny lifted the guitar over her head, set it into its stand, took the child's hand and walked out of the room. Cap, Matt and I waited. After a minute, maybe less, Lenny came back still holding Margo's hand. In her other hand she had a fountain pen.

"I'd just gotten out of a cab, was late for the gig because I'd been over in Jersey working with Smoke. At first I was just going to be the go-between, later they told me I had to take the gun in, pay the bribe to the two guards. They told me he'd be murdered in there. I had—"

"The cab," I said. "You were late for the gig."

She blinked, nodded. "I left my backpack in the cab. I realized it as soon as I'd turned the corner, ran back. He must have just gotten out of a cab, too. He had a Mets jacket on. I ran right into him. I remember because he was so polite, held me so I wouldn't fall, yelled for my cab to stop. I was lucky, the traffic was heavy on Hudson. I got my backpack."

"And when you turned back," I said, "he was gone."

"I wanted to thank him. But he'd just vanished. Then I saw this pen on the street right where I'd bumped him. He must have left so fast he never saw it or missed it."

I took the pen. It was a Mark Cross. An expensive pen with a gold monogram. A single letter: *G*.

"I watched for him to return the pen. I didn't see him for a week or so, then I thought I did outside the club one afternoon we went to reset the sound. But I only got a glimpse and then he wasn't there. Short, dark. I'd have said he was a good person, kind. You say he shot Rosa? Wanted to kill her?"

"He shot her, I don't think he wanted to. I think maybe he is a good man."

I got on the telephone to Lieutenant Marx. The police are a brotherhood. They couldn't be anything else. They live and die the same life. Next to the death of one of them, maybe the death of a prisoner in custody, the worst thing is a crime by a fellow officer. A lot don't want to even think about policemen being criminals, some don't care, but Marx is a different cop.

"You're sure, Dan?"

"I'm sure."

"I'll talk to the Captain. Stay on the line."

How much of our lives do we spend on hold? It was five minutes while I fidgeted, Lenny talked about the plan to break The Wind out of prison, and Cap, Matt and Margo watched us both.

"Okay," Marx came back on. "I'll pick you up."

Lenny changed into the corduroy jeans, turtleneck and boots of our first trip to New Jersey. Matt, Cap and the drummer would have to get a quick fill-in or go on without her. They didn't like it, but even Matt said nothing to her. Marx arrived alone. The trip would be low profile, unofficial for now.

"The Captain called Chief Reynolds in North Paterson. He didn't tell him anything except that I wanted to talk to him, it was important, had to be tonight, Reynolds said okay."

49.

CHIEF REYNOLDS LIVED in a modest ranch-style brick house in an old tract development from the post-World War Two days. He'd probably lived in the same house since he'd gotten his first promotion, the only sign of his status and greater affluence now was a second wing built onto the house for the private office where his wife sent us.

Reynolds saw me and Lenny.

"You said a private meeting.'

"They're part of it, Chief."

"Not here. Downtown in the morning."

I said, "The morning could be too late."

"I think you should listen Chief," Marx said.

Reynolds looked at each of us one at a time, then only at Marx. He nodded, stepped back and waved us in. It was a comfortable office. Couches, armchairs, a small wet bar, a large conference table with straight chairs, his awards, certificates and trophies on all the walls and in glass cases. Framed photographs of his whole career filled the rest of the wall space.

"The table," Reynolds said.

He took the high-backed chair at the head of the pale teak table, motioned for us to sit on the straight chairs around it. He watched unsmiling, not happy to see us there, but without a hint of any other emotion.

"The Captain thought—" Marx began.

Reynolds said. "With them here, Lieutenant, I suspect it has something to do with Sergeant Giannini and Fortune's case, so perhaps you had best let him tell it."

I told it all. From the plan to break Monroe out and ambush him to the hired gun chasing me through the streets of Greenwich Village. I told about Rosa and Giannini. I watched Reynolds the whole time. Giannini, Smoke and Loren O and the BLF, even the FBI, hadn't planned it all on their own. Reynolds' face showed nothing at first. As I laid it barer and barer I saw a pain behind the clear eyes, a darkening. He seemed to grow smaller as Monroe had grown smaller. When I finished, he sat there silently for some moments, looked straight ahead. When he finally spoke, his voice was darker, heavier.

"You could all be taking quite a chance."

"I don't think so," I said.

"Do I thank you for the trust, Fortune?" His eyes were angry that I dared to understand him, the honesty that was the dominant center around which all else he did had to move. "I hate Isaiah Monroe. I hate what he means in this country. I hate the dirt he's thrown at my men and my town in the newspapers, magazines, books. But if what you tell me is half true I'll petition for a new trial myself. You've told me, now show me."

I gave the details of the gunman and the FBI man, Cardenas, outside Lenny's apartment, Cardenas' clandestine visit to BLF headquarters and Monroe's story of the planned jailbreak. Marx listed all the evidence that pointed to the attacker waiting in the Oneida lobby. Lenny told him of Cap's and Matt's sense of being watched and how she had bumped into the man who looked like Giannini, found the pen. She gave him the pen.

"We've got the ballistics," Marx said. "I'd like to check out Giannini's guns."

"I think I could recognize him," Lenny said.

I said, "We know Rosa was arrested for demonstrating over here. My guess is that she met Giannini, got to know him."

Reynolds turned his head to look at each of us as we spoke. Then he sat and looked at the pen. "All I want is an orderly city where ordinary people can live in peace, work at what they want, do what they please as long as it doesn't hurt anyone else. I wish all this would go away, you understand? I wish all the troublemakers like Isaiah Monroe would vanish. Who needs them? Who wants them? I want peace and order. It's what everyone wants. Men like Monroe can only destroy."

"It depends on how you get peace and order," I said. "You can't lose what you want to protect, give up what makes life worth living."

Reynolds said, "A pen like this could belong to anyone."

"Why not start," I said, "by finding out who arrested and interrogated Rosa Gruenfeld."

Reynolds laid the pen on the table like a black scar against the pale teak, went to the telephone on his desk. It took some time at that late hour. After midnight when he started his calls, and past one before he finished. Mrs. Reynolds came in with a large urn of coffee and some sandwiches. She had seen a lot of late-night meetings, came to the rescue automatically. None of us would have thought we were hungry, but we all ate until there was nothing left, drank the good coffee until it was all gone, and Mrs. Reynolds took the urn out to make more.

It was past three before the first result of Reynolds' calls arrived. A sleepy female sergeant with copies of the arrest and interrogation records. Mrs. Rosa Gruenfeld, female Caucasian, aged eighty-six and eighty-seven, had been arrested for disorderly conduct, trespassing and resisting arrest three times in North Paterson. Detective Sergeant Giannini had been the interrogating officer all three times.

"The Good Gestapo," I said. "She liked him, so she remembered him. And she saw him in the Oneida that morning. If she tells Lenny, the whole plan to get Monroe goes up in smoke."

Marx said, "Maybe Miss Gruenfeld better go with your wife, Chief. We might need her to pick Giannini out of a lineup."

Lenny left the office and went into the house to help Mrs. Reynolds. Sergeant Giannini arrived at three-twenty. He had taken the time to shave and dress in a suit and tie under a worn brown topcoat. He was meeting his Chief. When he saw me his dark face paled, but he walked firmly toward us.

"You brought your weapons, Sergeant?" Reynolds said quietly.

Giannini shook his head. "No, sir."

"I told you to, didn't I?"

The swarthy policeman looked only at me. "Yes, sir."

"Then?"

"I lost them."

"All of them?"

"Yes, sir."

"You reported that?"

"No, sir." Giannini looked away from me for the first

time, looked toward Reynolds and saw the pen lying on the teak table.

I said, "It's blown, Sergeant. Monroe and Lenny Gruenfeld know, there'll be no jailbreak. Miss Gruenfeld can identify you, we know now it was you I saw around St. Vincent's. Smoke and Loren O will talk. Probably others."

He stared at the thin black pen with its soft matte finish, its gold trim, the monogrammed gold *G.* The silence had that lightheaded feeling of the early hours of a cold morning.

"Yeah," he said.

"Why, Paul?" Chief Reynolds said.

Giannini half smiled. "The Lieutenant told me to. Orders, right, Chief?" He seemed to think about that. "I guess I didn't have to, did I?"

The Lieutenant tells him it's orders from the Captain. It has to be done. Everyone knows Monroe is too dangerous to the community, maybe the country, to ever get out. The Lieutenant has nothing against the blacks, wants to see them become as good as the white man, rise out of their ignorance and poverty, but Monroe's the worst thing that could happen to the blacks. He's a violent, radical, godless outlaw, and there is a real chance he'll get a third trial.

Paul Giannini has lived in North Paterson all his life. He believes in small towns. They are the best places to bring up children, teach them the old values, have the comfort and security of friends and neighbors. He hates New York City and all the other big, dirty, cold, corrupt, cynical cities. He believes in The Law. He is a staunch Democrat, but he also believes that you respect whoever is elected, the man in the office. That's democracy.

He grew up on the Italian side of the city, went to parochial school, Catholic high school, St. Peter's Col-

lege in Newark for two years before joining the police. Married, the father of four children, he does not hate blacks but thinks people should stay with their own kind. He believes in separate but equal. He thinks everyone should have the same opportunity. He thinks if you work hard you will succeed. He thinks blacks and Hispanics are slow and lazy, prefer welfare to work, and that Italians, and even Irish, are harder working and smarter. He knows some blacks who work hard, are solid businessmen, lawyers, even judges. There are blacks on the North Paterson force, but Giannini and his friends do not associate with them off the job. It just happens that way. They go separate ways to separate sections with separate customs. Each to his own.

Isaiah Monroe is a deviant radical troublemaker and murderer who wants to destroy the world Paul Giannini was born into and accepts as the true, the normal, the good. God, Country, The Law. Giannini is afraid of chaos, of the different. Of change and the abnormal. He believes in what is, that the way things are is the way they should be. He worries about a man like Monroe being turned loose by radicals, and Communists, and black militants, and misguided bleeding hearts and stupid do-gooders.

So when the Lieutenant tells him that the Captain, and the FBI, and other authorities have decided Monroe and his violent plans are dangerous to the people of North Paterson and the country, if not the world, he does what he is ordered to do for the ambush plan. He works with Smoke and Loren O. He doesn't really trust their motives, but he's been a cop long enough to know you have to use anyone you can against criminals who too often hide behind the law. He acts as contact, go-between and one of those who watch Lenny Gruenfeld both on and off duty.

After the bumping incident when he lost his pen, he

lets others follow her for a week or so, and he does not report the loss of the pen. On the morning of Rosa's shooting he picks up Lenny at her apartment, tails her to the Oneida Hotel. He stakes out behind the lobby desk. Rosa comes out of the back corridor and sees him. She is surprised. She likes him, he has been kind to her, a good cop.

"Hey, Good Gestapo! What are you doing here?"

She comes behind the counter to see what he is doing, and he reacts. In an instant he realizes if she tells Lenny, if Lenny appears while Rosa is with him, the whole plan will be blown. So he shoots. Rosa falls. Giannini runs down into the hotel basement and out the back way. In North Paterson the Lieutenant is alarmed, but it looks okay. Lenny has not seen him, no one has seen him. The plan has to go on. Then they learn that Rosa isn't dead. They send Giannini back to finish the job.

Now Paul Giannini is in conflict. He is not a killer. The shooting of Rosa was in a real sense a kind of accident. He saw an immediate danger, he reacted. But now he is asked to kill in cold blood. His bosses have made a mistake. He can't do it. At least, not unless the old lady is a real danger. To be that she will have to regain her senses, be able to tell what happened. He comes to the hospital, but he only watches. He is seen, and he lets too much time slip away. By the time his bosses realize what he has done, send the hit man, it is too late. Johnny Agnew has been killed, and Rosa is under heavy guard.

"I didn't want to kill the old woman, it just happened, you know, Chief? I couldn't go back and kill her. I guess that was a mistake. It doesn't matter much, I blew the whole operation. You think he'll get out now? He's a real danger, him and the BLF. If that damned old Rosa hadn't spotted me. Maybe if I'd made sure she was dead the first time, but I couldn't, you know?"

Giannini talked, Chief Reynolds listened and said nothing. Marx had it on his pocket tape recorder, not that he could use it in court. Giannini wrestled in his web of conflicting values. Everything he believed pulled him two ways. The necessity for law and order and authority on one side, the sanctity of life and the individual and freedom on the other. Duty versus morality. Necessity against honesty. Right versus right. An impossible conflict.

It was well past dawn before we'd all gone into North Paterson, read Giannini his rights, got an official confession, hauled in Smoke and Loren O. They were sullen, but when they saw Giannini and his statement, they confirmed it all.

"Monroe think he bigger'n the BLF," Loren O said.

"I'm the leader, not any goddamned hotshot jock," Smoke said. "He doesn't even know what really counts in the fight."

They were getting ready for Lenny to pick Giannini out of a lineup when a lawyer roared in. Sent by the lieutenant and captain Giannini had implicated, he was defending them more than Giannini, raised hell with Chief Reynolds. Reynolds went nose to nose, redder and angrier and louder. Giannini sat apart by himself, ignored and irrelevant, his head down, his career over.

Marx finally asked about the hit man who'd killed Johnny Agnew.

"I don't know where he came from," Giannini said. "I don't even know why he killed that guy."

"Mafia," Smoke said.

I said, "Lieutenant, lend me your car."

If the hired gunman was Mafia, only one man could have sent him. And if I was right, he was on borrowed time.

50.

THE LARGE IRON GATE in the high brick wall was closed. At the early hour the wooded estates with their great houses sat silent in the spring morning sun, small leaves just greening on the bare branches among the evergreens of winter. There was a telephone in a wall niche.

"Yes?" A woman's voice, sharp and short.

"Mr. Keene, please."

"He doesn't talk to anyone before noon." It was the voice of a housekeeper.

I made it as harsh and urgent as I could. "He'll talk to me. Dan Fortune. Tell him."

"I really—"

"Tell him!"

There was a silence. It was short, Keene's smooth voice was annoyed. "Not now, Dan. Call me later. I—"

I said. "Giannini, Smoke and Loren O are talking."

This time the silence was longer. "The gate stays unlocked two minutes."

I got back into Marx's car, heard the click, and the gates swung open. I drove up the long blacktop drive. Keene stood on the porch of the imitation plantation house. He led me inside through the gracious antebellum entry hall, past the sweeping stairs up and the airy living room to the left, into the kind of large library where the gentlemen of South Carolina had planned the war they were going to win in three weeks or less.

He closed the door, swung around. He had a shotgun in his hands. Outside the windows a slim redhaired woman was loading suitcases and files into a silver

Mercedes. She hurried, looked back at the house.

"All right, what the fuck is this?"

"What you think it is," I said. "Time to cut and run."

He was in a pale blue jump suit too form-fitting for his thick chest and growing belly. A morning-at-home outfit. The bland face was redder than ever with anger. His hair seemed grayer, shaggy, not yet shaped into proper place for the best image. The permanent smile was gone, and the manicured hands moved in jagged gestures.

"I don't know what the fuck you're doing here, but you'll be going to the morgue unless you come up with some fast talk."

"I'm not your problem, Keene. Reynolds knows I'm here, and Lieutenant Marx from NYPD, but they're not your problem. Sergeant Giannini's told about tailing Lenny Gruenfeld, shooting old Rosa. Lenny, Smoke and Loren O have blown the ambush-escape plan on Monroe. Giannini named the Lieutenant, the Lieutenant named the Captain, the Captain will name you. They'll be here any time now, but that's not your real problem either."

His television-actor face had gone through the gamut as I talked, searching his mind for an answer, some escape. He held the shotgun in one hand. His free hand clenched and unclenched in the elegant library as if looking for something to hold onto.

"They're lying," he said, but his voice cracked. Even he didn't believe anyone would believe him.

"Your problem is the Mafia," I said. "That hit man you hired to get rid of Johnny Agnew, finish off Rosa in the hospital when Giannini went soft and burn me out when I became a threat. You're the Mafia connection. You can't do business in a lot of trades in New Jersey without dealing with the Mafia. You can't run towns or be chairman of a party. They've got the friends, the votes, the power, and you don't ask how they got the power, you just have to deal with it."

He licked his lips. "They'll deal with you. You screwed the whole thing! You ruined it!"

"They don't gain anything by killing me now. I've told all I know. But they gain a lot by killing you before you tell what you know. You're the only one who knows who sent that hired gun. You're the only one who can tie them into this."

The shotgun still in his hand, he picked up the telephone, asked for the police. He then asked for Chief Reynolds. I watched the redheaded wife finally climb into the Mercedes. She had two children with her, the briefcases. She and Keene had everything, king and queen of the hill, but I felt sorry for her and the children. It was all going to melt away like candy in a hot sun.

Keene hung up. "They're coming." He sat down on a pale brown glove-leather couch. "I ought to kill you."

"But you won't."

"Just for the pleasure of it. Just to do it."

"It would spoil the deal you're going to make."

He let the shotgun hang muzzle down in his hand.

"Why?" I said.

He said, "The fucking altar boy couldn't finish the job. That's what cost us. He didn't have to shoot the goddamned old Commie in the first goddamned place. Panicked, got trigger fever. I should have spotted him." He slammed his hand over on the arm of the couch. "Damn! Damn! Damn!"

"He believes what he was taught," I said. "The duty and the brotherhood. The government and the church. It made him do what you wanted, but it made him feel guilty, too."

"Christ! I should never have sent him back. I blew it, didn't I, Fortune? Let too much time slip before I called in the real muscle. Then they send me a fuckup who couldn't even get you. They send me a loser. My fucking luck."

"He got Johnny Agnew," I said.

He looked down at the shotgun in his hand, shook his head as if he still couldn't really understand how so much could have gone wrong in a perfectly good plan. "That son of a bitch tried to blackmail us. He'd seen Giannini tailing Lenny Gruenfeld, knew she sang for Monroe, put two and two together and called the BLF. They called me. He didn't know who Giannini was, but he had a good description, so I had to go to Marcello."

"That's his name? Your Mafia gun?"

"Marcello's the *capo.* The fuckup gunman is Dom, or Charley, or Vito, what's the difference? A new one all the way from Sicily. The big dons complain they can't hardly get good men from the States anymore, life's too easy. I should have had him waste Giannini, but the Captain wanted none of that."

"Kill Giannini," I said, "and you'd really have blown it. Reynolds would have followed that to hell and back."

We sat in the silent library waiting for the sound of sirens.

"Why?" I asked again. "Monroe is locked up tight. Most people have forgotten about him."

"Christ, Fortune, he's a time bomb. I've seen a psychiatric report on him. It's the scariest report I ever read. A third trial could get him out, for God's sake. And there's a good chance of a third trial the way the bleeding hearts and radicals and Commies keep hammering. You said it yourself, most people have forgotten what he did, the horror of it, the coldblooded killings. He could get out."

"If he's not guilty."

"Not guilty? He's an animal! You can't reason with him. He's a hurricane that could blow it all away."

"Blow all what away?"

"Everything we have! Everything we worked our asses off to get. We let them in the schools, the colleges, our world, and they want to change it all, push us out. Well they're not going to. They're not us, and they can't be. Halfbreeds and mongrels, most of them. Black, brown, yellow. Saying they're equal, even becoming Catholics. Monroe's the worst kind—educated, too much money, arrogant, attacking the whole way of life we built. He's a fucking cancer, and you cut out a cancer."

He sat there with the fear hanging out. Fear of losing what he had, of finding out that maybe he and his weren't that special after all. But that wasn't enough, not for F.X. Keene. That was the base, the abstract. What told him blacks and browns weren't human so it didn't matter what you did to them. But the Keenes of the world didn't act on the abstract.

"Monroe didn't kill those people," I said. "I know that now, and you always knew it. You helped frame him. If he's freed, the whole case has to be reopened and the frame comes out. There goes your empire, your power, your whole world. He's in jail, but he just won't go away. Each trial gets closer to the truth. So you and the others in the original frame decided to finish it once and for all. To the FBI, Monroe's a threat to national security, they don't want the frame to come out at this late date. To Smoke, The Wind's too much competition in the BLF. Giannini takes orders. The Mafia doesn't give a damn about Monroe, but want to do you a favor they can call in later. It's so easy. Monroe's dead, you're all safe."

"Got it all worked out, haven't you?"

"All except why you needed to frame Monroe back then in the first place. But that'll come out."

"Will it?" He raised the shotgun. "What if no one else figures it all out? Only you."

"Don't be any dumber than you have to." I stood up. The gun was beginning to get to me. "They'll dig it all up down to the last paper clip. Reynolds has to clean the department, and the FBI'll have to cover itself. You haven't killed anyone yet, you'll make a deal, cop a good plea, be out and building again in a few years. Kill me, they throw the book. Not to mention what the Mafia does."

As we faced off, the sirens began in the distance. I walked out. I felt my back crawl, men don't always act logically, but I made it to the door and along the entry hall and out across the porch to Marx's car. A State Police cruiser came up the long drive. The officer in the cruiser looked at me as we passed.

I saw the bloated face with the pale pink skin. The dead eyes and the stained, crooked teeth. I jammed on the brakes, rolled out of the car as I reached up and leaned on the horn. The blaring sound seemed to echo everywhere across the estate.

The State Police car screeched to a halt, the trooper jumped out. His uniform didn't fit. He held a long-barreled, silenced, very non-State Police pistol with both hands, took two sharp, spitting shots at me. Useless shots against a man behind a car. Wasted shots, and he seemed to realize this, turned and ran up the front steps of the mansion.

The two shotgun blasts blew him backwards off the porch in a shower of red blood and bone, the force enough to sprawl him spread-eagled on the blacktop beyond the steps, the long pistol still gripped in his dead hand.

Keene stepped out onto the porch. He held the shotgun. I stood up behind Marx's car. Sirens growled into the drive as the real police arrived.

51.

IT ALL CAME OUT, from the small panic shooting of Red Rosa all the way back to the original frame of Isaiah Monroe and Sam Johnson. Isaiah Monroe would get his third trial. He should walk out free at once, he hadn't killed anyone, committed any crime, but that's not the way the system works. We're quick to assume guilt, convict, but slow to admit we were wrong, sent an innocent man to prison for fifteen years, destroyed his life.

Marx laid it out for me. "Keene and the North Paterson lieutenant and captain were behind the frame. Keene was forcing kickbacks from party members who worked for the city, padding slum renovation contracts, taking Mafia payoffs, all the usual. The two cops were on Keene's payroll. Monroe and the BLF's activism was a danger, and Keene hated Monroe anyway, so when Monroe was picked up for the killings, he saw his chance. With the two officers on the inside, the rest of the NPPD glad to convict Monroe of anything, and most of the whites only too damned ready to believe, it was easy. Monroe's violent rhetoric didn't help. Judges don't like talk of guns and revolution."

It would go hard on Giannini, Smoke and Loren O, but the captain and lieutenant would get a plea bargain for lack of real evidence, and F.X. Keene would make a deal. The dead hit man, who had done all the actual killing and would turn out to have had no connection to anyone, had been shot in self-defense. Even I would have to testify to that. The Mafia wouldn't appear in the case.

"Old Roth won't testify against Carlos Arriba. We'll

need you," Marx said.

"How about Kevin Regan?"

"He broke parole, they're pushing it. I'll do what I can, but Fugitive Division is out to get him."

"Yeah," I said.

The North Paterson police captain and lieutenant would get fired, but little more. F.X. Keene would lose his position and, for a time, his rackets, serve a year or so or get off with probation and community service as a first offender who could afford the best lawyer. Regan would go back to prison, maybe return to his former life of crime. How much hope could one man hold onto?

"We'll need you on that TV converter box case next week," Marx said. "They're outraged, we're being unfair. Hell, doesn't everybody steal what they can from the boss?"

"Too many bad movies," I said. "When it's all over they get up and go home, have a couple of beers. They turn off the TV."

I reported to Lenny Gruenfeld, got my money. We drove up to see Rosa at the nursing home north of New Rochelle. Rosa was in a wheelchair in the corridor. One of fifty skeletons in wheelchairs, mostly women, slack-jawed, empty-eyed, confused, lost. Silent and pleading, or manic and babbling. Rosa looked up at us as Lenny bent and spoke directly into her face.

"Hello, grandma, do you know me?"

"Of course I know you. You're my mother."

I said, "Hello, Rosa. Are you okay?"

She blinked at my arm. "What have they done to you, Hans?"

"Dan Fortune, Rosa," I said. "We caught the man who shot you."

For an instant her birdlike eyes focused. "I know you! The Good Gestapo. What are you doing here? What . . ." The eyes faded, as open and empty as the mouths of infant birds. "They killed you, Hans. The horses. I hate them! We won, Papa. Don't, Mama, don't die. We . . . won . . . Papa . . ."

"Grandma," Lenny said. "Is there anything you want?"

But we had lost her. She sat hunched, staring, as if she could see the police horses that had trampled Hans Gruenfeld on the streets of New York sixty years ago. Or Sergeant Giannini behind the abandoned desk of the Oneida Hotel with a gun aimed at her only two weeks ago. The police she had faced all her life, the forces of power she had opposed all her life. No difference now, no time. All in an instant. No sense of who she was, or who she had been.

"She doesn't know any of it ever happened, does she?" Lenny said. She took the wheelchair, pushed Rosa slowly through the corridors crowded with the twisted old people waiting to die, clean halls that smelled of urine and feces, the smell no amount of scrubbing or disinfectant could remove, the odor of the beginning and the end of life. "Did she ever live, Dan? How do we know any of it happened? Does she know she ever existed?"

"We have to live as if it's real, as if what we're doing is worth something."

"For who? We'll all end like Rosa anyway."

"Maybe for other people."

"Like Rosa? Hans? Sam? It's not enough. My father, Flaco, F.X. Keene, perhaps they know more."

"They end up with even less."

We went on pushing Rosa. The mindless old woman babbled, slept, babbled again, until it was time to leave. We left her in a corridor insisting she had to wait in line to pay her bill, smiling good-bye to her mother and all her husbands. Red Rosa, who no longer knew who Lenin had been, or who she had been.

"I came from that old woman," Lenny said as we walked across the parking lot in the late sun of the spring afternoon. "Why, you know? To what purpose?"

"Maybe to try to find a purpose."

We were halfway to her car when I saw Cardenas get out of the dark blue Ford sedan, stride toward the entrance to the nursing home. Back in his blue three-piece banker's suit. I told Lenny I'd meet her at the car, cut him off.

"Going to shut her up?" I said.

He smiled. "She doesn't know anything about the Bureau, Fortune, but you never know when she might recover, be able to tell us something about subversives."

"Constant vigilance?"

"You got it."

"Looks like a new trial for Monroe. He's innocent, he'll get out."

"Probably."

"You don't care if he killed those men or not, do you? He's dangerous, a walking time bomb that threatens the status quo. He has to be rendered inoperative."

He looked over my shoulder toward the nursing home in the late sun. "He'll be guilty of something, Fortune, sooner or later. People like Monroe always break some law. That's why we make laws. We'll get him."

"Not Giannini, or Keene, or those two North Paterson police officers? Not even Smoke or Loren O?"

"Gianninis and Keenes come and go, they don't hurt the country. The Monroes'll destroy us."

"Wrong. It's the Keenes and Gianninis who'll destroy us in the end."

He shrugged, looked at his watch. "Hang in, Fortune, we'll argue it again sometime."

I watched him go off to find out if old Rosa could tell him anything to save the nation. He was right, it made no difference if Isaiah Monroe was guilty of this crime or not. That missed the point, asked for the facts, not the truth. The facts might prove him innocent, but the truth was something else. The truth was that a society did have to "get" a man like Monroe to protect itself. The truth was that anyone who refused to accommodate to the society in which they lived had to leave that society or, one way or another, be destroyed by it.

At her car, Lenny was waiting with the motor running. We drove out of the nursing home lot and turned south for New York. I told her about Cardenas, his words and my thoughts.

"Protect what you have," she said. "That's it, isn't it? The rest is indifference."

I could almost see the plastic shell slide shut again. The break that had been Rosa, the last try to connect to a world outside herself that had been Isaiah Monroe, closing like scar tissue over an open wound.

"What will you do now?"

"The band. Live as long as I can stand it." She drove fast in and out of the traffic as we neared the city. "We'll leave Margo with Alette. She's going to be alone for a time. They've got Neanderthal Nikolai under psychiatric examination. He'll plead all kinds of guilty, have therapy, spend a while in jail or a hospital or both. My brother Richard'll run the business."

"You're not worried they'll corrupt Margo?"

"I don't think it makes much difference. My father or Flaco or Rosa, it all turns out the same."

I could have tried to talk her out of it, but there didn't seem much point. A private universe of three that never stopped moving could be as good an answer as any. She dropped me at the Drake Hotel, where Kay had moved, didn't look back.

Upstairs Kay was packed. For both of us.

"We'll make it work, Dan. You'll see."

I saw Marty in my mind. In a man's shirt smeared by wood stains, her face dirty, her small body in torn dungarees, her hair in her eyes, the eyes bright as she worked over an old table she loved. A memory I've always carried with me, always will. Kay would not make me forget that memory, but she was making me wonder if maybe I could do it again. I wanted to love, and I wanted to live, and those are not always the same thing, but in those rare instances that really work, you can do both. Could I do both with Kay? I didn't know, but I did know that she was making me think you do get more than one big love in your life, or that maybe I hadn't had mine yet after all.

"I'll take a long look," I said.

I might as well live in California as find a new place I couldn't afford in New York. At least I could lie in the sun. Forget F.X. Keene and Isaiah Monroe both. Even try to forget Red Rosa.